WILD MAGIC

THE GATEKEEPER'S FATE: BOOK ONE

EMMA L. ADAMS

Never make a promise to a faerie.

I'd learned the above lesson before I'd learned to walk, and nowadays, almost everyone agreed that it was better to anger a faerie than to be in their debt. Despite this, there were certain situations in which it would really help if I had access to the magic the fae had once granted me in exchange for the promise which bound my family to serve them.

Like today, for instance, when I'd been tasked with shutting down an illegal fae gambling den run entirely by redcaps. Two fae greeted me at the doorstep, their sharp teeth bared in identical grins. Pointed ears stuck out beneath crimson hats marked with the coppery stains of old blood. They wore ragged, sack-like garments which hung off their spindly bodies, and they might have seemed as fragile as small children if not for the fact that one of them carried a serrated knife with a wooden hilt, presumably to prevent the iron from burning its skin, or that said knife was pointed at my leg, the highest part of me the creature could reach.

"Get out of my pub," growled the redcap. "Unless you'd like me to carve out your entrails and string them up on the walls."

"No, thanks." With one eye on the knife, I jabbed a finger over his shoulder. "That is the shoddiest glamour I've ever seen."

The room behind him appeared to be empty at first glance, but if I looked out of the corner of my eye at the grimy tables, the chairs were suddenly occupied by all manner of lesser fae. Hobgoblins drank pints of ale, hulking ogres and trolls too big for the barstools stood at tables that came up to their knees, and a redcap wearing an oversized trench coat he must have "borrowed" from a human stood on top of the bar and yelled out bingo numbers at anyone within earshot.

The second redcap's face fell. "It's the carpets, isn't it? I knew we should have gone for burgundy rather than crimson."

His mate shot him a disgruntled look. "That wouldn't have helped, dimwit. You can still see the bloodstains."

It wasn't the carpets that were the problem; the row of cages along the back wall was. Cages containing *people.* Hence my reason for being here. I didn't care if the fae wanted to gamble away their spare time in the human realm, but kidnapping the locals was against magical law and patently unfair to boot, given that most of them wouldn't be able to see past even the shakiest glamour. The odds of convincing a redcap to come quietly were lower than the odds of walking out of the faerie realm in the same state one walked into it, so I wasn't holding out much hope for rescuing the humans without turning those carpets an even deeper shade of crimson.

Keeping a careful watch on the knife, I edged forward and closer to the room. One step caused the illusion covering the tables to waver like a rippling curtain. Amateur, if you asked me, like putting a pair of wings on a troll and calling it a piskie. I'd once been able to conjure up better glamours in my sleep, but these days, I had nothing but the false authority in my tone as I said, "Release those humans at once."

The first redcap bared his teeth. "Why should we?"

"You're breaking the laws of this realm, for a start." I didn't expect that argument to hold much weight, and sure enough, both of them burst into laughter like a pair of shrieking hyenas. With an eye-roll, I reached into my pocket for a sealed container of iron filings and popped off the lid.

When I raised my arm and scattered the iron fragments at the redcaps' feet, the illusion masking the pub wavered before my eyes and then vanished altogether. The second redcap let out an indignant noise when one of the pieces of iron bounced off his spindly shoulder, leaving an ugly red mark behind. "You will pay for that, human."

"We could lock you up in a cage too," said the first redcap, his knife poking my knee through my jeans. "Once we've cut off a few limbs."

"Which one do you want to do first?" said his friend eagerly. "The left arm, do you think?"

"Both arms." The knife prodded at the joint of my arm. "I'll take the left, and you can take the right."

"I really wouldn't." Despite the sharp object digging

into the skin of my arm beneath my thin coat, I had to suppress a sigh of exasperation. "Do you know who the Winter Gatekeeper is?"

The redcap's grip on his weapon faltered. "The Unseelie Queen's most favoured human?"

I suppressed a snort with difficulty. Even as Gatekeeper, I'd hardly been "favoured" in any sense of the word, though it was true that Winter's monarch had even less regard for other humans than she did for me. "The very same. Did you know they say the Winter Gatekeeper can freeze the blood in your veins droplet by droplet or immobilise your neck until it snaps and takes your head along with it?"

There'd been a time when I'd had the magic to back up my threats, but as it was, the redcap's brief moment of panic came to an abrupt halt when his friend exclaimed, "There is no Winter Gatekeeper any longer! The curse was broken."

"That's right!" said the other in gleeful tones. "There's no such thing as a Gatekeeper."

Damn. Ah, well, it had been worth a try. "Who told you that?"

"Everyone knows," said the second redcap. "The Gatekeepers gave up their titles to stop the Courts from going to war. I wish that I could have feasted on the blood of that battlefield."

"Oh, if only," his friend said wistfully.

Bloody scavengers. Redcaps had once served my family and been loyal to the Winter Gatekeeper, but that arrangement had dissolved long before I'd become Gatekeeper myself. I hadn't known these fae were plugged into Faerie's gossip, but the breaking of the Gatekeeper's curse had been monumental enough to reach even the most remote locations.

Abandoning all notions of liberating the humans without bloodshed, I said, "Gatekeeper or not, I'm going to give you a choice. Let those humans go or die. I'll be generous and give you a second to think on your decision."

Silence spilled through the pub, the hoarse shouts of bingo numbers and general chatter fading as the patrons finally realised their illusion had lifted and their illicit dealings were laid bare for the world to see. Some rose to their feet, while the redcap staff dropped their drink trays and skittered over to join their buddies by the door until a line of them barred the way into the pub.

A couple of them shrieked when they trod on the scattered iron fragments with their bare feet, and the others collectively lost their shit. Within seconds, a wall of pointy-eared creatures with knives and sharp teeth stood between me and the cages, interspersed with angry patrons.

So that's how it was going to be.

I drew my iron knife from the handmade sheath at my waist. Unlike the redcap, I didn't need to protect myself from being burned by the metal—one of the few perks of being fully human—but everyone with a smidgeon of sense backed away from me. I turned the knife over in my hand and held it point-forward, clearing a path to the cages.

"Easy does it." I strode through their midst, my gaze trained on the miserable-looking humans. "See? Nobody gets hurt this way."

Still, it came as no surprise when one of the redcaps

tried to jump me from behind. My blade shot out, nicking the skin of his hand and causing him to drop his weapon. I'd barely left a scratch, but redcaps had a nose for fresh blood, and in an instant, a dozen pairs of eager eyes fixated on their friend. He hissed in annoyance, swatting away their grabbing hands, and then made another lunge for my leg in an attempt to trip me up.

I swung a booted foot at him, kicking him into the air and out of my path. Two more took his place, clawing at my legs, and instinct took over. A swipe of my knife brought a shower of crimson from their cut throats, and their bodies toppled backwards onto the floor.

Pandemonium broke out. The redcaps turned on their fallen companions with bloodthirsty cries, pulling off their hats in an attempt to soak them in the fresh blood. Turning my back on the unpleasant scene, I ran to the cages to free their unlucky captives. The redcaps hadn't done a particularly thorough job in locking the cages, and it didn't take long for me to pick the locks one at a time, occasionally sticking my knife in a redcap who got too close.

Even with their doors unlocked, the humans didn't budge, hunched and shivering with terrified eyes. Poor things. They might be smarter than their captors, but humans were so damn *vulnerable*. When they weren't walking obliviously into faerie traps, their slow reactions would do them in every time. Frustratingly, I knew that if I'd lost my Sight along with my powers, I might have ended up in the exact same position… except for one key difference.

The faeries hadn't taken away my knowledge of how to kill them.

I sliced open the throat of another redcap and threw the body into the midst of the others then reached through the nearest cage door and grabbed the occupying human by the wrist, dragging him out on shaking legs. "Go on. Run straight for the iron near the door, and don't stop."

As he broke into a jerky run, some of the others snapped out of their shock. I kept a close eye on them as they climbed out of their cages to make sure they didn't trip or get stabbed on the way out. When the cages were free of human inhabitants, I made to follow them, and a loud screech rose from somewhere behind me, causing me to pivot on my heel. One of the cages was still occupied, by a jet-black bird and not a person, its stubby clawed feet unable to get the door open. Shapeshifter fae? Or a bewitched human?

The crow screeched indignantly again, and I caved in. "I'll let you out, but you'd better keep that beak away from me."

I reached for the cage, and the bird beat its wings frantically at me as I picked the lock. The cage door sprang open and the bird toppled out, turning into a person as it did so. I staggered back under the weight of the lanky form of a teenage girl with long black hair, whose beseeching eyes looked up at me. "Help me."

Then she fell unconscious, her head lolling over my arm.

You have got to be kidding me.

I staggered away from the cage, nearly tripping over a redcap in the process. Most had fled or passed out, drunk on the blood they'd devoured, but I had to watch my step to avoid dropping the kid. She might have been anywhere between twelve and fifteen, and while she looked fully human in this form, she was either a shifter or half-faerie. I'd bet money on the latter, given the circumstances in which I'd found her.

Out in the street, the humans had scattered, their survival instincts finally kicking in. While I fully intended to send the authorities to clean up the rest of the mess, leaving the girl here as redcap bait was out of the question. I racked my brains for ideas as to where to leave an abandoned half-fae and came up with exactly one option, so I slung her unconscious body over my shoulder and made my way to Edinburgh's main half-blood territory. I figured she'd likely prefer to be with her fellow half-faeries rather than in a human orphanage, but even their own territory could be downright brutal on anyone who wandered in there alone.

I pushed open the thorn-covered gate to half-blood territory and headed to the house that belonged to Blaine Reyes, the person typically in charge of all matters involving abandoned half-faeries who had no knowledge of their parentage. Given the Sidhe's proclivity for ditching their half-human offspring without warning, there were rather a lot of them. When she'd spoken, the girl had had an English accent, so she presumably wasn't local, but it was hard to tell with the faeries.

Adjusting my grip on the unconscious teenager, I rapped on the wooden door with my knuckles. Blaine Reyes, a tall Summer half-faerie with silver hair and pale, elegant features, answered the door and raised his brows at me in surprise. "Holly Lynn? You need something?"

"Hey," I said. "Sorry to bother you, but I have an unconscious half-faerie kid I found in a redcap den. I didn't want to abandon her while I fetched the human authorities, but I figured she'd be better off staying here rather than with the humans."

"Let me see." He peered down at her face. "How do you know she's half-fae?"

"She shifted into a crow."

Blaine recoiled. "A crow?"

"Yes…" Had mentioning the shapeshifting been a mistake? I wouldn't have thought a pair of wings would be a deal-breaker, considering half the territory's inhabitants had claws or tails. "Why?"

"That is the Morrigan's daughter," said Blaine. "I won't have her staying here on our territory."

"What are you talking about?" The *Morrigan?* "How do you know whose daughter she is? She's unconscious, for crying out loud."

"The Morrigan's feral child has been sighted several times in the area recently," said Blaine. "By all accounts, she's a soul-eating monster who's a danger to all of us."

"She's a kid."

"Then by all means, leave her with the humans." He closed the door firmly, while the girl didn't stir, unaware of the rejection.

"What the hell?" I gave the girl's face a brief scan, trying to see the resemblance to the Morrigan, the shapeshifting menace who was feared by even most Unseelie faeries. I hadn't known the queen of the death fae had any children, much less half-human ones, but half-faeries could be surprisingly superstitious for beings who lived in a magically created section of the city fuelled by the magic of the Ley Line running through the heart of Arthur's Seat.

How had the daughter of the death fae's queen ended up in Edinburgh of all places? Admittedly, the Unseelie Court's darkest corner was hardly a decent place to grow up in, but I doubted the Morrigan had abandoned her in the human realm out of the kindness of her cold, shrivelled heart. Shaking my head, I turned my back on Blaine's house and began to retrace my steps to the gate.

I halted at the sound of rustling from among the nearby bushes. For a heartbeat, I thought I saw a pair of eyes watching me, but when I looked closer, nobody was there. Still, I knew if I left the kid alone here, she'd end up dead within hours, if not minutes. Wondering if I shouldn't have just let the human authorities take care of her instead, I carried her out of half-blood territory via the gates and resigned myself to leaving a teenage harbinger of death in my house while I went to report the redcaps to the local mercenaries who'd posted the job listing. I figured she couldn't do any harm while she was unconscious, at least, but it'd be a fine way to end the day if I got kicked out of my house for a brief act of kindheartedness.

As I turned the corner into my street, the wind blew a bright mass of leaves past me, painted in autumnal shades of orange and red like leaping flames. A shiver ran down my spine, and I quickened my pace until I reached home.

My house was a rental, shared with two mercenaries whose unpredictable work shifts ensured we rarely ran into one another—which was more than fine by me. I was theoretically part of the mercenaries' collective myself, but mercs were dull as shit to hang out with and were often as unscrupulous as the monsters they hunted. While their job was technically to ensure ordinary humans felt safe enough to sleep at night, the dudes I lived with were more interested in seeing how much loot they could smuggle out on the side, so the house was full of random crap like piles of jewels from trolls' lairs and pilfered faerie weapons. Meanwhile, their favourite activity was comparing the size of the teeth they'd pulled from monsters they killed and having mock sword fights that left holes in the walls and furniture.

The mercs wouldn't be happy with my new guest, but thankfully, nobody was in the house when I entered, so I carried her to my room without being waylaid. The cupboard-sized room contained little more than the most basic wooden furniture and the paltry belongings I'd managed to salvage from the ruins the faeries had left of my house after the curse had broken. I did at least have my own en-suite bathroom, so I stopped there first to clean the blood off my hands and face.

Even after several months, the muddy-brown eyes which stared at me from the mirror brought an unpleasant jolt. I barely remembered the days before my eyes had turned icy blue with Winter magic, while my forehead seemed bare without the swirling silver mark of the Winter Gatekeeper. Without the magical means to dye my hair black, it'd begun to fade back to brown, though I kept it short enough that nobody could tell.

Honestly, the biggest casualty from the loss of my magic was my fashion sense. These days, I lived in thread-bare hoodies and jeans and boots which became water-logged whenever it rained—which was often. At one time, I'd been able to use glamour to turn the plainest outfit into finery suitable for interacting with Sidhe nobles, but I'd settle for clothes which weren't riddled with holes and faded bloodstains and which didn't hang off me. I'd lost a good ten pounds or more since my last trip to Faerie, and given the tall, strong frame I'd inherited from my mother, half-starved was not a good look on me.

At least I had a roof over my head, which was more than I could say for my guest. She lay unconscious on the bed, her dark hair spilling like a waterfall over my pillow. If I hadn't known her for a half-faerie already, her fine glossy curls and porcelain skin would have given the game away. She made an incongruous sight on the sagging mattress of my secondhand bed, but this was all I had. The remnants of a life I'd tried to rebuild, as one might plant a seed to grow into a tree… while trying to forget the Winter faeries' tendency to strangle any life before it could take root in the ground.

When I looked at the sleeping kid, though, I had a hard time imagining her as an immortal devourer of souls.

2

I stood in a clearing surrounded by trees bare of leaves, whose branches had twisted to resemble contorted limbs. Frost coated the stiffened soil beneath my feet, and a semi-transparent sprite hovered in front of me with a thread of bright-blue magic shimmering in its hands.

"Will you take on the Gatekeeper's Trials?" asked the sprite in a high, reedy voice.

As if I had a choice. Either I accepted, or some other poor human got kidnapped in my place. Even the most self-interested wouldn't condemn another to suffer Faerie's wrath when they'd witnessed it with their own eyes.

"I will take on the Gatekeeper's Trials." As soon as the words left my mouth, the thread of blue magic left the sprite's hands and wrapped around my wrist like a bracelet.

"Your first trial begins immediately."

The sprite vanished into thin air, leaving me alone in the clearing.

Not for long. The air in front of me began to shimmer while I hovered on the balls of my feet. My fingers itched to reach for a blade that wasn't there, because the Sidhe hadn't allowed me to bring any iron weapons to the Trials. Instead, cold magic sprang to my palms, bringing a blue glow which frosted the air around me.

My opponent appeared in a white-blue flash, a shadowy form which vaguely resembled a person but without any visible features etched into the darkness comprising its facade. Chills swept in its wake, not from my own magic but from the deathly coldness the beast had brought with it.

A wraith. This couldn't be part of my trial, could it? Even in Winter, the Sidhe preferred not to acknowledge death as a possibility, let alone an inevitability, and a wraith was the unpleasant result of a Sidhe perishing without moving on to the afterlife. Instead, the wraith remained trapped, reduced to little more than rage and magic encased in a shadowy form barely resembling the fae it had once been. Shadowy hands reached out towards me, alighting with blue-white magic.

I focused on my own magic, and the cool rush of energy filled my hands. "You're not actually dead, are you? This is a glamour."

Faerie had an abundance of magical tricks at its disposal, and that this was a powerful illusion made far more sense than the notion of them letting an actual wraith into the Court to test the next Gatekeeper. Clouds of magic blasted from my palms, striking the fake wraith, but the attack made no dent in its shadowy form.

Instead, it looked straight at me, and the breath froze in my lungs when a pair of all-too-familiar bright-blue eyes met mine from within the darkness.

"Holly Lynn," whispered a voice I hadn't heard in a long time. "Holly... I've been trapped here for so long."

Nausea rose in the back of my throat. "Very funny. Stop pretending to be my mother and show your real face."

"This is my real face," whispered my mother's voice. "Don't you remember? This is how I was when we last saw one another."

"You're dead. More than dead." Oh, she'd *tried* to return from death, even going as far as to turn herself into a wraith and then possess her daughter in order to cheat the inevitable—but she'd failed. "Ilsa Lynn killed you."

"You should have taken her place," said my mother. "Her magic should have been yours. But you failed, and your own mother paid the price for it. You let me die."

"Stop that," I said quietly. "That's off-limits."

Nothing was truly off-limits to beings which could tear my worst nightmares from my mind and use their glamour to make them a reality. Yet despite the voice of reason screaming at me that this couldn't be my mother, she wrung the same reaction from me every damn time. The same dread and anger and shame.

"This is your fault," said the wraith. "You had the chance to help me ascend to glory even the Sidhe would never attain, and instead, you doomed me with your own hands."

"In case you've forgotten, you tried to kill me first."

I raised a hand, only to find my body stiffening with cold. While I'd been distracted by my mother's words, the fae's chilling spell had begun to immobilise me. I should have known better than to fall for an amateur trick like that.

"Join me, Holly," she whispered. "Join me in the afterlife."

A wave of cold washed over me…

———

I jolted awake to a deafening screech. Disorientated, I rolled over and smacked my head into a wooden post. Curses flew from my mouth while my scrambling fingers found the post to be attached to a bed. Right, I'd slept on a blanket on the floor and left the Morrigan's daughter asleep on my bed—which, in hindsight, might not have been a smart decision. When I'd returned from fetching my payment for dealing with the redcaps yesterday, she hadn't moved an inch, and since no healer would have gone near her, I'd settled for trickling water into her mouth in case she was dehydrated and then letting her sleep.

The girl lay flat on her back, screaming her lungs out, while her hands had shifted into the claws of a bird. She seemed physically fine… except for the claws, which dug into the mattress, scattering feathers everywhere.

As I leapt to my feet, she sat upright, her eyes flying wide open. "Help!"

"Hey." I moved into her line of sight, speaking in a soothing tone to reassure her that I wasn't a threat. "Are you okay? Were you having a nightmare?"

"You kidnapped me!" She bounced onto her knees on

the bed, her eyes—as bright as an Unseelie fae—brimming with indignation.

"I didn't kidnap you. You told me to help you," I said. "Do you have family?"

"No!" she yelled, her voice as sharp as a crow's screech, before drawing her knees to her chest and putting her arms over her head. "I don't need anybody."

"Right…" I froze when I realised she was crying, heaving sobs that shook the whole bed. I didn't quite dare get too close in case her claws came out again, so I crouched on the floor instead. "Is there anything I can do to help you?"

"No." She lifted her head, tears spilling from her vibrant blue eyes. "I'm the Morrigan's daughter. I don't need your help."

At least she knew her faerie parentage. That might have been awkward to explain. "I know you are. You begged me to help you and passed out in my arms, so I brought you home with me. If you want to leave, the door's that way."

The girl didn't move. Her skinny arms were wrapped around her knees, her gaze taking me in. "You shouldn't have brought me here. I might have eaten your soul."

"The thought did cross my mind." I rose to my feet, running my free hand through my sleep-rumpled hair, while her confused gaze followed my every movement.

"You're mad," she informed me. "You should be scared of me. I'm a monster who feeds on human souls."

"Yes, very scary." I rolled my eyes. "How old are you, twelve?"

"I'm almost *sixteen!*" she said indignantly. "I'm almost as powerful as the Morrigan, I am."

"Want me to take you to see her?" I didn't actually mean it—I'd need a substantial incentive to set foot in the Death Kingdom again—but she leapt to her feet with an outraged cry.

"Cut the bullshit," she said. "You can't take me to her. You're just a human."

"Yes, I can," I said, matching her childish tone. I hadn't signed up to deal with teenage faerie shenanigans at this hour of the morning. That was what I got for taking in strays. "Granted, I'd prefer *not* to go near the old bird's cave, but if that's the only way to get you out of my hair…"

"How do you know she lives in a cave?" Confusion seeped into her expression. "Who are you?"

"I'm the Winter Gatekeeper," I told her. "Used to be, anyway. I'm acquainted with the Death Kingdom and the Morrigan's lair."

"*You're* the Winter Gatekeeper?" she squeaked, the hostility on her face abruptly replaced by fear. "Really?"

Her reaction unsettled me. Did she not know I'd lost my title? "Yes… why?"

"Didn't you turn into a wraith and try to kill everyone?"

Oh. *Oh.* "No, that would be my mother. She was a real charmer."

The wraith's whisper from my dream lurked in the back of my mind, but the girl's snort of laughter displaced the lingering chill. "Yeah. I get that."

"Thought so." A knot in my chest I hadn't even known was there loosened. "I didn't get to do much Gatekeeping before the curse broke, mind you, but I'm human, not a wraith. I'm Holly."

"I'm Roseanne." She perched on the edge of the bed, her posture relaxing as if she hadn't been throwing a tantrum a short while ago. "I know you're human. I'm... half-blood."

"I know," I said. "And we've established that I didn't kidnap you, right?"

"Guess not." Her gaze darted from the discarded blankets in the corner to the battered rucksack in which I'd transported most of my belongings here. "This is your room?"

"Yes, but my housemates don't know you're here," I said. "I think they're out."

If they'd been in, they'd have banged on my door in annoyance when they'd heard her screeching. As it was, I knew better than to think they'd react with anything other than hostility to her presence, and I doubted Roseanne would want to know the other half-faeries had turned me away from leaving her in their care either. What to do with her?

"Okay." She fidgeted with the hem of her coat, which looked rather ragged. "We're in Scotland, right?"

"Last I checked." Where'd she even come from? She must have been living under the radar for a while if she'd heard of my mother's attempt at domination but not that the Gatekeepers had broken the curse, but she'd clearly been in dire straits even before the redcaps had captured her. "Are you hungry?"

She looked at me with bright eyes. "Starving."

"That I can help with." I walked out of the room and led her downstairs to the shared kitchen. "Better grab something to eat before the mercs come back in from their latest mission."

As I heated up some soup for both of us, I tried to figure out my next move. She wasn't hurt, which at least meant I wouldn't have to find a healer willing to deal with a half-fae shapeshifter, but she had nothing but the clothes on her back and was also a minor. A human orphanage wouldn't take her, while the half-faeries would never act behind Blaine's back and take her in even if they didn't care about her parentage. Maybe her survival odds would be better in Faerie, provided the Morrigan actually wanted her half-human offspring around, but that was debatable. She might not have even *met* her before.

I, on the other hand, had spent enough time delivering messages between the Morrigan and the Unseelie Queen to be reasonably confident that I wouldn't have any trouble getting an audience with the queen of the death fae. Whether she'd be willing to listen to me was another matter entirely.

I divided the soup between bowls and found that Roseanne had already devoured half the loaf of bread I'd put on the table. Picking up my own spoon, I sat opposite her. "You're English, aren't you? Why'd you come all the way up to Edinburgh?"

She spoke a few words indistinctly, swallowed her mouthful, and then said, "Wanted a change of scenery. Didn't count on the redcaps being here too."

"They're everywhere." I blew on my spoonful of soup to cool it down. "Where were you staying?"

She shrugged. "Around. I've moved to a new place every day. It was bad luck they caught me. I'm usually careful to put iron down to stop the faeries breaking into my hiding place."

I looked down at my soup bowl, guilt gnawing at me.

What kind of a life was that for a teenager to live? And Blaine Reyes had acted like *she* was the one I was supposed to be afraid of. Honestly.

Seeing my face, she frowned. "What?"

"Nothing." I scooped more soup out of the bowl. "You won't be seeing those redcaps again, anyway. I handed the survivors over to the authorities at the local mercenary guild."

"You're a merc?"

"Kind of," I said. "Mostly, I track down faeries who are breaking the law and report them to the authorities. If they're messing around with humans, I make sure they aren't able to do the same again."

Her brow wrinkled. "Why?"

"Because I have the Sight." That was the easy answer. "Not many humans can claim that."

The longer answer to her question was that I had a sense of obligation. After all, I'd spent a lifetime serving the very faeries who'd tormented humans for amusement, and the least I could do was make this realm a tiny bit easier to survive in.

"Guess not." She fidgeted in her seat. "I try to avoid them, but they always find me."

"Yeah… same." When you could see the faeries, it was almost impossible to hide that fact, and losing my Gate-keeper's mark hadn't made me less of a target for their mischief. Besides, it wasn't like I was remotely suited for any other career, since being the Winter Gatekeeper didn't come with the kind of skills one could use to retrain for any other job. My cousin Hazel had yet to find permanent employment, too, though the ex-Summer Gatekeeper at least had a normal family willing to help her out. My mother had been my only surviving close relative, and it'd been more than a year since she'd turned herself into a wraith to get back at the faeries for cursing our family and then made a second return from death to assist in an attempted coup against the Courts.

Really, it was no wonder I'd pitied the Morrigan's daughter. A harbinger of death and disaster was the perfect match for someone like me.

Once she'd finished devouring her food, Roseanne sprang to her feet. "What're you doing now?"

"Do you want to come and see the Morrigan?" I asked. "I meant it when I said I can take you there. Not easily, mind, but it's possible."

"No." She slumped back in her seat. "I don't want to see her. She said… she told me she never wanted a half-human kid."

That sounded like the Morrigan. "Then do you have anyone else who can help you out? I can't keep letting you stay in my room. If my landlord finds out, we'll both be in the shit, and my housemates will be back soon."

Someone hammered on the door, making Roseanne jump. "Is that them?"

"Better hide upstairs." I put the bowls in the sink. "I guess one of the mercs managed to get his keys eaten by a troll again."

Roseanne hurried back to my room and closed the door behind her while I went to answer the door. On the doorstep, I found a vaguely familiar half-faerie with bright-green eyes, tawny skin, and cropped dark hair. I'd seen him at Blaine's place before, and I groped around in my memory for his name. Brook? That sounded right, but

I couldn't begin to guess why he'd pay me a visit. Unless… he'd come to help Roseanne?

"Are you Holly Lynn?" he asked.

"Yes. Why?"

"You visited Blaine Reyes yesterday, did you not?" Without pausing for breath, he added, "He's dead. He was stabbed to death last night."

Ah… shit. "Who killed him? Not the redcaps?"

"Redcaps?"

"I found them on a mercenary job," I responded. "Not many survived, but the ones who did were taken in by the authorities yesterday."

"Nobody mentioned redcaps," he said, "but you were one of the last people to see him alive, so I wondered if you saw anything odd at his house."

"Not that I recall." Faeries could be bloodthirsty, but the guy rescued abandoned orphans, for the Sidhe's sakes. Who'd want to bump him off? He might have rejected Roseanne, but he'd acted out of concern for his fellow fae, not malevolence. "Might help if you were a bit more specific."

He gave a half shrug. "I don't know. Death fae, maybe. The killer got into his house without opening the door."

The memory of his words about the Morrigan's kid being a bad omen hit me like a blow. She'd been unconscious in my room all night, but if he'd mentioned her to any of the other half-faeries, they might have drawn their own conclusions about the timing of his death.

"Well…" I paused. "I thought someone was watching me from the bushes when I went to his house, but I figured it was just a piskie."

"Might have been," he said. "Come see me if you

remember anything else. I'm his apprentice, but I couldn't get anyone official to come and look into his death. The local authorities said fae murders aren't their area."

That figured. Most humans harboured a not-undeserved fear of the fae, and while a human's death at their hands might merit an investigation, the local police wouldn't see the stabbing of a local half-Sidhe at the hands of another fae as any different to those redcaps bathing their caps in one another's blood. "Tell you what, I'll drop by in a bit and see if there's anything I missed. Give me an hour, and I'll be there."

"Cheers." His sad gaze met mine. "I think you might be the only human who gives a shit about him."

I made a mental note not to mention our argument yesterday while I closed the door. Glad my human housemates weren't currently home, I ran upstairs to put some proper clothes on and brush my hair while Roseanne took a much-needed shower. After leaving her some of my old clothes to change into and warning her not to go near the mercs' rooms, I grabbed my shoes and coat and left for half-blood territory.

A number of half-faeries had gathered near the gate I'd entered through the night before, around Blaine's house. I didn't see any law enforcement, but the faeries were typically left to police their own unless they did something egregious enough to draw the local Mage Lords' attention. I walked past curious half-faeries from both Summer and Winter until I came to Blaine's house.

Nobody had closed the front door, so anyone who got within sight of the doorway could clearly see the body lying in the hall. Blood splattered the pale wallpaper behind Blaine's head, while the bone was visible through the gaping slash in his throat. Meanwhile, sprawling dark lines covered part of his face and neck, drawn in ink and not blood. I'd have noticed last night if Blaine had tattoos covering his neck and face. No, they were fresh, spreading from his throat to part of his exposed chest where his shirt had been torn open.

I veered through the gate, ignoring the elbowing, jostling crowd, and halted in the doorway to squint at the odd swirling markings on his skin. Those were witch symbols, the sort used in sacrificial magic.

Had someone slit his throat in a sacrificial ritual? It'd explain why Brook had mentioned the possibility of the dark fae being involved, but if his life had been taken in order to summon some ghastly beast from the dark realms between Faerie and Earth, it'd have rampaged through the city, leaving a trail of devastation which would be impossible to overlook. No shadowy beasts lurked in the shadows of the house. No hellhounds feasted on Blaine's dead flesh. The ink was wet, fresh, but its purpose remained inscrutable.

A hand snagged my elbow. "What are you doing in here, human?"

"Hey!" I dug my heels in, but a burly Summer half-Sidhe with a scar on his face yanked me out of the doorway. "What the hell, Sal?"

"You took in the child," he said. "Didn't you? The harbinger."

I suppressed a groan. Of all the people to find out about my unplanned visitor, it had to be a hothead like Sal Heywood, who was related to Blaine via some distant cousin or other. "She was unconscious until an hour ago. I couldn't leave her on the streets, Sal."

"She's a death fae," he said. "And that murder is the work of dark magic."

"It wasn't her," I said. "There's no way. Even if she hadn't been with me the whole time, those markings aren't a faerie's work."

His distrustful gaze raked over me. "Only a faerie could have got past the glamour on our territory."

Good point. What faerie would use one of their own as a sacrifice, though? In all my years of experience with the fae, I couldn't recall ever encountering one who used sacrificial magic beforehand. "Those symbols are the work of a necromancer. Or a witch, I guess, but it's usually necromancers who get into the bad stuff."

"How'd you know so much?" said the half-faerie. "Been into the bad stuff yourself?"

"My cousin works for the necromancer guild," I said, refusing to be goaded. "I bet she's seen markings like those before."

In fact, her boyfriend was a faerie-necromancer, able to use both kinds of magic. For all I knew, the killer could, too, and that was how they'd bypassed the glamour on Blaine's house.

He shook his head. "I wouldn't advise it. Better to leave them out of it."

"You want to catch the killer, don't you?" He must do, surely. Blaine had been his family, and besides, I'd bet some of the other half-faeries wouldn't feel safe in their own territory until they figured out who'd turned on one of their own. "It's that, or I tell the mercs. If they put a bounty on the person who did this, then there's a bigger chance of the culprit being brought in."

"We don't want mercenaries sniffing around the place," said Sal. "Anyway, if I were you, I'd send that kid away."

"That was the plan," I said, "but she didn't kill him. She was with me all night."

Would my word alone count as evidence, though? Most half-faeries would never believe in the innocence of the Morrigan's daughter. Hell, if they knew what the Morrigan was capable of, most *humans* wouldn't either.

Dammit. I needed to talk to my cousin.

3

I walked away from the crime scene, searching my phone for Ilsa's number. I hadn't spoken to her since the time she'd let me tag along on a mission which had caused me to realise working for the necromancers was decidedly not for me, but she was one of the handful of people I knew who had the Sight *and* a working knowledge of necromancy.

Okay, that was an understatement. Ilsa was one of the most powerful necromancers in the guild and no doubt too busy to bother with a case like this one. Murders were only the business of the guild if the victim had *unfinished* business… or death magic had been involved. Which it might have, but that didn't mean the half-faeries would consent to let the necromancers into their territory. Not when the victim was a faerie and, by all accounts, the perpetrator was too.

Got a free minute to talk? I hit send on the message to Ilsa and tried to ignore the sense of foreboding gnawing at my insides.

To say Ilsa and I had had a difficult history was like saying the Winter Court was a bit chilly. Not only had our immediate families once been allied to opposing Courts, but Ilsa had been forced to claim a talisman which granted her the magic and title of Gatekeeper of Death in order to banish my mother's angry wraith into the afterlife. Since my mother had bound me to a vow which prevented me telling anyone what she'd done, Ilsa had logically assumed the two of us were mortal enemies. Frankly, it surprised me that she'd forgiven me so readily, but then again, she'd got the better end of the deal as the one Lynn whose magic had survived the breaking of the Gatekeeper's curse.

I slowed my pace when I reached the cobbled street leading down to the local necromancer guild, thinking over my story. I'd ask for her help looking into those symbols, but there'd be no need to mention the teenage harbinger of death currently living in my room. That part was my business alone, and I didn't need to complicate things any further.

I spotted Ilsa approaching me in the opposite direction, wearing the long black cloak which comprised the typical uniform of the guild over her jeans. She'd tied back her dark-brown hair and combed her fringe to hide the spiralling lines of the Gatekeeper's symbol on her pale forehead, but the faint glow drew my eyes all the same.

"Hey, Holly," she said. "What did you want to talk to me about?"

"I don't know if you heard, but a half-faerie was murdered this morning," I said. "On their own territory."

"No, I haven't." Her expression clouded with worry. "Why? Is the victim's ghost causing trouble?"

"Not that I know of, but…" I scrambled around for the right words. "A necromancer might have been the killer."

Her eyes widened. "Why would a necromancer kill a faerie?"

"Not just a necromancer but someone who can see through glamour," I said. "They couldn't have got into the house any other way."

Understanding crossed her face. "A faerie-necromancer, you think? I'll ask River to see if he knows anything when he gets back from his mission."

So he was out. That at least would give me a little time to shake together an explanation for the other half-faeries if I did decide to take him and Ilsa to have a look around Blaine's house. "There were markings on his body too. They looked kinda like… sacrificial magic."

Ilsa swore under her breath. "Sacrificial magic? You mean someone sacrificed the victim to summon something?"

"If they did, it didn't stick around," I said. "Is sacrificial magic more likely to be witchcraft or necromancy?"

"Either." Ilsa's forehead creased in the expression she typically wore when she tapped into her vast stores of knowledge on magical theory. "Sacrificial magic is on the cusp between necromancy and witch magic, though symbols are more frequently used by witches. If you can get me a picture of the marks, I can hand them over to Jas, and she'll ask her witch friends if they can figure out the symbols' meaning."

"Let's keep that idea on hold for now." Now I remembered why I avoided asking Ilsa's help. While she might be far more knowledgeable than I was, half her contacts were spread across the country. The last thing I needed was to bring more trouble down on half-blood territory. "There's a killer at large, and the authorities are unlikely to take any steps to bring them in, so I'd rather keep this between the two of us."

Her brow furrowed. "Why wouldn't the authorities pursue the killer?"

"The victim was a half-faerie." Did I need to spell it out to her? "The killer left no traces, so even if a case is opened, it'll end up gathering dust. It's not like any of us can afford to hire one of the mages, and most mercs won't work for faeries unless it involves hunting rogues."

"Don't you work for the mercs?" she asked.

"Not officially." I only did jobs which nobody else was qualified for, the sort that required the Sight, and had no desire to join in with the posturing and other bullshit my housemates were mired in. Besides, there was too much faerie-related baggage in my history, and I still didn't know what to do with the teenage harbinger of death who might well have got fed up waiting for me to come home and taken off by now. I wouldn't blame her if she had. "So you don't think the necromancers will be able to help at all?"

"Oh, I wouldn't say that," she said. "Even if it wasn't a necromancer who did it, we have one skill that witches don't."

"Meaning…?"

"We can summon him back from death, of course."

I cocked a brow. "You think the half-faeries will let you summon his ghost in the middle of their territory? Do you think the *guild* will?"

Her lips pursed. "It doesn't have to be in the middle of their territory, but the longer that passes after his death, the lower the chances of summoning his ghost. Besides, I can theoretically do the summoning first and report later, since this isn't an official investigation. Not yet."

"Hey, if you're willing to bend the rules…"

"Don't make me regret it," she said. "First, we need a good place to do the summoning. Close to the scene of his death but away from witnesses."

"You can summon him that far away?" It must be another perk of being Gatekeeper of Death, because most necromancers had to practically be standing on top of a crime scene to call back the victim's unfortunate spirit.

"If I know his full name," she said. "Do you?"

"Sure." I could hardly believe I was agreeing to this, but no human authority or mercenary would think of summoning his ghost even if they actually wanted to get involved in a half-faerie murder investigation.

As for the Sidhe, they considered their half-human offspring as worthless as the rest of us mere mortals. Rather unfair, considering it was their dalliances with humans which caused the half-bloods' existence in the first place, but that was the Sidhe for you. They lured you into their palaces with promises of glory and then left you to rot in the dirt.

———

Ten minutes later, Ilsa and I stood beside a summoning circle comprised of twelve candles which my cousin dug out of the pockets of her coat.

"Does that thing have more than three dimensions?" I remarked as she arranged the folds of her coat.

"Sadly, no, but the designers deserve a pay raise." After

checking the candles were spaced at even intervals, Ilsa rose to her feet and snapped her fingers. All twelve candles lit themselves simultaneously, casting ghostly lights over her face as she spoke. "I summon you, Blaine Reyes."

For a moment, her words hung in the air, unanswered. Then a swirling current of smoke appeared within the circle, and the shimmering ghost of Blaine Reyes followed, identical to his living self aside from his new transparency and a shimmer that went beyond his silvery hair.

His gaze locked on me. "Holly Lynn? Back again?"

"Not exactly." *Please tell me he knows he's dead.* Ghosts often had trouble recalling their last moments. "What's the last thing you remember?"

"I don't..." He looked down at his transparent hands, and then panic flared in his eyes. "What happened to me?"

"You were murdered." I figured I'd get the bad news over with. "In fact, I think you were sacrificed."

"Sacrificed?" His eyes bulged, and if he hadn't been a ghost, I might have worried he was about to faint. "Why? How?"

"I hoped you might be able to tell us that." Ilsa stepped closer to the circle. "Can you tell me what you remember? Do you remember the moment of your death?"

Terror flickered through his gaze. "I can't. I can't..."

"You can't remember?" Ilsa asked. "We aren't going to hurt you. Nobody can."

What had scared him so much? I'd heard ghosts could be temperamental, but there seemed no obvious reason for this naked fear. Admittedly, getting murdered might have been scary enough on its own. "Do you remember seeing anyone in your house before you died?"

"No." He shuddered. "I remember... I woke in the night. I heard a noise. And then..."

"Then what?" asked Ilsa. "What did you see?"

"Nothing," he said. "I don't—remember."

A prickling sensation on the back of my neck made me turn my head. A breeze stirred a handful of leaves, blowing them down the street, past a figure watching us from a distance. A man with leaf-green eyes... which blinked once then vanished into the surrounding darkness as if they'd never existed.

I took a step back, and Ilsa glanced at me. "What is it?"

"Someone's watching us."

Ilsa's eyes widened. "Can you have a look? I can't remove the circle without banishing him."

"Sure." I ran to the street's corner, but the figure had disappeared long before I reached the shadows where I'd seen him. Nobody else remained in sight save for a lone jet-black bird perched on the cobblestones. As I took a step forward, the bird took flight in a sweep of wings, leaving nothing behind but a single black feather.

I studied the spot where it'd taken flight, part of me wondering if I was losing my grip. What were the odds that I'd run into two shapeshifter faeries in as many days? Did Roseanne have a sibling she hadn't told me about? No... the stranger's eyes had been vibrant green, not wintry blue.

Hadn't I seen a similar pair of eyes watching me from the bushes near Blaine's house last night?

After a moment's hesitation, I picked up the feather and carried it back to the summoning circle. To my dismay, Blaine's ghost had already vanished into the smoke, leaving only the candles behind.

Ilsa turned away from the circle. "Did you catch him?"

"No," I said. "I think he transformed into a bird and flew off."

"I should have tracked him through the spirit realm," she said. "I was too focused on the circle."

"Can you sense him now?"

"Wait a second." She held up a hand, her gaze turning vacant as she tapped into the senses which enabled her to see via the spirit realm. "No… no half-faeries in the area. If he flew off, he's beyond my reach."

"Great." I trod over to the circle. "Where'd the ghost go?"

"Timed out," she said. "He didn't let any more information slip about the murderer, but he had no recollection of those markings being drawn on him."

"So he *wasn't* a sacrifice?"

"I have no idea," she said. "Right now, I'm leaning towards no. If I knew which symbols had been drawn on him, I might be able to ask Jas for a more specific answer."

"If he wasn't a sacrifice, then someone who knew blood magic was involved in his death." I turned the feather over in my hand. "I'd like to know why someone was spying on our conversation with his ghost too."

"Want to use a tracking spell on that feather?" she asked. "Jas gave me some of her spare witch spells. They don't work on zombies, so you might as well take them."

"Cheers," I said. "Not sure if that guy was just a nosy bystander, but half-faeries aren't usually interested in watching necromancers at work."

Maybe I'd luck out and find the killer on the other end

of the tracking spell. Why else would someone be watching us? Unless... unless they were a spy for the Courts?

I shook off the thought. Why would the Court give a crap what I got up to? They'd washed their hands of me, and the feeling was mutual. No, this spy was acting alone, and I intended to track him down.

4

After Ilsa had departed, I examined the tracking spell, which resembled a bracelet made of green beads. I didn't have too much experience with witch-made spells, but this one was pretty straightforward. Laying the bracelet down on the ground, I flicked one of the beads, and it flashed bright green, followed by the others, while the bracelet expanded into a wider circle. I then tossed the black feather into the glowing lights before plunging my hands after it.

A vibrant green glow spread up my arms, and my vision tunnelled as an image filled my mind's eye, showing a cobbled street from above. The vision played without sound, and I flew down the road at a speed which might have alarmed me if I hadn't already suspected the fae spy had shifted into a bird. I followed the bird's path until it landed outside a building on a street corner with a gold-plated sign above the wooden door.

I squinted, trying to see the sign, but the vision faded until I found myself looking into the remains of the spell circle. The feather had vanished, the bracelet's beads collapsing into a fine powder. I had to hand it to Ilsa's friend Jas for creating a spell that even an amateur like me had been able to use.

I replayed the vision in my mind as I rose to my feet. While the streets looked different from ground level than they had through the eyes of a bird, I didn't find it too hard to retrace my flight's path until I found my way to a cobbled street lined with buildings which were mostly boarded up and abandoned.

Except, notably, for the one sitting on the corner. In the old world, it might have been a bank or office, with arched windows and the same worn grey facade as the rest of Edinburgh's Old Town. From the height of a human, I could read the gold-plated sign on the door, which said, The Goodfellow Detective Agency.

This had to be the place. "Goodfellow" had "faeries" written all over it, unless the owner was a fan of Shake-speare, but I'd already seen proof that the person I was following wasn't fully human, despite setting up shop outside of half-blood territory. I hadn't the faintest clue why a so-called detective would spy on us questioning a murder victim and then take off, but I kept one hand on my iron knife as I pushed the door open.

A faint bell tinkled as I entered a small room which contained a few pieces of plain wooden furniture and little else. Framed paintings adorned the pale walls, depicting woody clearings painted in Faerie's vibrant colours. As I walked, the paintings stirred to life, birds flitting across the sky, deer galloping into the bushes. *Nice glamour.* A much better job than those low-life redcaps had done… not that I'd be telling the owner *that* until I could be sure he wasn't the killer.

As I halted in front of the main desk, a tall man entered, the door opening and closing behind him with scarcely a motion. His eyes met mine, vibrant green with hints of gold, undeniably the same eyes I'd seen watching me from the alley near the summoning circle. The half-Sidhe's hair was autumnal coloured in strands of red and brown and gold, while his collared shirt and trousers were business casual, with no hints that he'd transformed himself into a bird to avoid being caught spying not long beforehand.

Seelie. A shapeshifter fae… with other potential hidden talents as well. I kept my hand on my knife as he studied me equally intently.

"Yes?" he said. "Can I help you?"

"You were spying on me." No point in beating around the bush. "Detective, are you?"

"Yes, I am," he said. "Did you want to hire me?"

Not if it was you I saw at the crime scene. My hand locked around the knife handle, and the smell of cut grass drifted across the room. The green of his eyes grew brighter, his magic reacting in anticipation of an attack. "Did someone hire you to investigate Blaine Reyes's murder?"

My question hung between us, unanswered, for a moment.

"I am sworn to protect my clients' privacy," he said. "Unless, of course, you have a confession to make."

So he wasn't going to outright admit to anything? Two could play at that game. "I can confess to helping my cousin to question the ghost of a murder victim and being rudely interrupted by a spy. Imagine my surprise when my tracking spell led me directly to you."

"Tracking spell," he said. "You're not a witch."

"Would it matter if I was?" I knew precisely what he was up to. His careful questions were intended to tease out the details of my own magical status and to figure out whether I was dangerous to him. I saw his gaze drop to the iron knife at my waist as he took me in, mentally pegging me as a mercenary. One with the Sight, anyway, because I doubted an ordinary person would have been able to stumble upon his place of work. To most eyes, it probably looked like an empty building.

A smile curled his lip. "Perhaps. Or not. You're human, yet you spend more time with the half-faeries than your fellow humans."

My shoulders tensed. How long had he been watching me? Detective or not, I intended to stop *that* as soon as humanly possible. Keeping my expression blank, I gave the room a cursory scan. "You don't seem to have many staff."

"I'm still hiring," he said. "I'm looking to expand my staff… and my client base."

Right. "Why Goodfellow, then? A joke? Or a nod to Shakespeare?"

"No, a family name."

My gaze snapped to his grinning face, and then the pieces slid into place in my mind. Who was the Summer Court's most notorious shapeshifter? "Puck? You're related to *him?*"

"The very same."

Damn. That would explain his unusual shapeshifting magic. I hadn't been able to recall any Summer Sidhe who could turn into crows, but Puck—aka Robin Goodfellow of the Seelie Court, the notorious prankster who'd caused trouble for the Sidhe for generations and whose legend had long outlived the man himself—could transform into anything at all. According to the legend, anyway. "I thought the original Puck disappeared."

"So the stories say," he said. "There's rather a lot of those. They say Puck can circle the earth in forty minutes and that even the Sidhe fear him."

"If that's the case, then this is a strange career choice." I indicated the room in general. "A detective, I mean. Among humans."

"I only see one human in this room, and she walked in of her own accord."

"Because you were spying on me." With that reminder, I forced my curiosity about how and why he'd come here to the human realm aside. He and I had another matter to settle. "While I was questioning a victim of a murder you won't admit to being involved with."

"Did you have permission to question his ghost?" he queried. "I wouldn't have thought the local half-faeries would have been inclined to allow a necromancer to speak to the ghost of one of their dead companions."

"You speak as though you aren't one of them." I'd had about enough of his mind games. "Which, if you aren't, I'd advise you to think twice before accusing *me* of going against their desires."

His smile was back. "Very well. Let us start our acquaintance again and try to refrain from any misunderstandings this time."

"You want me to forget seeing you spying on me?" I said incredulously. "Yeah, no. That's not going to work.

Even if you *are* a detective someone hired to investigate Blaine's death, sneaking up on his ghost is dubious at best."

"That was not my intention," he said. "I sought to speak with you anyway, but I little expected to find you two conducting necromancy on the victim. I confess to watching out of curiosity in order to see what you did."

He expected me to believe that bullshit? "You wanted to speak to me… why?"

"I heard you knew the victim," he said. "In fact, I heard you were one of the last people to speak to him before his death."

"Who told you that, Sal Heywood?" The scumbag. If *he'd* hired this guy, then I wouldn't put it past him to have passed on all his suspicions about me… and about Roseanne. "I spoke to Blaine last night. Then I went home. Anyone who was watching half-blood territory at the time can attest to that."

Like the person I'd seen watching from the bushes, for instance.

"You weren't accused," he added, "though I confess seeing you speak to his ghost made me wonder what he might have told you. Perhaps you and I might be of use to one another."

I tilted my head on one side. "You want to probe me for information, is that it? You're out of luck. The ghost didn't remember his death. If you *are* officially involved in an investigation, then you'll have to look elsewhere."

"Or you and I can agree to a partnership."

I narrowed my eyes. "Very funny."

"Not a joke," he said. "I think the two of us could make more headway if we worked together."

My gaze skimmed his face, which remained inscrutable. "What's in it for you? I told you everything I know."

"Not everything," he said. "Besides, it's not every day you meet a human with the Sight... and with a family member in the necromancer guild too."

Seriously? He didn't even know my name yet. "I'm not looking for a partnership with anyone, but I'm sure at least one of the other half-faeries will be happy to work with you."

Assuming you aren't the killer.

"If you change your mind, then feel free to drop by at any time."

"I doubt I will." It was bad enough that he knew Ilsa worked for the guild. I made a mental note to warn her in case he started hassling her as well. "What should I call you?"

"Call me Puck," he said. "And you?"

"Holly." I was already walking away from him, wishing I'd come here with a better plan. I'd hardly expected him to offer a partnership, but he was doubtless working some kind of trickery. Wasn't that what he was best known for? If I got involved with him in any capacity, I'd wind up with a horse's head affixed to my neck. No thanks.

Out of any other ideas, I headed home. At the house, I unlocked the front door and found my two mercenary housemates in the living room. They'd come back from their mission, and from the menacing expressions which crossed their faces when they spotted me, they'd learned of my visitor. In unison, they rose to their feet and sloped into the hallway to block my path. Two six-foot-something dudes with bulging muscles and the scars of mercs who'd taken too many risks were a terrifying sight to most, but it was hard to be frightened of regular people after the damage I'd seen the fae inflict upon humans.

"Hey," I said to them. "Can I get past?"

"You have a faerie kid in your room," said Maurice, who usually went by the name Meathead. "I saw her."

"I know," I said. "I saved her from redcaps yesterday, and I got called out on an urgent mission before I had the chance to figure out where to take her. She's an orphan." By human standards, anyway. I doubted it would help matters if I mentioned her mother was the queen of the death fae.

"She raided all our cupboards in the kitchen," said his buddy, Train. I had zero idea where his nickname came from and even less desire to know. "So you'd better get her outta here."

"I will." As if his mates didn't come over and raid the kitchen all the time, including *my* cupboards. "I'll pay you back."

"I hope you do," said Meathead. "The landlord doesn't allow faeries to stay here, y'know."

"I'm aware of that." I folded my arms, my hand inches from the hilt of my blade. "She's a visitor, not a paying guest. Can you please let me upstairs?"

I didn't generally need to resort to threats. The pair of them might collectively possess the common sense of a troll on a bloodthirsty rampage, but they knew another killer when they saw one, and they didn't need to see me at work to know crossing me would end badly for the pair of them. Sure enough, they exchanged brief glances then left the hallway without another word.

I sidestepped them both on the way to the stairs,

making a mental note to hand over the cash for the food as soon as I figured out how much Roseanne had taken. Reaching the landing, I opened the door to my room and found the Morrigan's daughter napping on my bed. For some reason, I felt a rush of relief to see she hadn't left, but when I saw the number of food wrappers littering the floor, I could guess why the mercs were so mad at me.

Her eyes opened when I closed the door behind me. "Where were you?"

"I had to run a couple of errands." At her expression, which suggested she didn't appreciate bullshitting, I added, "The half-faerie I took you to yesterday was found murdered this morning. I did a bit of poking around to find out who might have been responsible and had a run-in with a wannabe detective."

"You're investigating a murder?" She sat up eagerly. "Are you hunting down the killer yourself?"

"Not exactly," I said. "It's complicated. I'm not officially involved."

"But it's your job, right?"

"No… well, I deal with rogue faeries, but I have no idea what kind of fae the killer was."

My phone buzzed with a message from Ilsa, asking if I'd successfully found our spy yet. I'd intended to send her an update, but frankly, I had no idea where to start. How could I summarise Puck's offer in a mere text message?

"Who's texting you?" asked Roseanne.

"My cousin," I relented. "She wants to know about the detective I ran into. I promised to send her an update."

"Tell me everything." She sat expectantly on the bed while I typed out a vague message to Ilsa. "I want *all* the details."

I might have had second thoughts about sharing sensitive information with a kid, but my patience had all but eroded after my encounter with Puck, and despite his offer, I highly doubted I knew anything he didn't. Except for those markings possibly being linked to sacrificial magic. Ilsa had mentioned her friend Jas being able to translate the runes on the body, but I couldn't draw them from memory.

After dashing off a vague reply to Ilsa, I attempted to cobble together an explanation for Roseanne. "The victim's throat was cut, but everyone thinks a faerie was responsible because they'd need to be able to see through glamour to get into the house. That's all we know."

"And this detective?"

"He knows even less than I do," I said. "Not sure who hired him, but I told him to leave me alone, so he shouldn't be bothering me again."

I hope.

"So what are you going to do now?"

Good question. I sighed and looked down at the phone. "I need to have a look at the body again, but I bet they've moved it from the crime scene."

"Why d'you need to look at it?" she asked.

"There were marks on the body that my cousin's witch friend might be able to read." I turned off my phone and pocketed it.

Roseanne's shoulders slumped. "You're off *again?* You just got here."

"This'll be the last chance I'll have to get near the crime scene," I said. "The markings might point to who killed him."

"What if they already closed off the crime scene?" she asked. "Or took the body away?"

"I can get in if need be."

"Without getting caught?" She raised a brow. "I can get through small windows in my bird form, you know. You'll need a lookout."

Maybe… and the rate at which she was hoovering up all the food in the kitchen made me want to figure out a way for her to earn her keep. My resolve cracked. "Roseanne, want to come with me to see a dead body?"

She grinned. "Yes, please."

5

My offer put Roseanne in such a good mood that I had to warn her to tone it down when we got to the crime scene so as not to arouse suspicion. She shifted into a bird and flew out the window in order to dodge my housemates while I went downstairs and handed them enough cash to make up for the missing food. I'd have to live cheaply for a bit, but Roseanne's delight was amusing enough to make it worth the hassle.

When she shifted into human form outside, I rolled my eyes at her. "Most people don't get excited about visiting a crime scene."

Then again, she was a death faerie. They were about as morbid as the average necromancer. Roseanne shot me a pointy-toothed grin. "I want to catch the killer. I bet it's a shapeshifter."

Puck came to mind, but he wouldn't have taken the detective job if he was the person responsible for Blaine's death, would he? "I don't know. My cousin contacted

Blaine Reyes's ghost, and he didn't remember anything from his death."

She gasped. "Your cousin's a necromancer? That is *awesome.*"

"Not sure I'd use that word," I said. "Anyway, she's decided against telling the rest of the necromancer guild since the other half-faeries won't be happy, so try to avoid mentioning it."

"I'm not a snitch," she said. "I won't tell anyone."

I had no doubt she'd keep her word, or at least try to. She might be a kid, but she understood Faerie better than most teens her age. I trusted her a damn sight more than one of the descendants of Robin Goodfellow—that was for sure.

"Good," I said. "I just need to make sure we aren't going to run into any trouble with the other half-faeries. I'd rather nobody spotted us either."

Roseanne bounded alongside me. "Are those markings on the body related to necromancy, then? Is that why your cousin called his ghost?"

"My cousin thinks they're related to witchcraft or dark magic," I said. "She asked me to take a picture to send to her witch friend. That's why I need to see the body again."

"A witch killed him?" asked Roseanne. "I thought a faerie did it."

"So did I, which is why I want to know what the marks mean."

Blaine had died when his throat had been cut, of course, but it wasn't impossible to assume that the killer had drawn the marks on his body to cast a spell for another purpose. To throw us off the trace, possibly, but the person who'd drawn the marks must have known their meaning, surely. Blood magic wasn't something you screwed around with for fun.

Near the entrance to half-blood territory, I waited for Roseanne to shift into a bird before I found the thorny gate near Blaine's house and entered. Already, I could see the crowd had dispersed, everyone having gone home, and the door to his house was closed on the bloodstained hallway. Had they already moved the body?

As I beckoned, Roseanne flew to my shoulder, and I whispered, "Can you see if the body is in there?"

She let out a short *caw!* Wings flapping, she flew around the side of the house and circled it from behind before returning to me. A shake of her bird-head confirmed my suspicion.

"They must have taken him to the morgue," I murmured. "I know where that is."

The half-faeries' morgue sat on the far side of half-blood territory, an area most of them tended to avoid due to their prevailing fear of death in any form. Roseanne flew overhead while I walked down the winding path between trees which were in the process of shedding their autumn coating. Winter's magic had begun to creep into their territory with the changing of seasons, and fallen leaves dappled the path while birdsong filled the air and gave the impression of us being in remote woodland rather than the middle of the city. That was faerie magic for you. As pretty as nature and red in tooth and claw along with it.

Roseanne's crow form flitted from one tree to the next, occasionally disturbing a sleeping dryad which awoke with an aggrieved noise and tried to poke us with its branches. Just when I'd started to wonder if we'd picked the wrong direction, the temperature rapidly dropped as we came upon a square building nestled among the trees. The chill of Winter magic emanated from its walls, not surprising when the Unseelie drew strength from death energy. Not that anyone wanted to acknowledge that awkward fact aloud, which was why they housed the bodies of their dead in the middle of the woods.

I spotted a couple of security trolls and ducked behind a tree to avoid their patrol before retrieving a lock pick from my pocket. Once they'd passed out of sight, I tracked down the morgue's back entrance and picked the lock on the door, ducking under low-hanging branches as I crept into the darkness.

Roseanne flitted into the corridor behind me, but the absence of any light masked her from sight and made it impossible to tell where I was going. I'd bruised every limb on the hard stone walls before I found myself in a dimly lit room containing several long tables.

On each table lay a body of someone recently dead, preserved by Winter magic which encased them in ice which never melted. Blaine was easy to spot even with ice covering his face, which remained frozen in an expression of mild surprise, as though he'd begin moving again the instant the spell wore off. Shivering in the chill, I raised the camera of my phone to point at the symbols on his neck and chest which were visible through the ice, the inky lines black against his pale skin and hair.

After snapping several photos, the job was done. I retraced my steps to the back door, waiting for the security trolls to trudge past before slipping outside. I held the door open for a few seconds to allow Roseanne to fly out in bird form then closed it behind us.

I was just congratulating myself on my stealthy mission when a rustling noise alerted me to another person nearby. I tensed, preparing myself to face an aggrieved security troll, but instead, none other than Sal Heywood lurked in the nearby bushes. "What are you doing here?"

I racked my mind for an excuse and drew a blank. "I was looking for Blaine's body, but the crime scene was empty. I thought—"

"You broke into the morgue?" he said.

"I wanted to take a look at the symbols on his body, and nobody else was around to ask," I said. "I know someone—a witch—who might be able to identify the symbols."

"Keep the local covens out of this one."

You might have to worry about the necromancer guild, not the covens. I decided not to voice that part aloud, instead saying, "I won't let word spread beyond a couple of trusted individuals. Unless you know an expert on sacrificial witch magic?"

"Nobody said anything about sacrifices." His gaze fixed on a spot over my shoulder, where Roseanne sat on a branch. "You brought the harbinger with you to see his body?"

Ah, crap. I hadn't known he'd recognise her in her crow form. "She's been staying with me for the past day since nobody else would take her in. Including Blaine, for that matter."

"She's a bad omen," he said. "If you ask me, her presence caused his death."

"Don't be absurd," I said. "That's paranoid superstition and nothing more. She was with me when Blaine died."

"She's a harbinger of death," he said. "Even if she isn't the direct cause, misfortune follows her wherever she goes."

"You'll get plenty of that from me if you don't quit badgering her." I folded my arms. "She's a kid. Knock it off and leave her alone."

Sal shot her a glare. "That's not a kid; it's a killer in the making. Mark my words."

I took a step towards him, but Roseanne took flight in a shower of feathers and vanished into the canopy. "Harbinger or not, she's only a teenager, and it's not like Faerie is a shape-shifter-free zone. Unless spending too much time around humans has turned you against your own kind."

"How dare you?" Outrage twisted his features, the green light in his eyes brightening. "I should have *your* human visage turned into a permanent fixture here."

I reached for my knife. "Try me."

Magic blasted from his palms, and the nearest trees extended their sharp branches in my direction like grasping hands. I gave a diagonal slice with my knife, causing the branches to crumble into fragments, and he let out a furious hiss. "You dare to use iron against me?"

"You bullied a kid. I'd say you deserve what you get."

Roots sprouted from the ground at my feet, and I leapt back to avoid them. At one time, I'd have simply reached down and frozen his plants at the roots, but now, I had to awkwardly dance around them in order to get within striking range.

Still, it was worth it to hear his roar of fury when my

fist slammed into his nose. Blood spurted everywhere, and while my hand smarted from the pain, the explosion of blood knocked the fight straight out of him. "Back off, or I *will* use the iron next time around."

"What seems to be the problem?" asked a voice.

We both turned towards the newcomer as none other than Puck himself walked into view. How long had he been listening in? Long enough to form an opinion, evidently. I took a pointed step back, while Sal let his roots sink back into the earth, holding his bleeding nose with a hand.

"You're back early," he rasped at Puck.

Wait, they knew one another? Had Sal asked him to look into the murder? *I knew I was right not to trust the guy.*

"I thought it wise to tell you that Holly is working with me on the case," Puck said. "In case she neglected to mention that."

I stiffened. *So he is officially involved in the case?* More to the point, Sal Heywood had hired him? The burly half-faerie lowered a hand from his bleeding nose, his eyes roving over me. "That seems to be news to her."

"Nevertheless, it's true," said Puck. "I thought you two might appreciate my intervention before one of you got hurt."

Sal's face flushed. "I wasn't going to harm her. She shouldn't have walked into the morgue through the back door if she was working officially."

"Holly likes to live dangerously."

I shot Puck a warning look, but his attention was on Sal. Holding a hand to his bleeding nose, the half-faerie growled, "Don't do it again."

In a heartbeat, he vanished, leaving nothing but several droplets of blood behind him.

My gaze returned to Puck. "I had that under control."

"Of course you did." His brow quirked in amusement. "What were you doing, breaking into the morgue to look at the body?"

I scowled. "If you want a look yourself, then go right ahead."

"I don't think I need to if you got the information I need," he said.

"You're that confident I'll share with you?"

"Allow me to make a guess," he said. "The body was marked with odd symbols, resembling witchcraft or something of the sort?"

"How in the name of the Sidhe do you know that?" I said, disarmed.

"Because it's the third body in a week that's shown up with those markings on it," he said. "I can talk my way into the morgue if necessary, to see if they compare with the others, but I'm guessing you already have a picture."

"The third body?" I echoed. "Who were the other two?"

A smile played on his mouth. "Ah, now you're interested in what I have to say?"

My throbbing hand itched to give him a bleeding nose to match Sal's. "I'm interested in getting you off my back, but if this is the third murder in a week, we're looking at the work of a serial killer."

"Then let me propose an exchange of information," he said. "We both want something from the other. It should be an even trade, no?"

"You're making a lot of assumptions," I told him.

"Besides, you might trust my information, but I have no reason to trust yours."

"I can assure you that I keep my word."

If he'd been any other half-faerie, I might have believed him. Faeries tended to be true to their word, since while half-faeries could lie and the Sidhe could not, many of them acted as if the same rules bound them. Could I really take the word of a notorious trickster, though? "You want to swear a vow?"

Instinct yelled at me not to even consider the possibility. I'd escaped one faerie vow, which was more than most humans could claim.

"I'd prefer not to go to those lengths, but if it's necessary to satisfy you…" He trailed off suggestively.

"It isn't." I didn't need to be entangled with his so-called detective agency any more than I already was. "Look, I have enough allies. I don't need a partnership with a stranger as well."

"Yes, you have your necromancer cousin," he said. "Does she know the meanings of those symbols on the body, I wonder?"

"She has a witch acquaintance who can identify them." I was putting a lot of pressure on Jas and whoever her other witch friends were, but this guy was pushy as hell, and his insistence on dragging me into a partnership made me want to ditch the case and go after another redcap gambling den instead. "What do *you* get out of this, anyway?"

"Paid."

"That's not all there is to it." I was sure he knew more than he let on about these murders. He wouldn't be so cryptic with me if he didn't.

"My motives are my own, but I might share them with you if you tell me what you know."

I worked my jaw. I knew it was a bad idea to put any level of trust in him, but he knew of the other two deaths, and I doubted the other half-faeries would be inclined to share information as readily. "I'll take it under consideration."

"How long do you need?" he asked. "I imagine that the next body will show up in another day or two, given the timeline of the others, and if we put our minds together, we might be able to prevent another victim's death."

My brows shot up. "Guilt-tripping, are we?"

"Simply making an observation," he said. "I would add that I haven't been able to work out the nature of the killer myself, but the two of us together might be able to come to a conclusion."

If we found out the meaning of those symbols, then there was a possibility. Problem was, if he turned out to be right about the likelihood of another body showing up soon, then our time was limited.

"Give me your phone number," I said. "If I decide to share what I know, then I'll send you the same image I sent my cousin."

A gleam entered his eyes. "I accept."

Of course, I had to actually get my phone out then. He recited his number, which I inputted into my phone's contacts. "Done."

He gave a nod. "I'll hear from you later."

"Or not," I muttered under my breath, already turning away. I hadn't agreed to anything, but I felt like I'd lost a bet all the same.

I walked the rest of the way through the forest in a

foul temper, resisting the impulse to go and throw another punch at the dickhead who'd chased Roseanne off. I held on to the slim hope I'd find her at home, but there was no sign of her in my room in bird or human form. The mercs had gone out, but it looked like they'd got their wish after all.

Thanks a lot, Sal. He'd driven away the one person who'd seemingly been happy to spend an extended length of time with me without expecting anything in return. Kind of pathetic, since for all I knew, she'd only stuck around because I fed her. She was a teenager, after all.

I texted a photo of the markings on the body to Ilsa for her to pass on to her witch friends before eyeing Puck's new profile in my phone. He'd given me an offer that I'd be a fool not to consider. The odds of running into a half-faerie detective who happened to want to associate with me were low enough that I'd wonder if this was some kind of trickery if I hadn't seen the whole set-up for myself. I could do worse than see what evidence he had to show me. If he *was* pulling one of his notorious pranks on me, it could hardly be worse than anything I'd run into in the Winter Court.

After a long pause, I sent the image to Puck, too, hoping I wouldn't regret my decision.

6

In the middle of the night, I woke up to the sound of scratching against the window. My gaze picked out a dark, feathery shape in the shadows outside, scraping a claw on the glass pane.

No way. Half-sure I was dreaming, I pushed the window open, and the crow shook out its feathers and entered the room, shifting into Roseanne midway through and landing on my bed.

"Roseanne?" I whispered.

"Your windowsill is covered in iron fragments," she said indignantly, scattering feathers everywhere.

"Ah, sorry," I said. "It's to stop redcaps murdering me in my sleep. I didn't think you were coming back."

She shrugged one shoulder. "It's not fun sleeping outside."

"I guess it isn't." I wasn't dreaming. She'd actually come back. "Especially in the cold."

"I'm a Winter faerie." She flopped over onto the blankets I'd left out on the floor from where I'd slept the previous night. "I can't feel the cold."

"Nah, you can," I said. "You tolerate it better. Doesn't mean you can't feel it."

She blinked at me and yawned. "I dunno what that means."

It made sense to me, but then again, I was half-asleep. As I watched, bemused, Roseanne curled up and fell asleep at the foot of my bed.

I did my best to suppress the smile that threatened to spring to my mouth. Getting attached was a bad idea. I *knew* that. I also knew a kid her age was one push from flipping over to the wrong side and becoming one of the monstrous harbingers the other half-faeries already thought she was. She was resilient, but if her trust in me was any indication, she still possessed a kid's sensitive naivety. I didn't need to be the one to shake it out of existence, not when I remembered all too clearly how it had felt when life repeatedly kicked me down and yet the person who was supposed to be my protector was nowhere to be seen.

Letting Roseanne sleep, I checked my phone. No messages had shown up yet, but Ilsa was doing me a massive favour in getting those witch symbols checked out, considering I already owed her a debt I wasn't sure I'd ever be able to repay.

In the meantime, I did my best to fall back to sleep—and not think about the other unanswered message on my phone.

———

Roseanne and I were eating breakfast when my phone buzzed with a response from Puck. *Come to the office at 11. Bring the bird.*

Bring the bird? He'd seen Roseanne himself, and he'd overheard enough of my conversation with Sal that he might have guessed her identity, but why would he assume she'd come back, much less that she'd want to meet him?

Did he know she was the Morrigan's daughter? If so, he'd implied he wasn't working alone, so for all I knew, he might have an ambush prepared for both of us. On the other hand, what would be the point? The Morrigan cared as little for her half-human offspring as most of the Sidhe did, and if he was aware of my history as Gatekeeper, then he'd know that I was worth less than nothing to the Winter Court. Taking us as hostages would be a waste of energy for everyone involved.

Roseanne raised a brow at me across the table. "You've been staring at your phone for the last minute. What is it?"

"Roseanne, how would you like to meet the detective?"

She blinked. "I thought you weren't working with him."

"Change of plans," I said. "He told me there were two other murder victims who were killed in the same way as Blaine, and he might have some insights to share."

"So you shared your photo of the body with him?" she guessed.

"My cousin already sent it to the witches, while the half-faeries all saw the body anyway," I pointed out. "The witches stand a better chance of figuring out what the symbols actually mean than he does, besides."

"If you say so," she said. "Sure, I'll come. If he doesn't want me around, I'll go somewhere else."

Her tone was a little too casual. While she hadn't brought up yesterday's incident with Sal Heywood, she'd started projecting a feigned indifference that hadn't been there before, as though she didn't want to seem too keen to stick around in case it caused me to drive her away.

I understood why she felt the need to do that, but I wasn't deluding myself into thinking I'd be able to let her stay in my room forever either. My housemates and landlord would make that impossible, but she needed somewhere safe to stay, and I of all people couldn't offer her that. Maybe I'd think of an idea while we were out.

On the way to Puck's office, I told Roseanne the little I'd learned so far about the trickster fae-turned-detective, and she gradually lost her air of nonchalance and became as curious as ever. Her eyes roved over the sign on the door to the small office on the street corner. "Goodfellow? Is that—?"

"His real name? Haven't a clue."

I knocked once before pushing the door open. Two fae greeted me on the other side of the door. Puck stood behind the desk, talking to another half-faerie with medium-brown skin and black shoulder-length hair, dressed in a plain white shirt with the sleeves rolled up and dark trousers. He swivelled towards the door when we walked in, the green flecks in his hazel eyes pinpointing him as another Summer fae. "Hey there. You're the new girl?"

"I'm Holly," I said before Puck could speak on my behalf. Then I gestured to my companion. "This is

Roseanne. I hear you have some information on the person who murdered Blaine Reyes?"

"Straight to the point, aren't you?" The other half-faerie strode over to me, all casual grace, and extended his hand. "I'm Hawk, joint owner of Goodfellow Detectives."

I shook his hand warily. "Are you a descendent of Robin Goodfellow too? Is that why you set up this place together?"

"Not exactly." He eyed Roseanne. "She's a minor, is she?"

"I'm old enough to be here," Roseanne insisted. "It's not like this is an official investigation, right? You're not with the police or anything."

"Not with the police, no," said Puck. "We're an independent agency hired to look into a recent spate of killings, which Holly is keen to learn all about. As for you..."

"You said to bring the bird," I pointed out.

"So I did," he said. "You're full of surprises."

"Speak for yourself," I said. "In case you've forgotten, you're the one who backed me into a corner."

Hawk's gaze slid to his friend. "What did you do to her?"

"Want a list?" I studied Puck's face, which remained inscrutable. "Didn't you mention how you spied on me—at least twice—and you lured me here by implying someone else would get murdered if I didn't share what I knew with you?"

Hawk's brow pinched. "Puck, you didn't, did you? We're on Earth, not in Faerie."

"That's where you got your gilded tongue, is it?" I

tilted my head. "When did you move to Earth? Last week?"

"Not that recently," said Hawk. "We both left at the same time, though, and we are not affiliated with anyone there."

Did he mean to reassure me they weren't spies for the Summer Court? I'd assumed the Sidhe would have little interest in anything that happened this side of the Ley Line anyway, but the detective façade was as convincing a front as those redcaps' shoddy glamour. "All right. Then tell me what you know."

"About the murders?" Hawk said. "To start off with, I'm sure Puck told you Blaine's death wasn't an isolated case."

"He's the third victim that we know of," Puck said. "The others were found outside of half-blood territory."

"Were the victims human, then?" I asked.

"No, they were all half-faeries," he said. "Not everyone lives on their territory. Case in point—us."

"The killer is targeting half-faeries, then," I concluded. "Do you have any more information on the other victims?"

Hawk held up a folder. "We have their info here, as well as photos of the marks on the bodies."

He laid down the folder on the desk and opened it, revealing several photos. Since Puck didn't stop me, I crossed the room to the desk and peered at the pictures, which showed two different bodies from various angles. One victim was female, one male, and both had been killed by a single deep cut to the throat. Similar marks to the ones on Blaine's body covered their necks and upper chests—swirling glyphs drawn in bold inky strokes.

"See anything?" Puck stood closer to me than I'd expected, and it took all my self-control not to startle when his hand rested beside mine on the desk, moving the photos aside.

My gaze landed on an image of the first victim, zoomed out so it was possible to see more of her surroundings. Blood spilled from the wound in her throat onto the carpet of what I assumed was her house, and beside the crimson stain was a smear that resembled a footprint belonging to some kind of large animal. Based on the size and shape, a fae beast commonly found sniffing around dead bodies sprang to mind: a hellhound.

I looked up to see Puck's curious gaze on me. "What is it?" he asked.

"Is that a footprint?" I squinted at the smudged blood-stain, assuming it'd have been cleaned up by now. Hellhounds were more commonly found in the Grey Vale or wandering around liminal spaces between the human realm and Faerie, but they'd originated in the Winter Court. And like similar beasts of that nature, they gained power from being near death.

He peered at the image. "Interesting... that's not a human footprint."

"Looks like a hellhound," I said. In Summer, he might not have encountered one of those monstrosities, but they weren't rare on this side of the Ley Line, especially when there was blood and death around. "They're death fae. Might have been drawn to the scene..."

Or sent there. Though why anyone would send a hellhound to a murder scene when they'd already slit the victim's throat was beyond me.

The sound of a phone ringing cut through the silence.

Puck took the call while I moved to Roseanne's side and showed her the picture. "See that? Does it look like a footprint to you?"

"Where?" She peered at the image. "Yeah, it does. What did that?"

"I'd guess hellhound."

Her eyes bulged as the implication sank in. Before either of us could say another word, Puck clicked off the phone and swore under his breath.

"What is it?" Hawk asked him.

"Another victim," he said. "Looks like we're going back to half-blood territory."

———

Puck and I walked down the road towards half-blood territory. Hawk had stayed behind to watch the office, while Roseanne followed the pair of us until we came within sight of the gate, at which point she shifted into a crow and flew into the branches of a nearby tree. I assumed she planned to watch from afar, which was probably a smart idea. When I spotted Sal among the crowd gathering on the path inside half-blood territory, I found myself glad she hadn't come in.

Not that I particularly wanted to talk to him myself, so I ducked through the crowd, trying to see who the newest victim was—nobody I personally knew, or so I discerned from the whispers among the anxious half-faeries near the victim's house.

I stood on tiptoe, my almost-five-foot-eleven height coming in useful for once, and saw a smear of crimson on the doorstep leading towards the man's body slumped in the hallway. The position of the bloodstain suggested that the attacker had either jumped their victim at the front door or had been chased out, but the outcome had ultimately been the same.

"He wasn't taken by surprise like the others," I said in a low voice so that only Puck could hear me. "He fought back."

"He did." Puck was a shade taller than me, but he could have shifted into his bird form and moved closer if he'd wanted to. Instead, he waited until a gap appeared in the crowd, allowing him to glide to the front as smoothly as a fish through water.

I stuck close behind him and was rewarded with a clear view of the victim. Another difference from the previous murders leapt out at me: this guy's throat hadn't been completely slashed open. The wide crimson line went at a jagged angle from his collarbone to his ear, as if he'd attempted to twist out of the way at the last second. More shallow cuts on his face and neck suggested he'd done his level best to dodge his attacker, but he'd ultimately bled out.

The symbols on his skin were smudged at the edges, some unfinished and lopsided. Did that mean they'd been drawn on him before or after his death? In sacrificial magic, the markings needed to be drawn before the victim perished in order to have any effect, but the killer's ambush approach seemed to have backfired in this case.

Sal edged in behind me. "Where's your creepy little harbinger friend?"

"Gone, thanks to you," I lied. "I hope you're proud that you successfully frightened off a child instead of catching the killer now that a fourth victim has been claimed without a single harbinger in sight."

"What are you implying?" he growled.

"I would have thought it would be obvious," Puck said smoothly. "To anyone with a smidgeon of intelligence, that is."

"Say that again, trickster," he said. "I hired you to work for me, remember?"

"And you verbally and physically attacked my assistant."

Assistant? The glare I levelled on him was equal to the one I sent in Sal's direction. "Get your priorities in the right order, both of you. I'm going to take a closer look at the crime scene."

Sal's objection cut off when Puck stepped into his path, and the pair of them began to converse in low voices. I left them to it, taking the chance to enter the victim's front garden and approach the bloodstained doorstep. Pulling out my phone, I snapped a couple of photos of the body. He'd definitely fought back, while the smudged tattoos implied the act had been interrupted. Had there been any witnesses? No, I assumed, or else someone would have reported the attack.

I cast a glance over my shoulder. Sal and Puck had finished speaking, and the former looked mollified, if not entirely pleased. Puck, meanwhile, glided towards me with a notepad tucked under his arm.

"So you do take notes," I observed. "Like a real detective."

"I'm blessed with a somewhat better memory than most, but yes."

"So modest." I rolled my eyes. "Did you want a closer

look at the body, or did you want to leave that to your *'assistant'?"*

"Is that not what you're doing?" he said. "You're assisting me, and I am doing the same to you."

Faeries. "We're business partners. I don't work *for* you."

"I assumed you'd object to that word too."

"I thought Hawk was your business partner."

"He is."

His answer didn't tell me much. I'd wondered if they might be partners in more than the work-colleague sense, but it was difficult to tell. Since most faeries didn't have the same odd hang-ups about gender and sexuality as some humans did, I tended not to make assumptions, but while their preferences varied widely and they tended to view gender as a secondary consideration when it came to picking a romantic or sexual partner, they were usually drawn to their own kind and not to humans. Of course, there were some exceptions, like Ilsa's boyfriend River, but a half-faerie working for the necromancers was already an anomaly.

Whatever the case, there was no reason whatsoever for Puck to readily assume I'd step into the role of his colleague when I knew next to nothing about him. "Are you done here?"

"Yes, I think I am." He turned away from the body and made his way through the thinning crowd. "What do you think, then?"

I waited to reply until we were out of earshot of the others. "You mean about the murder?"

"What else?" He wore an expectant look.

I drew in a breath. "I think he fought against his attacker. It didn't go as planned, at least at first, but the killer ultimately prevailed. I take it nobody reported any strange noises?"

"Strange noises? On half-blood territory?"

"No need for the sarcasm, trickster."

His jaw twitched at the word. "Don't call me that."

"I didn't know it was a secret." Perhaps his position among the other half-faeries wasn't as secure as I'd assumed. "Look, I realise that there's often nighttime disturbances in this part of the city, but you'd think someone would have noticed a violent murder. From the blood outside, the front door was open at the time."

"Yes," he said. "It was."

"You think the killer was someone from half-blood territory?" It wasn't impossible, though where they might have been educated on sacrificial magic was a mystery to me. "Better wait for more proof before accusing anyone."

"I thought we might have a word with the victim himself too."

I stopped midstep. "You want to talk to his ghost?"

"If your necromancer cousin is willing to help, of course."

That was still far too presumptuous for my liking. "She might not be able to go behind the guild's back twice in as many days. Besides, I thought you wanted to stay in Sal's good graces."

"Sal knows he has nobody else willing to help him look into these deaths." He pushed open the gate out of half-blood territory, and when we stepped outside, Roseanne's crow form flew down to meet us.

"I'm going to take my notes back to the office," he said. "Give me an hour. You can ask your cousin for help in the meantime."

"Don't count on her saying yes," I said. "For all I know, she's banishing a zombie on the other side of the city, besides."

"If you're that keen to come back to my office instead, Hawk for one would be delighted if you stayed for lunch."

"No thanks," I said before Roseanne could shift back to human form and agree to his offer. "I'll shoot Ilsa a message, but don't blame me if Sal finds out and kicks both of us off the case."

"He won't," he said. "Besides, I think we both know you won't let this case go until you have answers, Holly."

I didn't dignify that with a response, instead texting Ilsa, telling her there was another victim and that if she had time, I'd appreciate it if she came to meet me as soon as possible.

Roseanne fluttered her wings and let out a wordless *caw,* to which Puck raised his brows. "No need for that."

"You understand her in that form?"

"Birds are easier to understand than people are," he said. "I'll see you later."

I waited to be sure he was gone before heading home. I'd rather he didn't know my address, because I had my hands full keeping my housemates from reporting me to the landlord for Roseanne's presence in my room as it was.

She turned back into a human as soon as we reached my road. "What a twat. He thinks you're work partners now?"

"He thinks I'm his 'assistant,'" I corrected. "He's deluded—I'll say that much."

I didn't think he was the killer any longer, though, unless he'd called us to his office to act as an alibi for this latest murder. But it sounded like Sal of all people had originally hired him to look into the deaths. Hawk didn't give me serial killer vibes either.

Question was, why did they want my help? Neither of them had admitted to knowing anything of my former status as Gatekeeper, but if they thought I might still have links to the Winter Court, it would explain their reticence to share information. On the other hand, they must know I no longer had the magic of the Winter Court at my fingertips, because I doubted they'd have let me walk into their office otherwise.

I'd do some more poking around later. For now, it was time to summon another ghost.

7

Ilsa agreed to meet me in half an hour, so Roseanne and I went to grab lunch first. We then made our way to South Bridge to wait for her, but as soon as Ilsa's cloaked figure came into view, Roseanne shifted into a bird and took to the skies.

"Do you have any idea how hard it was to shake off the rest of my patrol?" Ilsa halted beside me, looking out at the overgrown remains of what had once been serviceable train tracks. "I had to pretend there was a zombie outbreak at Calton Hill and then *send* the zombies there myself to back up my point. It's an easy job to handle, but they'll be looking for a necromancer who doesn't exist for the rest of the morning."

"Unless they figure out you're the one who did it."

"They won't," she said. "Those newbies aren't the brightest. One of them somehow set their own hand on fire while setting up a summoning circle yesterday. Anyway, your friend isn't here?"

It took a moment for me to realise she meant Puck.

"No, he went back home. I wouldn't call him a friend either."

"Yet you're working with him?" she asked. "What changed?"

"He's the detective the half-faeries hired to look into the murders, so he has most of the information on the other victims," I explained. "I went to his office to look at his files on the first two deaths when he got the call about the latest, so we both went back to half-blood territory together. Today's victim, though… he was different. It looked like he fought back against his killer, so I hoped his ghost might be a bit more help."

"Worth a shot, I suppose." Ilsa's gaze drifted past Roseanne's crow form perching on the bridge nearby. I doubted she'd be judgemental in the slightest, but if Roseanne didn't want me to reveal her, I'd respect her wishes. I didn't blame her for being wary of meeting anyone new, though considering Ilsa's own official title was the Gatekeeper of Death, a teenage harbinger wouldn't scare her in the slightest.

Once we'd crossed the bridge and found a suitable alley tucked out of sight, Ilsa set out the twelve candles in a circle and then performed the same magic as before, lighting the flames with a snap of her fingers. Then she spoke the name of the victim.

In seconds, greyness filled the circle, and the tall half-faerie ghost appeared within, hovering amid the fog. His limbs blurred as he spun around on the spot, thrusting an invisible weapon at an unseen target.

"Whoa, calm down," I said.

He rotated on his heel, almost tipping out of the circle.

"Can't you see I'm being attacked? Won't one of you help me?"

"You aren't being attacked," Ilsa said in apologetic tones. "It's too late."

"What?" He looked down at the candles by his feet and lowered his hand. "Who even are you people?"

"My name's Holly Lynn," I said. "This is Ilsa. She's—"

"Gatekeeper." He lowered his hands, his expression hollow. "I'm dead, aren't I?"

"Who killed you?" I opted to jump straight to the point. "I know you fought back, so you must have seen them."

He'd been fighting in his moment of death, in fact... but in response, he shook his head. "It was too dark to see my attacker."

Bafflement crossed Ilsa's face. "It was light outside, wasn't it? Weren't you attacked this morning?"

"Your body was found in the hallway, and the front door was open," I added. "Did you see them outside? Is that why you opened the door?"

"No, I heard them first," he said. "Inside the house."

A chill raced down my spine. "Your body was covered in markings when we found you. Do you remember them being drawn on you? Did the killer do that before you died?"

"It's a blur." His gaze was distant, empty. "I remember hearing an odd noise and going to investigate. Then... then... pain."

His ghostly hand touched his collarbone, free of the marks which had covered his body in death.

Ilsa shuffled closer to the circle. "What did you hear, exactly?"

Grey fog swirled behind his eyes. "Death. Creeping closer... I tried to run, but they caught me before I could leave the house."

"Who caught you?"

"Death." His voice sounded quieter, yet the alley's narrow walls picked up the echoes all the same. "Closer... so cold..."

"Shit, he's fading out," Ilsa said. "Do you remember anything else about your killer?"

"Were they fae?" I ventured. "What do you mean by 'death'? From Winter or from the Vale?"

"Death rides among us." He gave a visible shudder, and then his body dissolved into the surrounding fog. Greyness swirled in circles, undisturbed.

I watched the glowing candles for a moment, but he didn't return. "That was weird."

"Hmm." Ilsa's gaze went distant, and then she shook her head. "Nothing. He's gone."

"He remembered his death, but nothing substantial enough to point to the perpetrator," I said. "Did the person who killed him meddle with his sight or memory?"

"Possibly," said Ilsa. "If they anticipated a necromancer might try to talk to his ghost... but there's a dozen ways a faerie serial killer can mess with someone's perceptions using glamour alone."

"Or those markings," I added. "Have you got an update on those symbols yet?"

"Not yet, but Jas is looking into them," said Ilsa. "She can pass on word to the local covens too."

"Are you sure they won't tell everyone?"

"They won't, but does it matter?" she asked. "It sounds

like most of half-blood territory knows there's a killer on the loose by now."

"None of them has a word to say on those symbols, as far as I know." Then again, Sal seemed to expect Puck to handle the entire investigation himself.

"I'll head back to the guild to ask Jas." She crouched down to retrieve the candles. "I'll text you if she has an update, okay?"

"Sure." After waving her off in the mouth of the alley, I returned to the bridge, where Roseanne's crow form waited. "Coast's clear, but Ilsa won't care who your mother is, you know."

Roseanne landed at my side, turning human again. "You can't know that."

"She's a necromancer who's spent her life tied to Faerie, and she's met the Morrigan herself," I said. "She of all people knows not to judge a person by the actions of their parents."

Not just faeries either. Case in point… my own warped immediate family. Roseanne's brow puckered, but all she said was, "Where are you going? Are you gonna tell Puck about the ghost?"

"If I don't, he'll text me asking for an update anyway," I said. "Besides, we didn't finish looking at the evidence earlier."

In truth, I didn't know what else to do with my afternoon, short of going home and spending the rest of the day dodging my housemates. The mercs tended not to post any new job opportunities on Sundays, so I'd have to wait until tomorrow for another opportunity to score some cash. I might not get much further with the murder investigation until Jas got back to Ilsa with the meanings of those symbols, but in the meantime, Puck would appreciate an update, and *I* would appreciate some answers from him as to his own motives in getting involved in this case.

Roseanne didn't object to my idea, though it might be because she wasn't keen on the idea of potentially running into my bad-tempered housemates either. In any case, she walked with me back to the street corner where Puck's detective agency stood. I didn't bother to knock this time around, simply opening the door to reveal Puck and his friend talking to one another over the desk.

"No, Hawk," Puck was saying, his tone oddly serious. "This isn't the same as… oh, hey, Holly."

His usual casual smile returned as if it'd never left, while Hawk's expression smoothed out, not quite fast enough to hide that they'd been having a disagreement of some kind.

I crossed the room to the desk. "The ghost was barely more helpful than the last one, but I figured you wanted to know anyway."

"Ghost?" Hawk's brows shot up. "You summoned a ghost?"

"My cousin did." I'd assumed Puck would have told him, unless he hadn't thought Ilsa would respond so quickly. "She's a necromancer at the guild. Anyway, the guy's memory of his death was patchy, because it went all dark beforehand, and he was effectively fighting without being able to see his opponent."

"Dark?" echoed Hawk. "A glamour?"

"Or caused by those marks," I said. "Ilsa has a friend looking into those, but it sounds like the attacker sneaked up on him inside the house, and he went to the door in an attempt to escape. Otherwise, all he said was that 'death rides among us.' Whatever *that* means."

Roseanne stiffened at my side. "He means a death fae is doing this."

"Not necessarily," said Puck. "Most death fae don't need to use knives or magical symbols to inflict damage on someone."

"Any theories?" My gaze went to the photos on the desk, which had been newly rearranged into piles, and the folder that Sal had given him. When he didn't object, I scooted over and picked up the folder to read the scribbled notes.

"We've been assembling a list of the characteristics of the victims," said Hawk. "All the victims were Seelie."

"They were?" Most death fae were Unseelie, but half-faeries in this realm had little need for Court loyalty. Yet I didn't believe anyone in the Courts had done this. The Winter Court might not *like* Summer, but the mortal realm was the least of their priorities, and so were their half-fae offspring. Same with Summer, come to that.

"Yes," said Puck. "As to the murder weapon, we can discern that it was some kind of sword or knife. Not iron, of course."

Iron poisoning would have left visible greyish tints to their wounds, which had appeared clean-cut. An instant kill... except in the case of the final victim, who'd fought his fate to his last breath. A glance confirmed the folder contained no more information than I already knew, so I dropped it back onto the desk. "We already know the killer is half-faerie..."

As for their other half, though? Necromancer or witch, surely, since those markings wouldn't be known to regular humans *or* supernaturals. *I* sure as hell hadn't seen them before.

"Or so we assume," Puck said. "With no witnesses, we can only make guesses as to the nature of the magic they used on the victims."

"You don't say." Despite his casual air, a layer of tension lurked beneath his words. Did he assume I knew more than I'd let on, or was he hinting that *he* knew more than he was willing to admit to a mere human? Doubts prickled at the back of my mind. Was I making a mistake in trusting him at all? Sal had hired him, yes, but there wasn't an abundance of options on offer when it came to private detectives with the right skill set to hunt down faerie serial killers.

"As for the ghosts," he said, "I doubt we'll get any more answers from them, so there's no need to involve the necromancer guild in this."

I hadn't planned to, since the victims hadn't turned into ghosts of their own accord, nor had they otherwise held any links to necromancy. Yet his aversion to sharing made me wonder if he did have any suspicions he had yet to divulge. The killer had sneaked up on their victims, unseen, and shapeshifting would certainly have given them an edge on the stealth front. So would glamour, strong enough to turn day into night and as realistic as the landscape paintings glittering on the walls.

Roseanne shifted on the balls of her feet. "All right. Should we leave, then?"

"That's all I've got until my cousin comes back with an update from our witch acquaintance." I watched Puck's face for clues as to his thoughts on that, but his gaze resisted connecting with mine. "You'll let me know if you find anything else? We're supposed to be partners, after all."

That got a raised brow from him. "I thought you objected to the term."

"I do. Just wondered if you were paying attention."

Now he was, the gold spots in his green eyes dancing with amusement. "I'm glad you came to see things my way."

"Don't get too excited. If I run up against the witch covens' secrecy laws, they might put a geas on me and prevent me from telling you anything."

"What's a geas?" Hawk wanted to know.

"The witch equivalent to a faerie vow, minus the 'on pain of death' part," I said. "Witches can be pretty hard-core in their own way."

Enough to murder a half-faerie in their own home, though? I didn't know.

"I thought you didn't intend to involve the covens," Puck said.

"I didn't intend to end up working with you either, so I have the impression this investigation is not going to stay on the predictable side."

"I suppose not," he said. "Do tell me what your witch friend has to say, won't you?"

"As long as you tell *me* if you come to any more conclusions."

Since no more information was forthcoming, I turned away, feeling Puck's eyes on my back as I left the office. The instant the door swung closed behind me, Roseanne shook her head at me. "What the bloody hell was that staring contest about?"

"Mind games." *I think.* Bloody faeries.

"Huh," she said. "Who won?"

"That, I have no idea," I said. "I'm not sure our new friend is on the straight and narrow."

Roseanne snorted. "You don't say. He's a trickster faerie."

I frowned. "What do you mean by that?"

"Even us half-human faeries can't escape our natures," she said. "Why do you think they're so scared of us?"

"By 'they,' do you mean humans or faeries?"

She gave a shrug in reply, but I suspected the former. Nevertheless, if it was in my nature to be the Winter Gatekeeper, then did the same apply now that I'd lost my title and the magic that came with it? No. Roseanne didn't have to follow her mother's example, and *I* didn't need to emulate the wrathful woman who'd cheated death and come close to bringing two worlds to their knees.

I had to believe I could build my own destiny. It wasn't like I had much of a choice, after all, if the alternative to being the Winter Gatekeeper was being nobody at all.

I walked fast to shake off my thoughts, and it was only when the gate of half-blood territory came within sight that I realised my feet had taken me back to the crime scene.

Roseanne hovered behind me. "You want to talk to the half-faeries again?"

"Maybe I'll get lucky and one of them will answer my questions this time."

I didn't need to advise her to shift into a crow and hide from sight before I entered the half-faeries' territory. I'd prefer to avoid Sal whether Roseanne was with me or not, but if Puck was keeping secrets from me, I could do worse than gather more information myself.

As I walked down the winding path between the row of terraced houses which belonged to the half-faeries with enough cash to afford their own place, I noted that the door to the latest victim's house had been sealed, no doubt to stop any curious passers-by from wandering in. I backtracked to Blaine's house and knocked, and an instant later, Brook opened the door. "Holly. I thought I saw you wandering around outside."

"Hey," I said. "You live here now, then?"

"I was Blaine's apprentice, so I've taken over from him," he said. "I figured it was easier to stay here so I can keep a close watch on anyone who might want my help."

He must know he'd put himself in a vulnerable position if the killer came back, but then again, it seemed the murderer was capable of sneaking into their territory without anyone sensing them. Or hearing them. Blood-curdling screams ought to have woken even the heaviest sleeper, yet the victim's cries had gone unheard.

"Good idea." I debated asking if he'd help with Roseanne where his former mentor had refused, but I'd stand zero chance of getting answers from him about the murders if he kicked me out for associating with a harbinger of death. "Did Blaine know Puck at all?"

"Your detective partner?" he asked. "Can't you ask him?"

Maybe "partner" wasn't better than "assistant" after all. "I wanted to get an outsider's perspective, since I didn't know Puck before Blaine's murder. He was already looking into two similar deaths beforehand. I gather it was Sal who had hired him, but I imagine he must have spoken to Blaine at least once."

"That's true, but honestly, nobody else was going to

help us," he said. "I can't say I'm acquainted with the trickster myself, and Blaine told me nothing of their discussions."

They did know one another well, then. That couldn't mean Puck had killed Blaine, surely. It might account for my seeing him lurking outside Blaine's house that night if they'd met beforehand. Didn't mean he was guilty. "All right. Thanks for the help. We're having a trial run of our partnership, but I don't see us working together long-term."

"Good," he said. "Blaine may have been right to ask a trickster to help with these horrific deaths, but they rarely do anything out of more than self-interest."

He thought Puck was just in this for the money or prestige? I hadn't got that impression, but could I say anything for sure at this point? "I don't know what's in it for him. Has he been in this realm for long, do you know?"

I hadn't meant to start an interrogation on Puck instead of the murderer, but if there was the slimmest chance that the two were one and the same, I wouldn't mind ruling him out as the killer. Or at least learning how many of the half-faeries knew and trusted him.

"I'm sure he'd tell you if you asked," he said. "Blaine told me nothing, Holly. If you want to ask more questions about the murder, you'll have to take it up with Sal."

That figured. "He's not my biggest fan. Would he want to know that all the victims so far have been Seelie?"

"Probably not," he said. "Half our territory is Seelie. Unless you want to question all the Unseelie, which won't make you popular."

"I'm blaming nobody without proof," I told him. "As for Sal…"

He cleared his throat, and I heard a twig snap behind me. The dickwad was right *there,* listening to our conversation. I rotated on my heel, smoothing out my expression.

"As for me… what, exactly?" Sal tilted his head on one side. "Where's your detective boss?"

Boss? That was a thousand times worse than "assistant" and "partner" put together. "He didn't hire me. Technically, *you* hired both of us. Anyway, he sent me here to ask a few questions about the victims."

"I gave him everything I have," said Sal. "You're poking your nose where it doesn't belong; that's what you're doing. You're not one of us."

His words dove under my skin, but they barely left a faint scar. "Your gratitude is overwhelming. I might remind you that I used to work directly for the Courts, which makes me more qualified for this than you are."

Brook cleared his throat from behind me. "Sal, try not to let your dislike of humans alienate one of the few allies we have. Holly has at least tried to help us find the killer, which is more than I can say for most."

"Exactly." It was nice to have *one* person argue in my favour. I shot him a grateful look then glared at Sal. He gave me a sour look before walking away. "He's the one who hired someone to investigate at first, right?"

"Yes, but…" Brook hesitated. "Be careful who you make alliances with."

What did that mean? Did his mistrust of Puck go beyond his reputation as a trickster, or was his comment more directed at my friendship with Roseanne? "I'll keep that in mind."

I turned away, wondering when the half-faeries had become so divided. At one time, most half-faeries in this realm had hero-worshiped the Courts, and they'd all been on the same side by default, but after the landslide of disasters in the last few years, it was hard for most of them to summon up any optimism that the Sidhe would ever come to their aid. Except for the lucky few who'd been contacted by a Sidhe parent in Faerie, of course, but most would never see the realm of their ancestors. Granted, Ilsa's boyfriend River had been offered a home in Faerie and had picked the necromancer guild instead. I had to admire his nerve, though he'd never been bound to Faerie by a vow like I had.

When I neared the gate out of half-blood territory, Roseanne landed in human form beside me. "That Sal is a complete arse."

"It'd serve him right if he's the next victim." I pushed on the gate, which stirred beneath my grip. I let go swiftly as the thorny vines comprising the gate moved of their own accord, sealing the way out and forming a wall of knife-like protrusions.

I moved into a defensive stance, pulling out my weapon. "Who's out there?"

A rustling sound was our only warning before the thorns leapt forward like arrows loosed from their bows, skimming the tips of our heads as we ducked to avoid them. The vines followed, lashing like tentacles, but my knife sliced through them with ease. Thorns snagged my bare hands, but I ignored the pain and kept slashing, the iron slicing through the branches until the magic fuelling their growth left them blackened and bare. Roseanne's hands transformed into bird's claws to help me clear a way out, and I let her climb ahead of me before following with my knife in hand.

I swore softly when we touched down on the other side, having left a human-sized gap in the half-dead thorns which had once formed the gate. If the killer got in again, it was entirely the fault of the dickhead who'd weaponised the security against us. "Fucking Sal."

"That attack was aimed at me." Roseanne's shoulders hunched. "I shouldn't have come with you."

"Don't be ridiculous," I said. "I was the one doing the interrogation, and the other half-faeries don't trust me because I'm human. Nothing new there."

"Brook does," she said. "I bet the others did, too, before you met me. They have a genuine serial killer among them, and yet they hate me more."

"They don't hate you personally, they just have an irrational fear of death," I said. "Which is the same reason they avoid the guild. If Ilsa visited them, they wouldn't treat her any different."

"Bullshit," she said. "They fear the Morrigan more than they fear the necromancers. They know she's an evil, soul-eating monster. Why wouldn't they think the same of me?"

All the possible replies died in my throat. "They're mistaken."

"Doesn't make it any less true," she said hollowly.

My phone buzzed and interrupted my reply. Ilsa had messaged me. *You're in luck. Jas has an update for you at the guild.*

8

The necromancer guild, a tall brick building in Edinburgh's Old Town with magical wards shimmering up and down its front walls, was supposedly out of bounds to the public. So when Ilsa pushed open the oak doors and indicated for me to follow her, I half expected to get mobbed by a group of angry people in cloaks. Instead, most people glanced at Ilsa and utterly ignored me. Made a change from being attacked by thorns; I'd say that much.

"There's been dozens of new novices coming in and out of the place in the last few weeks," Ilsa commented in an undertone. "Sometimes they stay. Sometimes they don't. Nobody pays much attention to newbies."

"Good." I assumed bringing in a crow would be a step too far, so it was probably for the best that Roseanne had flown off as soon as I'd mentioned I'd be meeting Ilsa. My cousin had reacted to my scratched arms and torn sleeves with nothing more than a raised eyebrow, which was fine by me.

Ilsa led the way upstairs to the necromancer guild's archive room, which resembled a small library contained in a single room. The smell of old books drifted from the countless ancient tomes crammed onto the towering shelves, while a single desk and chair sat in the front.

Ducking back out the door, Ilsa said, "I'll be back in a minute."

My objection died in my throat as a young woman with long dark hair and a lip piercing stepped out from behind a shelf and laid a heavy-looking textbook on the desk. She was short, barely five feet if I had to guess, with pale skin and bangle-shaped witch spells on both wrists. I hadn't known the necromancer guild allowed witches to practise their own brand of magic on the property.

"You're Ilsa's witch contact?" I guessed.

"That's me," she said. "I'm Jas. You're Ilsa's cousin Holly, right?"

"Yep," I said. "I'm told you have experience with blood magic symbols?"

"Not long ago, mentioning blood magic in public would have got you arrested by the Mage Lords," she said wryly. "Ilsa said you missed all that."

"All what?" I shook my head. "You know what—it doesn't matter. You know what those symbols mean, then?"

"Some of them," she said. "I had to ask Asher, which was kind of tricky, because he and Isabel are travelling around with the Council of Twelve, talking to the various witch covens in England at the moment. So I sent him the pictures."

I had no idea who either of those people were, but at this rate, the photos would be halfway across mainland

Europe by next week. "Can you tell me what you know, then?"

"Firstly…" She pulled out the wooden chair and sat behind the desk. "What do you know about blood magic?"

"Not a ton," I acknowledged. "Ilsa told me a little, but all I know is that it works by drawing magic-infused symbols directly onto a person."

"Blood magic symbols are more… I guess you'd say more *direct* than a regular spell," she said. "They're also too powerful for all but the strongest witches to control. To use blood magic, witches usually draw the required marks on themselves and imbue them with a part of their own magic to activate their effects. So if I drew the symbols for 'speed' and 'strength' on myself, I'd temporarily become faster and stronger."

"What about drawing them on other people, then?" I asked. "It wouldn't be fuelled by that other person's magic if they weren't a witch… so you'd have to use your own. Right?"

Jas shifted in her seat. "Using true blood magic requires a special kind of ink which is hard to get hold of. The ink is a catalyst all on its own."

"What kind of ink is that?"

"Blood," she said. "Hence the name 'blood magic.' That way, you don't have to cut the marks directly into your own skin. Instead, you can draw them on the walls or the floor…"

"Or another person," I finished. "Got it. Whose blood is the ink made out of, then?"

Was that even legal? I'd assumed witches were the more law-abiding out of the non-fae supernaturals, but perhaps not.

"I can't believe Ilsa didn't tell you," she said. "I know you've been in Faerie, but you must have seen…"

"Seen what?"

The door swung open, and Ilsa came back in, accompanied by a tall half-faerie with short, curly blond hair. River, her boyfriend and the second-most-powerful necromancer at the guild, gave me a curt nod.

"Hey, River." Would he really be willing to help us? I'd been effectively an enemy of his Court on several levels until recently, after all, but his lack of hostility implied he didn't hold it against me. No doubt Ilsa had had words with him before I'd arrived here.

"Ilsa said you thought the killer you were searching for might be a necromancer," he said.

"Or a witch," I said. "Due to the symbols drawn on the bodies. They were killed by having their throats cut, but we're not sure if it was sacrificial magic or not. I was about to ask Jas about the difference between blood magic and regular witch magic. Both involve symbols, right?"

"Yes, but blood magic isn't widely known or studied, and it's almost always used for an illegal purpose," said Jas. "There's even one symbol which can resurrect the dead."

"Isn't that just necromancy?"

"No. The symbol prevents the body from rotting and leaves it in total control of the person who put it there."

"So they don't decay like the regular dead," I said. "Wait… that's not one of the marks on those bodies, is it? Because they're still in the morgue."

"I don't *think* so," she said. "It's not among the marks in the photos you sent me, anyway. If the killer was trying to create zombies, there are easier ways."

I made a mental note to double-check the pictures

Puck had of the other victims all the same. "The symbols were drawn before or after their deaths, so I guessed they might be a hint from the killer."

A killer leaving the hints in the form of symbols even most witches couldn't read wasn't much of a strategy, either, but maybe there was method to the madness.

Jas picked up her phone and held it up to reveal the photo I'd sent her, using her free hand to indicate one of the symbols. "That one means 'sightless' or something of the sort. Essentially, it takes away the sight of the person who wears it."

"The victims were blinded so they couldn't see their attackers." That would explain the ghosts' confusion. "Clever of them. Neither of the ghosts Ilsa and I spoke to remembered seeing anything… which I guess proves the symbols were drawn on them before their deaths. How'd they stay oblivious, then?"

"With this one." She indicated another marking. "Temporary paralysis. The killer must have sneaked up and drawn that symbol first, which bought them enough time to draw the others."

"Seems pretty intricate for a faerie serial killer." Definitely methodical too. The killer had a pattern they wanted to follow.

Jas put down her phone. "I only figured out one other symbol, and honestly, even Asher was confused on the meaning. It's ambiguous."

"In what way?" I queried.

"The symbol means 'absorb' in the glyphs of the ancient witch covens," she said. "Or maybe 'siphon.' Not sure what it was used to do, though."

"I thought maybe they wanted to absorb the victim's

life energy," said Ilsa. "I can't think of a life-drinking fae which wouldn't find it easier to take that energy from a living person instead, though. No need for an elaborate set-up."

"Rituals involving life energy aren't unheard of," said Jas. "Also, if you kill a necromancer in any fashion, their death unleashes a ton of spiritual energy. Perhaps something similar happens when a faerie dies too."

"Their magic leaves their body," I said slowly. "Unless they stay around as a ghost. I didn't think to ask either of the spirits if they lost contact with their magic…"

"Most don't keep it beyond death," Ilsa said. "Especially Summer faeries. It's rare enough in wraiths."

Yeah. Winter magic was strengthened by death and decay, but they didn't need to kill someone to get a boost of magic. They just needed to stand on some fallen leaves or a dead plant. If the victims had been necromancers, then their moment of death would have caused a magical surge, but to my knowledge, none of them had been.

A shiver broke out on my skin. "So the killer wanted to… wanted to absorb their magic somehow?"

"Maybe," said Jas. "I don't know much about the relationship between faeries and death except that it isn't a nice one."

"I think a death fae is doing this." I looked between her and Ilsa. "You definitely don't think it was a summoning? There was a hellhound footprint at one of the scenes…"

"A hellhound?" said Jas. "You didn't say."

"Hellhounds can be summoned with a droplet of blood, no symbols necessary," said Ilsa. "Fetching a hellhound is the most basic kind of summoning. If it was a mass summoning, though, the easiest way to go about it would be to generate the energy from killing a witch or necromancer, preferably on a spirit line."

Spirit lines. How close was half-blood territory to the Ley Line? Not far, because the fae needed to be near their realm in order to access their magic, but not directly on top of it either. I didn't know if Ilsa's theory held weight, though necromancy did gain power in the mere presence of death… and so did Winter magic.

On the other hand, there were less conspicuous and complicated ways to boost one's magical power than to commit ritualistic murders.

"I don't know whether or not I should be concerned that you've thought about it in this much detail," Jas remarked to Ilsa. "Lucky I know you're not summoning hellhounds on the weekends."

"I'd rather not know if you are," I supplied. "Maybe one was drawn to the crime scene and then bolted when people showed up. Jas, will you be able to find the meanings to the other symbols?"

"Possibly, but even the witches don't know them all," she said. "The person responsible must be well versed in the glyphs of the ancient witch covens, more even than—"

At that moment, the door opened again, and Ilsa stepped aside to let in her brother, Morgan, along with his boyfriend, Lloyd. Everyone shuffled back to make room, while Morgan shot me a grin, his dark hair like a bird's nest and his cloak too big for his skinny frame. "Hey, Holly."

"Where's Pepper?" Ilsa asked him.

"Keir took him for a walk," said Lloyd, a tall black guy with locs whom I vaguely remembered as being Jas's best friend. "That puppy worships the ground he treads on, I swear. You're still stuck on archive duty, Jas?"

"For now," said Jas. "I didn't expect the boss to be *that* angry about me blowing a hole in the wall of my room. Your room's on the other side; it's not like I'm going to use a spy hole to ogle strangers."

"You nearly singed my hair off," Morgan said accusingly.

"I didn't expect the spell to have that much explosive power," Jas said sheepishly. "Is the boss around?"

"She's on the prowl." Lloyd eyed me. "I take it you didn't get her permission to bring in a visitor, Ilsa?"

"No, but it was easier to show Holly our research in here," said Ilsa. "I'll walk you to the door, okay?"

I nodded, relieved to get out of the cramped space and away from her friends' natural camaraderie, which always made me feel out of place.

"Sure you haven't changed your mind about joining the guild?" Morgan asked.

I didn't dignify that with a response. Instead, Ilsa and I headed downstairs to the guild's front doors, thankfully without running into the notoriously fearsome Lady Montgomery on the way out.

"Don't tell me you think he has a point," I told Ilsa. "You know how much of a disaster my trial at the guild was."

"It wasn't *that* bad."

"I'm not a necromancer." The irony wasn't lost on me. If I was going to have any kind of magic left after I'd lost my Gatekeeper's abilities, I'd hoped the type that actually did run in the family would show up, but I remained without an ounce of necromantic magic at my disposal.

Roseanne, on the other hand, had magic which was closer to death magic than any other faerie's, and she could also see spirits, which would make her a better fit for the guild than me. Then again, after seeing how the half-faeries and other supernaturals had treated her, I wasn't certain that encouraging her to sign up when she turned sixteen would result in anything other than more heartbreak.

As though conjured up by my thoughts, the crow-shape of Roseanne flew to meet me outside. Ilsa watched, her brow furrowing. "I've seen that bird before."

"It's not a raven," I said. "Not like Arden."

I referred to the familiar who'd belonged to both sides of our family and whose magic now resided in the Gatekeeper's book Ilsa carried in her pocket.

Would it really matter if Ilsa knew I had a new death-faerie friend camping out in my room? I opened my mouth to speak, and Ilsa's phone buzzed, prompting her to pull it out of her pocket. "Dammit. I have to run."

"Trouble at the guild?"

"There's been a wraith sighted in the city, which usually means I have to deal with it."

A wraith. The word sent a bone-deep chill racing down my spine, and from the expression on Ilsa's face, she remembered my mother's wraith form trapped between life and death. Yet Ilsa hadn't been there when I'd found her body sprawled on the floor of the study, her ghostly form wreathed in magic which had followed her into death itself.

Every second of that day was carved deep into my mind—from the moment of discovery to the fear which had chased me downhill in my flight to the nearby village to find a necromancer able to rid me of her ghost. Yet none of them had been able to do more than trap her in a circle of candles, while Ilsa had been the one who'd banished her wraith beneath the gates of Death.

I forced the image of her furious, inhuman face from my mind and kept my tone casual. "Where'd it come from?"

"The Grey Vale, probably," Ilsa said. "Most of them do."

"Is it more common now?" Most Sidhe who died in the Grey Vale ended up trapped and consequently turned into coalesced bundles of magic and helpless anger, but I didn't know if the same was true of those in the Courts. My mother hadn't been Sidhe, of course, but she'd had the magic of the Winter Court at her disposal, and that same magic had enabled her to stay far past her sell-by date.

"I wouldn't say they're common," said Ilsa. "Most Sidhe in the Courts don't become wraiths. It's the outcasts who do, and the Vale is full of far more dead Sidhe than any of them want to acknowledge."

"Good luck," I told her.

On that happy note, we parted ways. I might have offered to help, but without any magic, I'd only get in the way. Only the strongest of faeries or necromancers could handle a wraith, and even then, the Gatekeeper alone had the power to banish them to the afterlife.

Roseanne shifted into a human again when we reached the end of the street. "Are you going to tell Puck about those symbols?"

"I have no idea." I rubbed my forehead. "He's not being forthcoming with any of his own theories. To tell you the truth, I'm starting to think I should go it alone."

Yet he was the one the half-faeries had hired, not me,

and this case was rapidly spiralling into something I had no business being involved in. My first priority ought to be getting some cash in the bank, so I opted to drop by the mercenaries' place in the hopes of finding a job which might cover my bills for the week. Roseanne fired eager questions at me about Ilsa and Jas as we walked while I buried my hands in my pockets to warm them. The cold air had turned bitter, a reminder that autumn was upon us and the Winter faeries' magic would only get stronger as the seasons changed.

A particularly icy blast of air rammed into me, and I dug my hands into my pockets. "Damn, that's bloody freezing."

Not natural cold either. My head snapped up while Roseanne took flight with a shriek as a patch of darkness swirled above the road, turning into the vague semblance of a person.

That must be Ilsa's wraith.

Cold air radiated from the shadow, catching Roseanne's bird form in its path. She fell out of the sky, screeching, before transforming into her human form and landing in a crouch. Swirling brightness coalesced around the shadows, its white-blue sheen confirming the chill was definitely Winter magic. The wraith had been one of the Unseelie when it'd been alive.

The real question: How much of its magic did it have left?

Roseanne's skin bubbled as her hands transformed into claws, and she hit out at the wraith, but her clawed hands simply passed right through it. So did my iron knife, though I held it defensively in the hopes of holding the wraith off long enough for Roseanne to make a getaway.

"Run!" I warned her, but she didn't budge. "Roseanne, run."

The wraith's power wrapped around us, and I reached in vain for magic that was no longer there, images flickering behind my eyes.

I stood in the clearing of the Winter Court, watching the dark form of a wraith descend upon me...

I opened the door to the study of the Winter Lynn house, finding my mother's inert corpse lying on the carpet with a malevolent shadowy form hovering above, beckoning with a crooked hand...

I reached for the Gatekeeper's book, feeling the tempting call of its magic...

I blinked frantically, willing the images to leave me be, but they dug in with sharp teeth.

"Get away," I whispered, cursing the weakness in my own voice. "Whatever it is you want, you won't find it here. Go back to the Vale."

The wraith lay atop us both, its icy form smothering and unbearably cold. At my side, Roseanne let out a wordless scream of terror.

"Go beyond the gates of Death!" Ilsa's voice yelled.

My cousin ran into view, faster than I'd seen her move before, with the Gatekeeper's book open in her hands. A torrent of magic blasted from its pages and smacked into the wraith, pushing it away from Roseanne and me.

The icy paralysis lifted enough for me to pull Roseanne out of the way, grimacing at how cold her skin was. A bolt of energy pulsed from the book in Ilsa's hands, and the outline of a pair of gates appeared in midair, beckoning the wraith into the world beyond this one. The wraith faced her, its shadowy hands reaching out as though to cling to the land of the living—but in vain.

There was no resisting the call of the Gatekeeper.

The gates enfolded the wraith from behind, and it vanished within. At my side, Roseanne collapsed into a shuddering heap. I crouched to check on her and then straightened upright to face my cousin. Nothing remained of the wraith but a lingering chill in the air.

"Should have known it'd sneak over here to get a taste of death energy." Ilsa indicated the nearby cemetery, which had slipped my notice until now. "Nasty creature. You okay?"

"Sure." I'd got off lightly, all things considered. "Thanks."

"You're welcome." Ilsa's gaze flickered over to Roseanne, and then she checked her phone. "I have to go. Is she…?"

When her gaze dropped to Roseanne again, I mouthed, *I'll explain later.*

Ilsa responded with a look which said, *You'd better*, and then walked away.

I, meanwhile, dropped to a crouch again. "Roseanne?"

She groaned. "No…"

"It's okay," I said, attempting a soothing tone. "The wraith is gone. Is it the first one you've seen?"

Roseanne gave me a wild stare. "Didn't you see it?"

"What does that mean?" Then it hit me that the wraith must have shown her a vision too. Some of them fed on emotions like fear and anger and used their insidious magic to create visions by drawing on their victims' most unpleasant memories. "We should get home. The beast isn't coming back."

"But you didn't... why aren't you running away from me?"

"Why would I do that?" I frowned. "If it's about what the wraith showed you, I didn't see. Wraiths of that sort tend to draw out particular memories from each of their targets."

And I had plenty of horrors of my own for it to feed upon.

Her mouth parted. "Oh."

"Come on home, and I'll cook us a hot meal," I said.

My words snapped her out of her funk, and she followed me without complaint until we reached the house. I only had instant noodles, hardly gourmet, but she eagerly followed me into the kitchen after I'd checked my housemates weren't around. Then she sat at the table and watched me cook, fiddling with a loose thread on her coat. "I... saw my mother."

"Oh?" I stood by the pan, inviting her to continue her explanation. "The wraith showed you visions with the intention of distressing you, no doubt to fuel its own power."

"I know," she mumbled. "She... the Morrigan... did awful things."

"So did *my* mother," I said. "She turned into a wraith in a bid to steal the Sidhe's magic and nearly blew up the Ley Line in the process. My cousin banished her to the afterlife, but she was tenacious enough to cling to the gates of Death until she had the opportunity to return. Then she possessed me in order to help the Seelie Queen in a failed coup to steal the throne of the Summer Court."

"She possessed you?" Roseanne's eyes widened. "Seriously?"

"Yeah." Ghosts typically couldn't possess living people, but my mother had been nothing if not exceptional. "Only for long enough to snag a new body. Unfortunately for her, it backfired in her face."

"Oh." She looked down at the worn surface of the table. "Mine swore a vow to someone she shouldn't have. And he… he forced me to swear a vow to him too."

Despite the heat of the oven, goosebumps pebbled my arms. The pan was bubbling over, so I took it off the stove with shaking hands. "I think I know exactly who you mean."

It'd been pure luck that I hadn't been Gatekeeper at the time of the catastrophe which had resulted in the end of the Sidhe's immortality, but the Morrigan had played a major part in causing it. I hadn't known Roseanne had too.

Roseanne gulped down a breath. "He forced her to obey. He forced me too…"

I studied her until she looked up and met my eyes. "You can tell me, Roseanne. I won't judge you."

"He made me kill my human father." As she broke into sobs and buried her head in her hands, I left the pan and walked to her side. "He had me set these awful creatures loose, and they tore him to pieces. I thought the—the Huntsman was telling me the truth, but every word he said was a lie."

Oh, damn. Her story was worse than I'd imagined. "What did he say?"

"He promised me I'd get to be immortal," she whimpered. "He promised all the half-faeries would. Instead, most of them died, and their immortality source broke because of him—because of me."

"I'm sure that's not true." *Gods.* I'd heard the stories from my family about the breaking of the source of immortality, and most seemed to agree that a Sidhe called Fionn, also known as the Huntsman, had been responsible. He'd bound the Morrigan to his will—and, it seemed, her daughter too. Some of the stories had said he'd been attempting to create an immortal army, but they'd neglected to mention he'd tried to make *half-faeries* into said immortal army. And it was pretty clear that most of them hadn't survived.

Except for Roseanne. No wonder she was reluctant to trust anyone at all... until, for some reason, she'd latched on to me, perhaps because my own hands were as blood drenched as a redcap's hat.

"It might as well be," she mumbled. "Fionn died. He deserved to. But I have to live with what he made me do."

"It's not your fault." I fetched some plates and began doling out our meals. "He caused the faerie invasion too. He was trying to conquer our realm."

"Yeah," she mumbled. "When he captured my mother, he was trying to do the same, but his plan failed and cost the Sidhe their immortality."

"Serves him right, if you ask me."

A sudden thought hit me like a lightning bolt. The Sidhe's immortality had been fuelled by the same source used in the most potent illegal blood magic... and it was only now that I remembered Hazel had once mentioned a similar kind of magic had sustained the Gatekeeper's curse.

The originator of our family's bond with the Courts, etched in symbols we'd once worn on our own skin, had been in the blood of the original gods of Faerie. The Ancients.

"*A wraith?*" Puck watched me from behind the desk in his office with apparent genuine surprise.

"That's what I told you." The following morning, I'd dismissed my better judgement and messaged him about my conversation with Jas and Ilsa at the guild yesterday and then figured I was better off explaining it in person. I hadn't thought the wraith was the part he'd fixate on, but he'd probably never set eyes on one before. "Near the mercenary guild of all places. Glad it didn't get inside, or else I wouldn't have been able to earn any cash this week."

As it was, I had a job on my schedule for later that morning, and while I wasn't looking forward to dealing with more faerie bullshit, the dire state of my finances prevailed. The rate at which Roseanne was consuming the contents of my cupboards was enough of a motivator in itself.

"How did you get rid of the wraith, then?" Puck asked.

"My cousin banished it," I said. "Anyway, she had an

update on those symbols on the victims' bodies, courtesy of her witch contacts. One symbol blinded the victim's sight to their attacker, and the second paralysed them, presumably so the murderer could complete the inking without being interrupted."

"Any others?" said Hawk.

"A third signalled some kind of absorption," I said. "Jas wasn't sure on that one, but if the killer was trying to siphon the victims' magic, then it would explain the intricacy of the set-up."

"I've never heard of a witch wanting to absorb someone's magic before." Hawk wore a grim expression, a contrast to Puck's apparent nonchalance.

"Blood magic is versatile, or so I hear," I said. "Sounds like it's a new innovation… or rather an old one which has come back in vogue in recent years. Anyway, that's all we've got. What're your thoughts?"

I opted against mentioning the other theory which had occurred to me yesterday… that the witches weren't the only ones who could use blood magic to achieve their own ends. Not that I'd necessarily call the Sidhe's form of immortality "blood magic," since it didn't involve writing symbols… just immersing themselves in the lifeblood of a slain god.

Yeah. That was the Sidhe's dirty little secret: they owed their immortality to their deceased predecessors. The Ancients had all but been driven to extinction by the Sidhe themselves, which gave their current predicament a nice kind of irony, but the gods' magic had predated—and created—Faerie itself. More to the point, the very language of the Ancients brimmed with power, and merely speaking or writing a single word brought that magic roaring to the surface. Speaking an Invocation, a spell written by the gods, would drive any regular mortal to madness—but the original Summer and Winter Gate-keepers had evaded that consequence by wearing the mark which bound them to Faerie itself on their foreheads.

None of us had known the mark had belonged to a god who'd once formed the foundation of the faerie realm itself until Hazel had shattered the curse and caused our marks to vanish, but my finger could trace those swirling lines from memory, and they did bear some resemblance to the symbols the killer had left on those bodies.

If the markings were inked in the blood of the gods, it amplified their potency, but it seemed absurd to think that a run-of-the-mill serial killer might have been able to get hold of a tool containing the blood of a slain god, much less that they'd know their language. No, the victims' deaths had been inflicted by someone who lived in the human realm and were unlikely to be connected to the Sidhe *or* their deceased gods, but the thought clung like a burr nevertheless. When neither Puck nor Hawk offered another comment, I raised a brow at Roseanne. "Wow. Am I the only person here who did their homework?"

"You already told us the meanings of some of the marks, and we don't have contacts among the local covens to figure out the rest," said Puck. "Our theory that the killer intentionally blinded their victims was proven correct, and the paralysis explains how their attacker was able to intricately mark their skin before taking their lives. What we have yet to determine is how the killer accessed their victims without being sighted by anyone else."

"Nobody else has been killed overnight, then?"

"Not as far as I'm aware." Puck's tone was harsher than normal, and despite his impeccable appearance, the faint shadows under his eyes were hard to disguise even with glamour. Hawk looked similarly sleep-deprived. I found myself wondering what they'd been doing if not looking into the murders. "I have yet to hear from Sal, save for an update that he saw you snooping around half-blood territory again yesterday."

"I take it that 'snooping' was his word, not mine?" I glanced at Roseanne. "He also attacked us with thorns on our way out."

A shimmer of amusement entered his eyes. "What did you do to him?"

"Absolutely nothing at all," I said, annoyed. "I visited Brook, who's moved into Blaine's vacated house. He doesn't seem to be a fan of yours either."

I'd spoken without thinking, but Hawk frowned. "What does that mean?"

Maybe I ought to have avoided the subject. "He just said he didn't know you personally, like Blaine did. Don't take it as an excuse to go and hassle him. He didn't do anything wrong."

Puck and Hawk exchanged unreadable glances before Puck said, "No, we don't know one another. I'm curious… did you ask him about me?"

Crap. Why had I mentioned him at all? "He already knows we're working together. I'd appreciate it if you stopped telling everyone that, because it's pretty clear you have no trust in me whatsoever."

"I might say the same about you," said Puck. "Your cousin's ability to banish wraiths is hardly a common one, even among necromancers."

I wished I hadn't mentioned the bloody wraith to begin with. It had nothing to do with the case, and besides, he ought to know Ilsa's Gatekeeper status if he knew who *I* was.

Or did he? He'd presumably been in Faerie the whole time I'd been Winter Gatekeeper, but while the Courts were generally pretty good at keeping their secrets from one another, the Gatekeepers had been common knowledge. Not that the Sidhe would ever have dared to *admit* that we were useful to them, but it was hard to hide the presence of the one family of humans permitted to enter Faerie.

If he'd been hiding under a rock for the last few years, though, I didn't have the time to enlighten him on everything he'd missed. "If you want to know, ask Ilsa yourself. In the meantime, text me if you change your mind about sharing your theories with me. I have to go and deal with a sluagh in someone's garden shed."

"A sluagh?"

"Thrilling, I know." I headed for the door. "Also, let me know if anyone else dies."

No reply followed, so I left the office with Roseanne trailing me. I was pretty sure I'd just closed the doors on being officially involved in catching the fae serial killer, but I'd been spending way too much time in Puck's office lately. If he had a change of heart about sharing his insights with me, then I'd reconsider, but it was far better to get out before our arrangement became more complicated than it already was.

"Don't tell me to go home," Roseanne said. "I can help you with this merc job of yours."

"You really want to turf a sluagh out of someone's shed?"

"Yes." At my raised brows, she said, "It's not like I've never seen them before. Besides, I'll be old enough to sign up to join the mercs as soon as I'm sixteen."

"Well… all right." It wasn't going to be an exciting morning, but she wanted something to occupy her time, and it might help both of us forget our lingering disquiet after yesterday's encounter with the wraith. Knowing most half-faeries and even some Sidhe wouldn't have been able to deal with it didn't make me less annoyed at myself for almost getting killed—and Roseanne along with me.

We walked for about half an hour before reaching the terraced house belonging to the unfortunate guy who'd had his garden shed taken over by death faeries. The middle-aged man responded with little more than an indifferent grunt when he opened the door and I explained what we'd come for, so Roseanne and I didn't bother hanging around to chat. Instead, we headed through the back door into the garden and approached the little wooden shed near the fence. Even from a distance, the chill of death magic radiated from it, and shadows crept underneath the door.

I reached for my knife. "Roseanne, want to kick the door down?"

"Sure." She strode up and kicked at the wooden door and then transformed into a bird and flew back to my side.

The door swung open, revealing that the sluagh had

completely moved in on the place. Half-solid, half-ghost, they were a bitch to take down but nothing on a wraith. I couldn't see much more than a swamp of shadows within the shed, so I'd need to lure it out.

"Hey, dickhead!" I called out. "Why're you hiding in a human's shed? Too scared to show your ugly face?"

Not my most original taunt, but I wasn't in the mood for a drawn-out job. I just wanted the beast gone, my payment in hand, and something in this accursed week to go right for a change.

Roseanne landed at my side, in human form again. "Hey, twatface! Get out here, or I'll set your shed on fire."

The sluagh didn't move, so I reached for the container of shredded pieces of iron I kept in my pocket and then flung it into the shed.

The beast stirred, rearing up to avoid the shards of iron, and emerged from the shed in a wave of rippling shadows. Extended to its full height, it resembled a vaguely humanoid figure except more shadowy and semi-transparent. As it shook off the last of the iron fragments, I readied myself to strike.

My knife slid right through the beast as though it wasn't there. With a curse, I yanked the weapon out while Roseanne hit out with her clawed hands and managed to get in a strike which drew blood. The beast shifted from corporeal to ghostly quickly enough to make it a pain in the arse to land a hit.

Rearing back, I drove my knife into its spine or what-ever the equivalent was, and with a horrible screech, the beast collapsed into a heap of shadowy flesh. Gotcha.

"Holly!" Roseanne said. "Something else is moving in there."

My gaze snapped up. Even with the sluagh dead, the inside of the shed remained coated in darkness. As I watched, a tentacle inched towards the dead body of the sluagh. Ugh. There must be a death stealer in there too.

The death stealer resembled a bruise-coloured octopus with a suction-like mouth teeming with sharp teeth which could drain the life from someone in a heartbeat or rip their skin off depending on their mood. Emerging from the shed, it spat a mouthful of inky-black slime across the garden. I leapt back out of range, while Roseanne shifted into flight. The glob of slime hit the ground with the force of a small bomb, several flecks striking Roseanne in midair and others splattering the shed and the side of the house. Roseanne shifted to human again and dropped back to earth, rolling over on the grass in an attempt to rid herself of the slime.

"Roseanne!" I sidestepped an all-too-mobile piece of slime myself and kept my knife in hand as I ran at the death stealer.

My knife flashed out, sinking into an oncoming tentacle and slicing it off. The beast swung on me, mouth brimming with teeth, and I cut off another tentacle. The iron poisoning spread rapidly through its slimy form, and when I reached its side and stabbed into the top of its head, its body sagged like a deflating balloon.

"Ugh." Roseanne shuddered, struggling to pull a piece of slime off her arm. More inky blots covered the entire right side of her body in a sticky web. "Creepy fucker."

"Hang on. I'll get rid of it." I stuck the knife carefully into the biggest piece of slime on her leg, which began to flake away like dead skin when the iron touched it. "Haven't seen one of those in a while."

Death stealers had been kicked out of the Courts for being too creepy, if the Sidhe had the right to define such terms. This one seemed to be alone, because nothing else leapt out of the shed. I squinted into the darkness. "Got a light?"

"No…" Roseanne kicked another piece of slime off her foot.

"No worries." I reached for my phone and turned on its light. While no more death fae lurked within, a rotting body lay on the shed floor. A male half-faerie, judging by his pointed ears. No wonder the death faeries had been drawn to the place. Did the owner have any idea he was here? The body appeared to be several days old, and a familiar series of markings covered his neck and chest.

I spun on my heel and ran back to the house to find the owner while Roseanne hurried to catch up. My heart hammered in my chest, my grip on the knife tight.

The man sat on the sofa in the living room and cast a glance at me without acknowledging my dirty appearance. "You done?"

"Aside from the dead body, yes."

He swung his gaze in my direction. "Didn't you clean up the dead fae?"

I raised my knife. "Don't play the innocent. There was another dead body in your shed. Did you put it there yourself?"

The man's features shifted, turning elfin, while he shrank somewhat below the height of a regular human. Leaping off the sofa, he brandished a serrated knife at us.

"What the hell are you?" Roseanne's claws came out.

"I think the question is, what are *you*?" Glee filled his voice. "A harbinger like you will be very useful as bait. Or maybe I'll gut you instead and let the other death fae feast upon you."

"You bastard." I ran to meet his knife, but he flung it at Roseanne instead. I veered into her path, and the knife sank into my own arm. Not deep, but it sent a shock of pain up to my shoulder and caused my own grip on my weapon to falter.

"Holly!" yelled Roseanne.

A bolt of feathers shot past my head and collided with his face. The faerie staggered back, while his adversary transformed into a snake, rearing up with fangs bared to strike. My vision wavered, and when the faerie swung his knife at the serpent, it transformed again, becoming leaping flames the colour of autumn leaves.

Puck? Whomever it was, they'd left my path clear, so I lunged past the fire and decapitated the faerie.

What I hadn't counted on was the second blade concealed in his hand, which sank into my ribs as his lifeless body fell to the ground.

"Fuck." The knife hadn't stuck, but the crimson stain rapidly spreading across my chest told me he'd cut deep. I stumbled towards the door, vaguely aware of Roseanne saying my name. "Let's get out of here."

"Not if you bleed to death on the way," she said. "Holly…"

"C'mon." I kept a hand on my side in a futile attempt to stem the bleeding and concentrated on putting one foot in front of the other. "I'm not going to get taken out by a death fae unawares."

"I *am* a death fae," said Roseanne. "And Puck is right there."

I groaned, and a shadow fell over me from above as my knees hit the ground.

"Just bloody perfect." I glared up at Puck, my vision wavering as I attempted to stand. "If you wanted to take credit for the job, then you're out of luck."

"That's not why I'm here." Concern laced his voice. "Holly… you're bleeding. A lot."

"You don't say." I pushed upright, trying to ignore the numbing sensation in my right side. "Been there, done that."

"Holly!" Roseanne's face had gone chalk white. "Don't you have… I dunno, a healing spell? Whatever it is humans use?"

"It's not a deep wound."

"Looks like it to me." Roseanne stared down at me. "You saved my life."

"Guess I did." My vision blurred, but a sweep of wings caught me in their grip before I hit the ground. Frankly, I didn't know if it was Roseanne or Puck who was carrying me, but when darkness became absolute, everything ceased to matter.

S al's angry voice snapped me out of my doze. "Get her out of here."

"She's injured," said Puck. "I know you have healing abilities."

He'd brought me to Sal? Seriously? I'd have raised an objective if I could speak, but I couldn't do more than feebly move a hand. The world swam around me, a blur of colour and light.

"I'm not healing her," he said. "You could have taken her to anyone else."

"You're the only person with this skill I know of," Puck said. "Consider it a favour which may be repaid equally at a later time."

A lengthy pause ensued in which I did my level best not to pass out again. "I'll hold you to that."

A current of warmth washed over me, dulling the pain in my side. Within several seconds, I began to feel more alert, while the pain faded more and more with each passing moment. My vision came back into focus, and I became aware of someone carrying my limp body over a threshold into a dark room. A soft surface cushioned my back, and when the haze lifted from my eyes, Sal was walking away. "I expect you to hold up your end of the bargain, Puck. Find those killers."

"Naturally," Puck said from somewhere in the nearby darkness. "Holly… you're awake?"

"Yeah." My vision flickered at the edges as Sal's healing magic continued to do its work. "You should know… we found another murder victim in the shed."

"What?" Puck's voice sounded distant, and I forced my head upright to avoid losing consciousness. The room was dark enough that the only part of him I could see was his eyes—green flecked with gold and wide with disbelief.

I fixed my gaze on him. "The sluagh and death stealer were there for a reason. A dead half-faerie's body was in my client's shed, marked with the same symbols as the others. Someone ought to take care of that, but I'm a little tied up."

He swore under his breath then left the room at a swift glide. I heard him waylay Sal and speak to him in an urgent voice while I fought to hang on to consciousness.

Within moments, he returned to my side. "What else did you see?"

"No more bodies if that's what you mean." I lowered my head against the cushions. "I don't know how long he was there, but I assume the faerie in the house wanted to lure in his next victim. I don't think he was the actual murderer, though. He went down too easily."

Puck's mouth formed a curse in the fae's lilting language. "That job was bait to lure in the next victim. You might have been killed."

"No shit." What would that faerie have to gain if he wasn't the person marking and sacrificing his victims, though? Unless he was their ally, of course. Sal's words came to mind. *"Find those killers."* Sal thought there was more than one killer... but did Puck too? "Why'd you come after me?"

"I regret letting you leave the way I did," he said. "You brought me valuable information, and I dismissed you."

"Wow." I closed my eyes and opened them again. "Must be the blood loss talking, but I think you just apologised to me."

"I thought..." He trailed off for a moment. "This case is more dangerous than I initially anticipated. I thought you were human, but..."

"But what?" I pressed. "You know who I am."

"I know your name, Holly." The way he said my name brought a start of surprise, perhaps because he spoke so softly and without the undercurrent of hostility I'd come to expect. "I can't say you've told me much else about yourself, have you?"

"Isn't the name enough?" I dragged myself into a sitting position, using the cushions for balance more than I'd have liked to admit. "How many other families have the surname Lynn and the ability to see the fae?"

"Lynn. Gatekeeper." I saw the moment the truth slid into his eyes, and his evident shock pushed the last of the dizziness from my limbs.

"Yes." I leaned forward in my seat. "Where in the world have you been for the past few years?"

"Believe it or not, not every corner of Faerie has access to the same information," he said. "I haven't heard anything of the Gatekeepers in a long time."

"You must have been living underground." Not the Grey Vale? Or the borderlands? No, both of those places had played a big enough role in recent events that word would have reached him. Maybe he'd been hiding in a liminal space instead.

"Something of the sort," he said. "Your cousin…"

"Ilsa is Gatekeeper of Death, the only member of the Lynn family to still hold her title and her magic."

"That's why she can banish wraiths."

"Among other things." If he wanted to target my cousin as a potential business partner instead, he was out of luck. Ilsa would never let him get her into trouble with the guild, and she'd know from my mistake not to trust him to keep his word.

He'd come back for me, though… and he'd saved me from bleeding out. Maybe Brook had been wrong. Puck wasn't just in this for himself. But what else was he after if he hadn't known my past as Gatekeeper? If he didn't know my mother had schemed against the Courts and that my Sight was my last souvenir from the life I'd once had?

"There were two Gatekeepers," he said. "Summer and Winter. One for each Court."

"Where did you think I got the Sight?" I asked. "Did you think I was part faerie?"

"You speak as though it's a bad thing."

"It isn't." I spent all my time around faeries and knew more about them than I did humans… with him being one of the few exceptions. "You've seen me fight with an iron blade. I'm as human as you can possibly get."

"It was seeing you fight that made me wonder if you were fae."

What was I supposed to say to that? "You don't last long as Gatekeeper unless you know how to fight against the Sidhe."

"Was that your job?"

"Only if they misbehaved." I turned my attention on my shredded top, checking on the wound. Not a trace was left. Sal did have a gift for healing, then. "Nah, the Gatekeepers were more peacekeepers. Our role was to stop the Sidhe's temper tantrums from catching humans in their path. Given the state of this realm, it's safe for you to assume we screwed up royally."

"You're not Gatekeeper any longer."

I'd had a rough enough day without explaining *that* epic clusterfuck. "No. My cousin broke the curse and saved us all. Yippee."

"Did you just say 'yippee'?"

I rubbed my forehead. "Look, I just came close to bleeding out. Should I send someone to pick up the body from the shed? They should get in there before the mercenary cleanup crew makes a mess of the place."

"I sent Sal," he said.

"You told him what to do? And he listened?"

"I'm told I'm quite charming."

I snorted.

"Was that a laugh?"

"What favour did you promise him?" His words urged me to let down my guard, but I couldn't forget that he'd turned his back on me not so long ago.

"Whatever he asks for. I doubt it'll be outside my capabilities."

Another snort. This time he grinned while I shook my

head at him. "Charming indeed. Don't let your head get stuck in the door frame on the way out."

His brow arched. "You're kicking me out?"

"I want to clean up before I head home." In fact, I was in a living room I was fairly sure belonged to Sal, which was weird to think about, especially as he wasn't in. My legs were a little shaky, but I had to hand it to Sal—he'd healed me despite his dislike of me and the company I kept.

I found a bathroom through a nearby door, where I washed my hands and face. I'd have to change out of my bloody clothes when I got home, but keeping Puck out of my sight made it easier to think clearly. I'd be having words with the mercenaries—that was for sure—but they had zero control over who sent them job listings. Had that guy who'd posted the job ever been human, before the faerie had taken his place?

Had he been working with the killer? The presence of the body in his shed certainly indicated that was the case. I hadn't asked if the victim had been Seelie, like the others, but I'd probably have to wait for them to identify him first. Then Puck and I could—

No. Not "Puck and I." We weren't partners. I'd already established that. Yet he'd convinced Sal to pick up the body, and… dammit, why did he have to save my life and complicate everything in the process? I'd never truly established he wasn't involved in the murders himself.

I pressed my hand to my forehead. Five dead, all marked with the same symbols. The clues rattled around in the back of my mind, refusing to connect. If the killer was indeed absorbing the victims' magic at death, how many more would they need to kill before they were satisfied?

I found Puck waiting outside the bathroom when I left but not Sal. He must be fetching the body from the shed or dealing with the clean-up crew.

"You're still here?" I asked. "Where's Roseanne?"

"No idea," he said. "She disappeared after I brought you into Sal's house."

"She might have gone home." Given our last experience together on half-blood territory, I wouldn't blame her for keeping out of the way. "My house, I mean."

"I'll walk you there," he said.

I hadn't the energy to argue. "Fair warning, I have two mercenary housemates who might ambush you and want to compare the size of their swords with yours."

"The size of my *what?*"

I gave an eye-roll. "I meant that literally. They collect monster teeth and weapons and spend all their free time comparing… stop laughing at me."

Honestly. The blood loss didn't help, but Puck was not making it any easier by snickering like a twelve-year-old. "I'll accept the risk if it means I get to see your room."

"I'm the one suffering from blood loss, not you." What did *that* mean? "Stay outside and behave yourself."

He laughed behind me as we walked the short distance to my house. Unfortunately, Meathead was in the process of unlocking the door, and he stopped to ogle me as I walked into the front garden. "How'd you end up covered in blood?"

"Bad job." I waited for him to go in first so I could head upstairs and look for Roseanne without giving away that she was still here.

Meathead eyed Puck, taking in his pointed ears and green eyes. "You brought another faerie home?"

"I have no intention of intruding on your hospitality," said Puck in such polite tones that he sounded like a totally different person to the guy who'd spent the last few minutes laughing over unintended sexual innuendo. "I simply walked Holly home."

Meathead grunted and walked into the hall, kicking mud off his boots.

I leaned in to whisper to Puck, "Let's just say they aren't taking kindly to me taking in a harbinger of death."

"You really took her in, then?" he asked, his voice scarcely a murmur.

"I'm figuring out a plan. It'd be easier if people didn't keep trying to kill both of us." I avoided his gaze, abruptly wishing he was still poking fun at me instead of asking serious questions. "Wait out here. I'll be back in a second."

I darted into the hallway and headed up to my room, unlocking the door. At once, it became apparent that Roseanne wasn't there. I crouched to check under the bed in case she'd hidden in her crow form, but no signs of her materialised. She hadn't come back to the house at all.

"Roseanne?" I called, keeping my voice low enough not to be heard downstairs.

No response. With a sinking sensation in my chest, I locked up again. Then I left the house and found Puck waiting outside. "She's not home. Where'd you last see her?"

"Outside Sal's house," Puck said. "She disappeared as soon as he answered the door."

Had the other half-faeries driven her off their territory? It wouldn't surprise me if they had, but after our close call earlier, I wanted to make sure she was safe. "I'd better check half-blood territory. Sal tried to attack us with thorns the last time I took her there."

"Is she truly the Morrigan's daughter?"

"Of course she is. Why?" I turned on my heel and began to head back to half-blood territory at a fast stride.

Puck kept pace with me easily. "I wondered why the others were so afraid of her."

"It's superstitious bullshit," I said fiercely. "She has absolutely nothing to do with the murders, death fae or not."

He didn't reply, which only fuelled my annoyance. I reached the gate to half-blood territory and nearly collided with Brook on his way out.

Brook glided out of my path, his mouth pulling in a frown. "Holly. Is it true that you found the body of another half-faerie in a human's home?"

"Did Sal tell you?" I guessed. "The human turned out to be a faerie in disguise, and the body had been in his shed for days. Sal has gone to pick up the body and bring it back to half-blood territory. Have you seen Roseanne?"

"Who?" he said distractedly.

"The half-faerie kid who was with me last time I came here," I said. "She can turn into a crow…"

"The harbinger?" he said.

I tensed at the word. "Or so they call her. I got stabbed while fighting the fae hiding in that human's house and needed Sal to patch me up, and Roseanne ran off while I was recovering."

"I assume she's around," he said. "I'm going to meet with Sal myself, but I expect he'll want you to update him on what you found at the house."

"I already did." Puck stepped in. "We'll speak to him again later if need be."

"No bloody chance," I muttered while Brook ran off with a hurried "goodbye." "He'll probably assume I'm in his debt for life after he healed me. Anyway, where the hell is Roseanne?"

My nerves stood on end, not at all helped by the reminder that death fae had been loose in the area and that most people would sooner believe Roseanne was working with the death fae than against them. At least the gate had been restored to its former state after the mess I'd been forced to make of the thorns, so I entered at a fast pace, keeping both eyes open for any jet-black crows sitting in the trees. If she was still covered in death-stealer slime, she'd have trouble shifting, so maybe she was in human form. There had to be an easier way to find her...

I halted and dug in the pocket of my coat, finding the spare tracking spell Ilsa had given me. All I needed to activate it was something of Roseanne's, and a quick inspection of my sleeve found several long dark hairs which definitely belonged to her.

Puck raised his brows. "Are you sure that'll work?"

"It worked on you." I put down the bracelet-shaped spell, which expanded into a circle at my touch, and then dropped the hairs into it.

"So that's how you found me," he mused.

Before I could reply, the spell ignited in green and sent me plunging inside a vision of half-blood territory. I recognised the road running parallel to the territory as I walked down the street... or rather, Roseanne did. My gaze was on the fence circling the territory until a shadow fell over me from behind and a large hand lifted me into the air.

A scream tore from my lungs, unheard, as the hand gripped the scruff of my neck and carried me down the nearby road, away from half-blood territory and around a corner. The roads blurred with the speed of our movement until a shimmering line appeared in the air before us, stretching in each direction like an invisible rope. The dark shapes of houses on the other side of the line faded before my eyes, to be replaced by a path winding between trees which looked grey and washed out… trees taller and more unearthly than any I'd seen in this realm.

Then my captor moved forward, carrying me through the invisible line and into the forest beyond.

Impossible. My shock jolted me out of the spell. "No. Fuck. Not there."

I leapt to my feet and ran towards the gate to half-blood territory, following the route I'd seen in the vision. Puck called my name, but I ignored him, picking up speed around the corner. I hadn't a hope of matching the frantic pace of the person who'd taken Roseanne, but I already knew where I'd find the road where the Ley Line cut through the city.

The invisible barrier between this realm and Faerie barely existed from my perspective, hardly a shimmer in the air, but if I squinted, the shimmer darkened enough to give the impression of a transparent path…

Puck hissed out a warning. My eyes snapped open again as a shadowy tentacle reached for me, and I whirled around, grabbing my knife. This death stealer was half-gone already, its tentacles flattened as though something heavy had trodden on it, but it attempted to latch on to me all the same. I hit out with my knife, and Puck transformed into a leaping flame. The tentacle ignited like a pile of dry leaves, while a coughing laugh came from the bushes near the dying beast.

I ran over to the noise, where a redcap lay in the undergrowth, his body squashed in a manner similar to the death stealer, as if a giant beast had trampled him flat. When he saw me, he gave another wheezing laugh.

"Who did that to you?" *They took Roseanne.* Whomever it was, I needed to find them.

Blood bubbled up from his mouth. "Death... death rides among us..."

"Hey." I crouched beside him. "Tell me who took Roseanne."

"The harbinger is theirs now." His laughter faded to silence, his sightless eyes staring up at the sky.

"Who's they?" I demanded. "Damn you. I have to know who took her."

"Holly." Puck's voice radiated concern as he strode over to me. "What did he say?"

"They took her to Faerie." My voice trembled. "Some death fae captured her and took her to Faerie—to the *Grey Vale.* Through the Ley Line."

And they'd trampled their own kin on the way through. Rather harsh of them, but I shouldn't expect any less from Vale fae.

Why would they take Roseanne? She'd already said her evil mother didn't want her... but if she did? The last time the Morrigan had been wronged, she'd nearly unleashed the apocalypse on the human realm.

"Holly." Puck reached for my arm, but he stopped

short of touching me. "Holly, going into Faerie would not be a wise idea."

My hands clenched. "It wouldn't be the first time. Besides, it's not your decision to make."

I turned my back on the dead fae and strode away, thinking hard. Only the Sidhe had the ability to cross between realms, which painted Roseanne's kidnappers as Vale rogues and made it near impossible for me to figure out a way to follow her. Few half-Sidhe had the ability to cross between realms. If Puck was one of them, I'd owe him more than I could repay in a lifetime if I asked him to take me there. There had to be someone else…

River. Ilsa's boyfriend. He had a faerie talisman, which allowed anyone in his company to cross into Faerie through anywhere on the Ley Line. Not to the Grey Vale, but I'd figure that part out later.

I pulled out my phone and called Ilsa. It rang a few times, and then, to my intense relief, she picked up.

"Holly," she said in a muffled voice. "Hang on. The signal is shit in here. What is it?"

"Urgent question," I said. "Can I borrow River for a second? I need his help to get to Faerie."

11

eath rides among us. The words echoed in the back of my head like a mantra as I explained the situation to River and Ilsa. They'd agreed to meet with me at a supernaturals-only café near the necromancer guild, which at least spared me the risk of getting caught inside the guild's base at the worst possible time.

"No," said River in response to my request. "I have an invitation to the Court, not to the Grey Vale. Only a Sidhe can send you there, and there's no guarantee they'd let you come back."

"I'm aware of that," I said. "I wouldn't ask if it wasn't an emergency, but death faeries kidnapped Roseanne."

"Who's Roseanne?" asked River.

"Her friend," Ilsa ventured. I could tell she didn't quite buy my story about how I'd accidentally acquired a death-faerie roommate, but it wasn't like Roseanne could back me up at the moment.

"She's a half-faerie," I explained. "Half death faerie,

which is why the other half-bloods don't give a shit about her. Neither does anyone else."

Except me.

River's expression clouded. "My talisman… it can't take you to the Vale."

"Nor mine," said Ilsa. "Yes, the Gatekeeper's book can theoretically cross realms, but—"

"No," said River firmly. "It nearly killed you the last time you tried it. Your talisman is designed to open the gates of Death, but the Vale isn't part of Death *or* Faerie."

"It used to be." The Vale had once belonged to Faerie, before the Sidhe had decided to exile their own gods and had ripped a part of their own realm away in the process. As a result, the Vale was a literal death trap in every sense of the word and consisted of endless forests of trees which never aged, death fae who even the Courts wouldn't accept, and abandoned relics of the gods which were more than likely to kill the person who picked them up. Most Sidhe barely acknowledged the place existed, and as River rightly claimed, going to the Vale did not guarantee walking out again in one piece.

Ilsa's lips pressed together. "If one of the Sidhe transported you into the Vale, you wouldn't be able to navigate the place. You'd need a talisman—and any Sidhe already in there would have total control over its paths."

Meaning I'd likely run into a trap the instant I set foot there. What use was a lone human against the dark beings which had survived the worst Faerie had to offer? Yet abandoning Roseanne to a brutal death would be etched on my conscience forever. Dammit, I'd once been Winter Gatekeeper. I must have some leverage left over from my years of running around doing favours for the various Sidhe of the Winter Court.

"Then take me to Winter."

Ilsa's brows rose. "You want to ask the Unseelie Queen for help?"

"No. The Morrigan." It was a wildly risky plan, but compared to potentially getting stranded in the Vale for the rest of my life, I'd take it.

"You want to speak to the queen of the death fae?" asked River.

"She's Roseanne's mother," I said. "Roseanne already told me the Morrigan has zero attachment to her half-human offspring, but maybe I can make an appeal to her conscience."

"Does she have one?" said Ilsa.

"Probably not." If anything would stir her to action, though, her daughter being captured by Vale rogues might be it. "Might be worth a shot. I'm all out of better ideas."

River studied me. "I can take you to the path between the Courts, but you'd have to walk to Winter yourself. You'd also have to find your own way back."

"I can do that," I said. "I know the Unseelie Court like the back of my hand."

Certainly better than anywhere in the mortal realm, anyway. Ilsa's gaze caught mine, and I detected a flash of pity that I didn't care for in the slightest. I'd have preferred to go it alone, not stoop to begging for her help, but without another route into Faerie, I had no choice.

Morgan walked into view, holding the lead of the fluffy black faerie dog which immediately drew the attention of everyone in the café. A half-dozen people cooed and fussed over the puppy before he reached our table, at which point the puppy spotted me and tried to hide behind Ilsa's legs.

"Hey," said Morgan. "You want to get into Faerie?"

"You told the whole guild?" I asked Ilsa.

"No, she told me," said Morgan.

"Isn't that basically the same thing?"

Ilsa snorted. "Fair point, but most of the guild doesn't know anything about Faerie. They certainly wouldn't get in your way. Nor will I, but I'm going to stand by my point that it's a bad idea."

"I never said it wasn't," I said. "I just need someone to get me through the Ley Line. I can figure the rest out myself."

"Take Pepper with you." Morgan attempted to coax the faerie dog out from under the table. "He knows Faerie."

"Didn't he try to run away the last time you brought him to the Death Kingdom?"

"You're going *there?*" Morgan said. "Not to see that creepy Morrigan?"

"I never said I made sensible life choices."

He handed me the end of the puppy's lead. "Take Pepper with you. He's good to have around in a crisis."

He doesn't like me. The words died in my throat as the puppy shuffled out from under the table at Morgan's command. Maybe having backup wouldn't be a bad idea, but entering Faerie in the company of a dog which was as likely as not to run off and leave me stranded seemed a risky venture.

"All right." I took in a breath. "Better not delay, then."

River and Ilsa exchanged glances before getting to their feet, and our group left the café. Pepper made two attempts to escape on the way, earning more fuss from strangers at the tables near the door, but he seemed resigned to his fate as we walked away from the guild and towards the half-faeries' part of the city.

The Ley Line cut through the heart of the city, and I could theoretically cross into Faerie at any point, but I hoped it might give me a better shot at finding Roseanne if I followed the exact path of her captors. At one time, I'd been able to access Winter via a gate next to my family's home on Faerie's doorstep, but now I had to rely on the faerie dog to steer me in the right direction.

When we neared half-blood territory, none other than Puck walked into view. When he stopped in front of me, the others stared at him, recognising him as fae.

"Holly," he said. "You should know—the other half-faeries are looking for you."

"What do they want with me?" Seriously? If it wasn't about the fact that kidnappers had grabbed Roseanne right outside their territory, I wasn't interested.

"To question you about the body you found in that shed. They're worried—"

"If they think Roseanne is the one who put it there, I'll invite them to shove their words where the sun don't shine as soon as I get back from rescuing her from Faerie."

"That's not it." His bright-green eyes were unusually serious. "Death fae have been found in other places in the city. There are rumours."

"They can wait." I nodded to the others. "Come on, let's get this done."

"What body in a shed?" Morgan asked. "You never said you found a body."

"Was it like the others?" Ilsa asked curiously.

"Yes, with the same marks and everything, but that's

not the point." Why had Puck chosen now to show up and derail me? "You can all go and talk about the murders to your heart's content once River gets me over the Ley Line to Faerie."

"I'm not going to talk about the murders," said Puck. "I'm coming with you to Faerie."

"What?" I blinked at him. "You don't even know where in Faerie I'm going."

"The Courts?"

"No, the Death Kingdom."

I thought *that* would push the ridiculous idea out of his head, but he said, "Very well. That's fine."

"Are you serious?" said Morgan. "Nothing about that place is 'fine.' It's a fucking nightmare."

"Yes, it is." Ilsa looked at Puck as though she thought he had a screw loose, and I was inclined to agree. "Are you sure you aren't planning to turn on Holly and stab her when her back is turned?"

"Good question."

"You'd believe so little of me?" he said. "After I saved your life?"

"He saved your—?"

"Okay, that's enough bullshit," I said, interrupting Morgan's question. "Puck, you're welcome to come with me. I might need help keeping hold of our guide."

The faerie dog whined and tried to grab Morgan's leg, but he gave him a gentle shove in my direction. "Pepper, I know you don't want to go, but it won't be for long. I'll be here when you get back."

"So will we." Ilsa waited with Morgan, while River stepped up to our side.

"Ready?" he said.

"Sure." To the others, I added, "I'll see you soon."

"Good luck," Ilsa said.

Too late to turn back now.

The question remained, though, of whether Faerie would deign to leave me alive and unharmed when I was no longer their Winter Gatekeeper… or if I'd end up facing the same fate as the other humans unfortunate enough to wander into their midst.

River stepped through the invisible line, and Puck and I followed, with Pepper the faerie dog bringing up the rear. The air rippled around us, the street disappearing and the houses blurring into a solid mass.

The next thing we knew, we stood on a path which wound between large oak trees. River turned back to face me, his green eyes brighter in the blazing sunlight. "Here you are. I'd offer to wait on the path, but given the way time passes here…"

"Don't worry about it." I held Pepper by the lead. "Our guide will get us out."

Assuming Puck *didn't* stab me in the back when it was turned. With his bright hair and eyes, he fit right in here among the towering oaks and the vibrant leaves, but I wasn't fooled by Faerie's pleasant facade. This was the main path which connected Summer and Winter, and since we were closer to the Summer side, the vibrant flowers and evergreen trees almost masked the poisonous deadly brightness which waited like a Venus flytrap ready to devour us.

On the right-hand side lay the main route into the Winter Court, our destination. I turned my back on Summer's brightness and hoped the Death Kingdom was in the same direction as it had previously been. A flash of light told me River had left us. Pepper gave a whine.

"I didn't know you knew any half-Sidhe with access to the Courts," said Puck.

"That was River, Ilsa's boyfriend."

"Your cousin," he said. "The Gatekeeper."

"Of Death. Hell of a title, I know." I began to walk down the path, coaxing Pepper to walk with me. "I'm the one who even faerie dogs are afraid of, though."

"Really?" He crouched beside the puppy and laid a hand on his fluffy head. "What's the problem?"

I looked down at him, bemused. "You understand him?"

He'd understood Roseanne in her bird form too. How many more skills did he have which he hadn't shared yet? They'd come in handy in Faerie, but the question of his trustworthiness lurked out of sight like alluring flowers hiding a deadly poison. He'd agreed to help me where the others hadn't, but I didn't begrudge them that choice. I owed them, not the other way around.

When he rose to his feet, the puppy had visibly relaxed without him saying a word. "Animals are easier to understand than people."

"I agree with that one." I decided not to add that animals tended to mistrust me as much as humans did, but at least their behaviour was readable. More so than humans... and certain half-faeries. "Right... it's this way."

"You've been here before," Puck observed.

"Yes, I have." Now that he knew I'd been one of the Sidhe's two Gatekeepers, he had a fifty-fifty shot at guessing which one, but all doubt would vanish once we reached the Winter Court. "Would you have been able to enter Faerie without River?"

"No," he said. "Not without an invitation, and I am not in favour with the Courts, you might say."

"You and me both." I kept a hand on my knife as I continued down the path, adding that to my mental list of facts about him. He wasn't in Faerie's favour or among the few half-Sidhe with the privilege of truly belonging to two worlds.

"You didn't part on pleasant terms, then?" he asked.

I glanced at him. "We didn't part on any terms at all. The curse broke, and my access to the Courts cut off automatically."

"Seems harsh," he remarked.

"Blame my cousin Hazel, not me."

While I'd been running errands for the Unseelie Queen, Hazel had been trying to solve the Erlking's murder, and she'd ended up stumbling upon a hidden community of Summer Sidhe who'd gone into hiding while their queen plotted to steal the throne of the Summer Court. The Aes Sidhe also happened to be the originators of the Gatekeeper's curse, but some trickery on behalf of the Erlking of Summer had seen to it that future Gatekeepers had served Summer and Winter instead of them. That was our role—to be passed like toys among the Sidhe, who hardly cared if they broke us.

Ultimately, Hazel had ended the curse in a desperate gambit which had thrown us both out of Faerie, but while she'd had the chance to repair her relationship with Summer, I hadn't set eyes on the Unseelie Queen since our brief meeting at the new Erlking's coronation several months ago. I hadn't a clue how the rest of the Court would receive me, but I found myself keeping a hand on the hilt of my blade as we walked.

"You carry iron here," Puck remarked. "Is that wise?"

"Winter fae usually don't mind." They'd use any underhanded method against me, given the chance, and now, I had no other advantages left at my disposal. "Except the Unseelie Queen, but I have zero intention of visiting her today."

"Good," he said. "The Unseelie Queen and I are not friends, but the Morrigan and I have no history, good or bad."

"I find that hard to believe."

He chuckled under his breath, and we walked until the trees shed their meagre coatings of leaves and their branches warped into twisting shapes like contorted limbs. When I'd possessed Winter magic, the ever-present chill in the air had invigorated me, but now, it bit at my skin and sapped my energy. I tugged my coat tighter around myself and kept walking, taking care to keep outside of the route which led to the centre of the Winter Court.

Instead, I veered onto a well-trodden path which led uphill between bushes which were spiked like dismembered claws and thick trees which blotted out the light. Puck didn't seem bothered by the closed-in path, but while he wasn't visibly armed, he must have had a weapon or two hidden away somewhere.

"Watch out for banshees," I warned him. "If you hear wailing, strike first."

"I'll keep that in mind," said Puck. "I'm sure every corner of Faerie has its charms, but this one seems somewhat lacking."

I took a wild guess that *he* hadn't been here before. "It beats the Grey Vale by a fair margin."

The banshees were the worst part aside from the Morrigan herself, with a tendency to act out their own premonitions of death by ripping their victims to shreds. While some poor soul's bloody entrails were strewn over the nearby plants, the first noise we heard was a deafening crack like a tree being torn up by the roots.

I went for my knife as an ominous creaking noise came from among the nearby trees. Then one of them tumbled forward, its heavy form heading right for our group.

I ran forward, fast, and the branches slammed into the path inches from where we'd been standing. When Puck and I skidded to a halt on the other side, a giant beast appeared from the gap where the tree had stood—an ogre, towering over us with blood streaking its stone-like skin.

The ogre bared its craggy teeth at us. "I will feast well on the two of you!"

"Not if I can help it." I brandished my knife, but the ogre reached for my companion instead.

His hand grasped empty air when Puck vanished, and a shower of leaves slid from the ogre's grip. As the beast spun around in confusion, the leaves drifted back to earth, and Puck appeared from their midst, safely out of reach.

"Nice trick." I leapt forward, slashing upward with my knife.

The iron cut deep into the ogre's chest, and blood fountained over my hand. Grimacing, I withdrew the blade, but the ogre was slow to see its upcoming death. It hit out with its fist, knocking me flat, my knife flying into the bushes.

"Shit." I crawled over to the bushes to fish out the weapon while Puck shifted into a snake and slithered between the ogre's giant hairy feet. His fangs sank into the beast's ankles once, twice. My heart caught in my throat when the ogre stamped its massive foot, but Puck took flight in the form of a bird before descending upon the ogre's head. Claws sliced into its eyes, eliciting a bellow of rage.

I removed my knife from the spiny bush and leapt at the ogre's slumping back, my blade sinking into its spine. The momentum sent the beast staggering forward, while Puck took flight out of range before turning human again. The ogre's heavy form hit the path with a thump which rattled the nearby trees and brought down a shower of twigs.

"Nice job." Breathless, I resheathed my knife. "You have no end of tricks, don't you?"

Instead of replying, Puck glanced behind us. "Where's the puppy?"

"Oh, crap." I made for the nearby patch of trees, my heart sinking in my chest. "Hey, Pepper?"

No reply came, but Puck caught up to me in a gliding step. "Are you sure you want to leave the path?"

"I'm fairly sure Ilsa and Morgan are capable of sending a ghost to haunt me for eternity if they find out I lost their pet. That's worse than anything Faerie can throw at me."

Wandering into the forest was a bad idea in a wild area like this one, but it was that or have to sit here calling out, "Here, doggy!" like a fool for the next few hours.

"They did send him to guide you." Puck walked behind me into the mass of shadowy trees.

"Why are *you* here, then?" I asked him. "Seriously, there's nothing in this for you. Is there?"

"Is it hard to believe that I thought it unwise for you to go to Faerie alone?" he said.

"You and everyone else." I scanned the dense trees, seeing no signs of the puppy. "Can you use your animal speech trick to find the puppy?"

"No need." He simply pointed to the end of the dog's lead, which lay in the mud at my feet. I picked it up and followed the trail until I found the faerie dog shivering under a bush.

Puck crouched down beside the bush and reached out a hand while I watched in bemusement as he expertly coaxed Pepper over to him.

No end of tricks indeed. I just hoped they'd be enough for both of us to make it out of here in one piece.

12

I held Pepper's lead firmly as we walked, but he didn't try to run again until a familiar horrible smell hit us as we ascended a small hill which brought us within sight of the Morrigan's lair. The stench of newly dead bodies mingled with decay and coppery blood, and I gripped the lead to discourage him from running off. "I don't like it either, Pepper, but this is our destination."

"I'll take him," said Puck, "while you talk to the Morrigan. This is her home, isn't it?"

"Unfortunately, yes." I handed the faerie dog to him as we walked down the hill towards a large moat comprised mostly of piled corpses of dead fae. Crimson water flowed between the pile of mangled bodies, while a bridge led across to a giant mound of stone and mud in the centre. "She lives in there."

"How delightful," said Puck.

"Isn't it?" I said, trying not to breathe in. "Let's see if she's in a good mood."

While Puck coaxed the reluctant faerie dog to stay at

his side, I crossed the bridge and did my best to ignore the smell of rot lingering around us. The Morrigan wasn't just a soul-eating monster: she presided over the territory which the dead passed through on their way to the afterlife or whatever lay beyond. Sometimes, she ate their souls instead, depending on her mood.

One of her ogre security guards stood between us and the cave where the Morrigan made her home. A tad jumpy after my encounter with his fellow ogre earlier, I rested a hand on my knife when the large ogre looked down at me. "State your name."

"Holly Lynn," I said. "Winter Gatekeeper. You already know who I am."

"You aren't the Gatekeeper any longer," he said.

Tell me something I don't know. "I seek an audience with the Morrigan regardless."

He indicated Puck. "And him?"

"I'll wait outside, if you don't mind," said Puck. "Go ahead."

"Just make sure you don't fall into the water," I warned before turning back to the ogre. "No funny business, or I'll stick you with my knife."

And on that promising note, I walked into the Morrigan's cave. A group of jet-black crows flew over my head, prompting me to duck, but they didn't attack me. In truth, I wasn't entirely sure what to expect from the Morrigan. The last time I'd been here, I'd accompanied my cousins to help them find out if she was helping the Seelie Queen with an attempted coup. She'd turned out to be innocent that time around, but she'd also refused to help in the battle which had followed. It was anyone's guess as to how she'd react to my current dilemma.

Small fae which resembled fireflies gathered in clouds on the ceiling, casting faint streams of light upon the being hunched on the throne in the cave's centre. The Morrigan's craggy face hadn't changed an inch, with her silver crown the only splash of colour against her dark attire. When she sat upright, her body was more bird than human, with her large black wings clamped to her throne by the same iron chains which held down her clawed arms. A testament to her power—iron sapped her power but didn't kill her like it did the other fae. Even chained in iron, she was a force to be reckoned with, and now, I no longer had the protection of the Unseelie Queen to keep her from striking me down with her army of crows.

Nevertheless, I kept my expression free of any fear as I walked up to her throne. Her gaze lingered on my forehead and the mark that wasn't there any longer, and she released a cackle of laughter. "The Winter Gatekeeper returns. How fortuitous."

"What's so funny?" I kept my tone dispassionate, masking my annoyance.

"I told you myself that your ancestors' mistakes would have consequences, didn't I?" she said. "I wish I had witnessed the fallout of Thomas Lynn's sacrifice. I heard it was… explosive."

That was one way of putting it. Both queens who'd been fighting over Faerie had died when Hazel had broken the curse and set us both free. As to why the Morrigan found that so amusing, it was anyone's guess. "We're none the worse for it. Our family is free from the curse."

She rattled her chains. "Nobody is free. Some chains are simply more visible than others."

Whatever *that* meant, I had no desire to spend longer in here than I had to. "Morrigan, I wish to ask for a favour. Your daughter is missing, and I believe she's been captured by death faeries and taken to the Vale."

"My daughter," she said. "Which daughter would this be?"

"Roseanne," I said. "You've met her, haven't you?"

"You know my half-human offspring are all the same in my eyes," she said. "I'm surprised she lived long enough to fall prey to the Vale faeries."

Ugh. I could see why Roseanne hadn't felt particularly kindly towards her.

"She was captured by death faeries," I repeated. "I believe they're holding her hostage and that they have plans to use her for nefarious means."

"She is weak compared to me," said the Morrigan. "She is already as good as dead. Better to let her perish, mortal, rather than linger on."

My hands itched to punch her in her beaky face. Had I really expected anything else from the goddess of death, though? "Surely there's something you can do to help her. You didn't exactly rush to her rescue when Fionn had her captive, but now—"

When I spoke the Huntsman's name, she rose to her full height, or as tall as she could stand with iron chains weighing her down. Her wings extended, causing a deafening clanking sound to echo around the cave. "The Huntsman rides no more. He is no threat to me or to anyone."

I cringed at the noise. "I'm aware of that."

Fionn, the Huntsman, had sealed the Sidhe's fate in more than one way, with his failure spelling the end of the

Vale faeries' attempt at a second invasion as well as the Sidhe's immortality. Up until then, the Sidhe had been reborn into new bodies upon physical death after bathing in the cauldron of resurrection, but these days, the Morrigan and her kin alone held true immortality. Her magic made her an exception to the usual rules but not her half-human offspring. Roseanne was mortal, vulnerable, and alone.

The Morrigan sat down again. "Does the Unseelie Queen know you're here?"

"No," I said. "I came here to ask for your help, not hers. If there's anything within your power you can do, then I'd be grateful if you could help me find your daughter."

"You want to make a deal?" she said. "I might consider helping you find your harbinger if you do something for me."

"Like what?" Tension gripped my shoulders. The Morrigan might not be able to harm anyone in her current state, but that didn't change the fact that she'd worked with Fionn in his second gambit for power and had slaughtered countless humans in battle at his command. Granted, Fionn had been controlling her against her will, but after she'd been slain, she'd been reborn to find herself a prisoner at the hands of the Unseelie Queen. If she asked for her freedom back, I'd never be able to grant her request. "Tell me what you desire before I make my decision."

"As Gatekeeper, you used to deliver messages from me to the Unseelie Queen," she said. "I wish for you to give her a letter on my behalf."

"Seriously?" There must be a catch. "Can't one of your crows deliver it?"

"The letter contains delicate information, mortal," she said. "I'm sure you understand why I cannot risk it falling into the wrong hands."

"Yes, I do." It seemed a simple request, but I'd hoped to escape without visiting the Court. Still, if it gave me the sliver of a chance of getting Roseanne back, I'd accept her offer. "If I deliver this letter for you, will you assist me in rescuing your daughter and ensure that neither of us comes to harm in the process?"

"I will."

The vow hit me square in the chest like a forceful blow. I staggered as a current of sharp magic rushed through my body, a semi-transparent line appearing in midair and connecting me to the Morrigan. Damn if it didn't feel like taking in a deep breath after suffocating in a dark cave. I'd rather chew off my hand than admit so to her face, but from the glint of amusement in her eyes, she'd seen more than I wanted her to.

One of her crows flew down and deposited a slip of paper in my hand, folded into a complex pattern I doubted I'd be able to undo on my own.

The Morrigan shifted on her throne. "When I hear of the letter's delivery, I will send help for my daughter, Holly Lynn. Look for my crow."

Hearing my name from her mouth brought a tug at the invisible connection between us. A vow which would tear me to pieces if I failed to uphold my end of the bargain. Good job I had no intention whatsoever of going back on my word.

I emerged from the cave, gripping the letter in my hand like the lifeline it was—for Roseanne, anyway. Puck and the faerie dog waited for me on the other side of the bridge, so I walked across without looking down at the murky waters or the bodies piled within.

Puck's brows drew together as I reached the other side. "You were successful?"

"I have to deliver a letter to the Queen of Winter," I said. "If I manage to do that, the Morrigan claims she will help search for her missing offspring."

"You made a deal?" he said. "You must know what that means?"

"A vow, I know." Most wouldn't be flippant about such things, but I'd been born with a vow etched into my very existence. When Thomas Lynn had made a deal to serve the Courts, his entire family line had fallen under the same vow since he was mortal and the Sidhe were not, and it'd taken centuries for anyone to undo the curse. This vow, on the other hand, was a simple exchange. One favour for another.

Puck eyed the folded scrap of parchment. "Then for both our sakes, I hope it isn't a trick."

"It isn't." I knew the Morrigan's scratchy handwriting. "I used to deliver letters between her and the Unseelie Queen all the time."

"That doesn't strike me as a fun way to spend one's time."

"This used to be my job," I told him. "I might have been a glorified messenger bird, but at least I had a purpose."

What the hell had I said that for? I'd already told him too much, but the Morrigan's vow tugged at me with every step and made it hard for me to judge my decisions. Bad timing, considering I still had to speak to the Unseelie Queen.

Puck glanced in my direction as though gauging a

response to my accidental outburst and wisely decided on silence. Damn that vow, tugging at my chest and reminding me of the magic which had been ripped away from me when the curse had disappeared into the void.

Returning to the path, we retraced our steps towards the main part of the Winter Court. Since Faerie's paths moved around at random, it wasn't long before we were in unfamiliar territory, and while the smell of the rotting corpses in the Morrigan's lands faded, the chill in the air and the presence of decay lingered. A paradox, maybe, given that nothing new ever grew from the hard soil, but that was faerie logic for you. In Summer, nothing ever died and new life was in constant abundance, so it figured that Winter would have to be an exact contrast. At one time, it might have been different, but no Sidhe either remembered or acknowledged a time before two Courts had dominated their realm. Now that they were no longer immortal, those few lingering memories would pass out of existence soon enough, I didn't doubt.

The sound of beating hooves on the path drew me to a halt. A Sidhe lord rode into view, tall and angular and dressed all in black with gleaming silver buttons on his coat. His dark eyes contrasted the usual bright blue of a Winter Sidhe, while he wore his glossy black hair tied back. His horse was jet black, too, and as swift and sleek as all faerie horses. When I'd been about ten, I'd tried to ride that horse and been thrown head first into a snow-drift, but his gaze showed no recognition at the sight of me.

"Lord Lyle." Relief seeped into me at the realisation that I'd brought us closer to the Court than I'd expected. "Take me to the Unseelie Queen."

His cold eyes looked down at me. "What is a mortal doing in our realm, I wonder?"

"Don't pull that one, Lord Lyle." *Oh, come on.* "There's no need for the selective amnesia. I have a letter from the Morrigan for your queen."

"Then give it to me." He held out a hand without dismounting while his horse sniffed dismissively at me.

"I have to meet her in person." I didn't offer him the letter. "As per the Morrigan's request."

"Then that is your risk to take, mortal." He gripped the horse's reins again, and it broke into a gallop until Sidhe and horse alike had vanished into the surrounding trees.

"Is he normally that friendly?" asked Puck.

"Maybe he fell into a redcap's nest." Or was pissed off that his Court had lost its one loyal human. "Believe it or not, he used to be one of the *least* bloodthirsty Sidhe here in the Court."

Lord Lyle shared the Sidhe's general disdain towards mortals like me, but his lessons had saved my neck in the Unseelie Court several times. I'd have been lying if his dismissal didn't sting a little, even though I understood why the Sidhe would rather pretend they'd never once relied on the aid of humans.

Puck coaxed Pepper out of the bushes—the faerie dog had hidden when the Sidhe lord had shown up—while I turned in the direction Lord Lyle had approached us from. "The Unseelie Court's that way. You should probably stay here."

There was zero chance of a Seelie trickster fae getting in and out without being turned into an ice statue, but I'd already accepted the Morrigan's offer, and I'd have to see through my side of the bargain if I ever wanted to see

Roseanne again. I'd just go into the Court, deliver my letter, and leave. Simple.

"I'll wait for you here, then," he said.

"Right." His gaze was unreadable, and while I might have warned him not to stay within sight of the Sidhe, he had a dozen ways to hide from sight with little effort. "If I'm not back in half an hour, you might as well go back to Earth."

"What?" he said. "Don't suggest—"

"Believe me," I interjected, "if Lord Lyle is anything to go by, the Winter Queen won't be falling over herself to get me to stay in her company. I'll be back before you know it."

And with that, I left him behind and headed into the heart of the Winter Court.

13

Winter's beauty was sharp as knife blades frozen in ice, and the memories of its winding paths cut equally deep. My route took me past sprawling estates blanketed in snow and through patches of trees covered in jewelled snowflakes. My gaze lingered on the clearing where I'd accepted the vow which bound me to take part in the Gatekeeper's Trials to become Winter Gatekeeper, the place where I'd faced an illusion of my mother's wraith and had been officially ranked as equal to a Sidhe.

Now? Faerie's denizens refused to even look me in the eyes. Even Lord Lyle, who'd overseen my training, wanted nothing whatsoever to do with me. I found myself breathing hard as I walked, anger churning inside me, until I reached a familiar road lined with sharp-leafed plants which resembled giant holly leaves, adorned with blood-red berries.

My mother had told me she'd picked out my name the day she'd come here to tell the Unseelie Queen she was pregnant with me, when she'd been speared by one of those plants deeply enough to scar. *And I wonder how I turned out the way I did.*

I took care to avoid the spear-sharp leaves as I walked towards a large mound coated in pure-white snow which never melted. The mound contained the Unseelie Queen's home as well as the beating heart of the Court, and two large ogres guarded the entryway while groups of pointy-hatted redcaps and scaly hobgoblins traipsed in and out, carrying orders back and forth among the gentry. There didn't seem to be a major event like a revel on, but the Unseelie Queen liked to show off her presence to other Sidhe, in contrast to the Erlking of the Seelie Court, who was notoriously reclusive. Or he had been before his death. I didn't know if his replacement was the same.

I halted outside and addressed the ogres. "I have a letter from the Morrigan to deliver to the Unseelie Queen."

Both of the ogres looked down at me, while the nearest group of redcaps removed their pointed hats with eager expressions as though prepared for the inevitable bloodshed when a human had wandered into their midst. My free hand rested on my iron knife when the ogres didn't move to allow me to enter. I was well aware I wasn't dressed for an audience with the nobility, but short of pilfering an outfit from a noble or begging someone to throw a glamour on me, I didn't have any choice but to walk in there wearing my jeans and jacket and hope that it wouldn't get me turned into an ice statue.

"The Morrigan requested I deliver the letter to your queen in person," I told the security ogres. "I'd advise you not to disappoint her."

The ogres exchanged glances then shuffled to either side to allow me to enter the tunnel beyond them. The redcaps donned their hats again, scowling as though I'd personally let them down by not getting murdered in front of them. At least they had the good sense not to attack me openly, but I kept one hand on the hilt of my knife as I strode into the cave.

I kept my head high, as though I wore the circlet above the symbol on my forehead which gave me the power to summon ice to my fingertips and to gain strength from these very walls. In fact, this was the first time I'd walked through the doors into the Winter Court and not felt the rush of energy emanating from its core. Nevertheless, its raw beauty remained, its ceiling covered in glittering icicles while the illusion of a starry night sky hung over-head. Glittering stalagmites jutted from the floor, shining as though imbued with frozen starlight, and nobles wandered around dressed in finery which put the stars to shame. Beautiful and lethal—those were the hallmarks of the Winter Court.

And within it all, the Unseelie Queen sat on a throne carved from ice, decorated with twin chimeras which wrapped around each side of the chair, their leonine paws placed on the ground and their tails intertwined behind the Unseelie Queen's shoulders. I kept my gaze on the back of her chair and sidestepped a group of redcaps serving drinks as I made my way towards her, trying to ignore the rush of self-consciousness every time I passed an immaculately dressed member of the Sidhe gentry. At one time, I'd have taken my time selecting an outfit from among my glamoured wardrobe which would best fit my mission here, and while no fine clothing could cover up my humanity, I'd never felt so out of place.

I halted when one of the nobles barred my way. "What are you doing here, human?"

"I'm here to deliver a letter from the Morrigan to the Winter Queen, by her personal request."

Like Lord Lyle, he knew perfectly well who I was, but he and the female Sidhe at his side both looked at me with cold, sparkling blue eyes. "You dare to bring iron into our midst?"

"You never had a problem with me using iron in defence of your Court." The act was getting old. Some of the nobles had known me since I could barely walk, for crying out loud. "Besides, I simply came here to deliver a letter from the Morrigan."

"What does *she* want, I wonder?" He held out a hand for the letter.

"I don't know. I didn't read it." I didn't want to know, frankly. Whatever the two wrote to one another had resulted in enough tantrums on both sides for me to be perfectly happy remaining ignorant. Especially now, when a Sidhe temper tantrum might legitimately end in my unwelcome demise.

"Then give it to me," said his female companion.

"Oh, don't be tedious," said a light, chilling voice.

My spine stiffened as the queen's cold voice pierced me from head to toe. The two Sidhe nobles rotated to face the room's centre, where the Unseelie Queen lounged on her icy throne. Her dark hair spilled over her shoulders like a waterfall, and her porcelain skin was the same shade as the snow which covered the floor, while her ice-white dress glittered with silver jewels. More jewels studded her ears and hung around her neck, but the brightest light shone from the carved sword which rested against her throne, never more than an inch from her reach: her talisman, wreathed in the bright-blue glow of Winter magic, and the centre of the Unseelie Court's power.

The air fled my lungs as her impossibly bright eyes fixed directly upon me. I sucked in a breath, my hand trembling against my will as I removed the letter from my pocket.

"Give it to me." She beckoned with one hand.

I walked towards her. Even without the invisible vow tugging at me, the sheer force of her will made it impossible to resist. I halted before her throne, extending a hand to offer her the letter.

The Unseelie Queen plucked the parchment from my hand and unfolded it in a casual flick of the wrist. She read the letter in silence while I tried not to look too closely at her vibrant face. It was generally hard for mortals to look upon the Sidhe, and years in their company hadn't quite dimmed their effect. The Sidhe were beautiful, yes, but with an inhuman quality which reflected what the person who looked upon them found the most stunning and terrifying in equal measures. Without the protection of my Gatekeeper's mark, the dangers were as stark as crimson blood on white snow.

"Interesting." The Unseelie Queen lowered the parchment. "Very interesting. And what did she promise you in return?"

Was I really that transparent? "Did I mention a promise, my queen?"

"I see her mark upon you. I dislike it."

Her words ignited a spark of fear in my chest. When

the queen of Winter disliked something, she then disposed of it by her own hand. When a harpist had displeased her at a revel, she'd had her redcaps tear him to pieces before ripping out his hair to string the harp of his replacement. Another night, a hobgoblin was a touch too slow to bring her a glass of elf wine, so she'd lopped off his head and forced every other hobgoblin in the room to wear one of his teeth on a string around their neck as a reminder for the rest of the evening. Those were just two of the incidents which had been permanently etched into my brain from the Unseelie Queen's revels.

Swallowing down my fear, I said, "I asked her to help me find her daughter. The Morrigan's half-blood daughter. Nothing more."

"The Morrigan's half-blood daughter?" She sat up a little straighter. "Oh, the little harbinger who the traitor Huntsman took a fancy to? The girl is lucky she hasn't been found yet if that's the case."

She has been found. By dark fae in the Vale. Not that I'd be telling *her* that. I hadn't known she'd been aware of Roseanne's unpleasant history with Fionn the Huntsman either.

"Yes, she is," I said. "I should take my leave."

She folded the letter in her hand. "If you find the girl, then do tell her to come and talk to me, won't you?"

Why does she want to see her? Not for any good reason, I assumed. "If I find her, then she'll come back with me, or else the Morrigan's side of the vow will remain unfulfilled."

"Ah, but your vow says nothing about the girl returning to you, does it?" she said. "No, I imagine it doesn't. The Morrigan has no love for her half-blood kin, after all."

Her tone indicated she was in one of her capricious moods. If she liked, she could order me to bring Roseanne directly to the Winter Court and then torture her to death. I had to divert her attention, and fast. "Maybe not, but I doubt you have much use for her either. She lives in the human realm and has never been to the Courts."

"Ah, but she betrayed us all the same." Her soft voice belied the anger glittering in her eyes. "Summer may have forgotten, but I have not."

My blood chilled. "She was controlled by a vow. Fionn bound her, the same as the Morrigan, but she was a child and completely powerless. Now, all she wants is to be left alone."

With every word, the blue glow in the Unseelie Queen's eyes brightened, while the temperature dropped until my quickening breath fogged the air. *Shit.* This was all going wrong. I'd grown too used to freedom, to not having to watch my tongue, and I'd forgotten how uncompromising the Sidhe were when it came to getting what they wanted.

"The Morrigan was justly punished for her crimes, but her daughter was not," she said. "The Huntsman stole from me, and that I will never forgive. Nor will I pardon any who served him."

Her words froze the breath in my lungs, while the bright-blue glow in her eyes made me acutely aware of my own powerlessness. Not that I'd ever stood a chance against her even when I'd had the magic of the Winter Court at my fingertips. The Unseelie Queen was the most powerful individual in Faerie not just because of her position but because she'd won the talisman by slaughtering all the competition.

"If it is the Morrigan you wish to speak to, then I would gladly tell her myself," I said carefully. "The Morrigan does not forgive the Huntsman either."

"The Morrigan forgets that she is not as eternal as she thinks despite being the eldest of us."

What the hell was that supposed to mean? It didn't surprise me that the Morrigan was older than the Sidhe—while they'd lived for hundreds of years, most hadn't been around during the downfall of their gods some thousand years prior—but she was the only one who'd kept her immortality after the destruction of its source. Being a death goddess ensured she was reborn upon physical death, and while I'd never exactly questioned her on her history, I gathered that she'd seen the rise of the Courts and the Huntsman's betrayal as well as the recent loss of immortality and its resulting shockwaves throughout the Courts.

I had zero idea what the Unseelie Queen expected me to say to that, so I kept quiet until she spoke again. "I think we have left the harbingers alone for too long. Why should that child not be mine?"

"If it's a harbinger you desire, surely an adult one would be of more use, and one who lives in Faerie," I suggested. "There are a large number of banshees who I'm sure will be happy to serve you."

"The girl is nearly an adult by now, is she not?" she said.

Unfortunately, she was right. Back home, Roseanne wouldn't be considered a legal adult until she turned eighteen, but Faerie cared little for technicalities, and it wasn't like the Morrigan's daughter had any kind of guardian who might stand up for her—not that anyone who stood between the Unseelie Queen and what she desired was likely to live long anyway. Why she even wanted a harbinger was entirely a mystery, but I'd definitely underestimated her lingering hatred of the Huntsman despite his death in battle and the Morrigan's subsequent imprisonment.

Whatever the case, I could see where this was going. She'd take Roseanne under her metaphorical wing, and whether she survived or not, I'd never see her again.

"I didn't come here to sell a half-human girl into servitude," I said. "I will deliver a response to the Morrigan's letter for you as a favour, if it's what you desire."

"You think you can offer *me* favours?" She rose to her feet, towering over me, her eyes aglow with magic. "You owe me more than you can ever repay, mortal."

"I owe you?" Dread sank its claws into me. "I'm no longer Gatekeeper. The vow was broken."

"I might claim your mother's actions left you in my debt, regardless of whether the vow remains intact or not."

To my horror, twin spirals of glittering ice shot from her hands and struck my booted feet, solidifying until I stood rooted to the spot. *Fuck.* I tensed, part of me wanting to grab my knife, the other part of me knowing it'd mean instant death. If I died, Roseanne was doomed.

"My queen." My voice was brittle, an ice sheet on the verge of cracking. "I—"

The Unseelie Queen waved a hand, and the ice crept up my legs until they were numb from the knees down. "I liked you better with blue eyes."

My heart contracted with fear while my legs numbed and the ice crept higher and higher, past my waist. As it reached my hips, the sound of pounding hooves cut through the cave, echoing from the walls.

"Your majesty!" said a breathless hobgoblin. "Lord Lyle is here to see you with an urgent message."

The Unseelie Queen's beautiful face twisted into a scowl. "Bring him in."

The hob's gaze went to me and the icy coat spreading up my body before he ran out of sight. To my intense relief, the ice's spread halted before it reached my face when two Sidhe entered the room, one of them being Lord Lyle.

Alongside him strode a female Sidhe in similar dark attire. Her bright-blue eyes shone with Winter magic, a similar glow surrounding the sword strapped to her waist, and her long travelling cloak glittered with gemstones. What was her name again? I groped around in my memories and came up blank.

"Lord Lyle," said the Unseelie Queen. "Lady Rive. To what do I owe the pleasure?"

That's her name. Lady Rive, one of the more prominent Sidhe who ruled over a fair portion of the Winter Court—partly because her predecessor, Lord Avalin, had managed to get himself exiled to the Grey Vale and perished there.

Lord Lyle's gaze went to my frozen body for a second and then back to his queen. "There have been more… incidents on the Path of the Dead."

"Elaborate," she said.

"I believe the beasts of the Wild Hunt are trespassing in the Court," said Lady Rive. "They're attacking livestock, savaging our horses, and generally causing mischief."

"Then drive them off," she said. "With force."

"We have yet to set eyes on any of them," said Lord Lyle. "I believe they're searching for the Hunt. Or perhaps for the former Huntsman, though he rides no more."

"I believe the time has come to name a replacement," said Lady Rive. "It's past due, in fact."

Whoa. I was pretty sure I wasn't supposed to witness this discussion, but Lady Rive hadn't noticed my presence, and the others didn't particularly seem to care. The former Huntsman's death had left a void, everyone knew, but was there a point in ferrying souls down the Path of the Dead if the source of immortality no longer existed?

Then again, I suspected some of the Sidhe had kept seeking an end to death even after the loss of their immortality. How could they not, when immortality had been part of the Courts since their inception and had permeated every part of their lives? Considering the immortality source had been the blood of their predecessors, though, it wasn't easily replaced. If any of the gods still lived, they were keeping their distance, and with good reason. Regardless, the replacement Horseman might well find themselves saddled with that responsibility.

The Unseelie Queen studied the two Sidhe before her. "We will discuss this further. Come with me."

After picking up her talisman, she strode out of sight through a tunnel at the back of the cave, followed by Lady Rive. Lord Lyle, meanwhile, turned to my frozen form. "Holly Lynn."

"Lord Lyle." My breath fogged the air. "You remember my name now?"

"Coming here was a mistake," he said. "I told you."

"It was this or break a vow with the Morrigan," I told

him. "Is it true that there's trouble with the former Wild Hunt?"

"Yes, and it's not any of your concern."

"Might be if I'm going to be an eternal ornament in the Court," I said through chattering teeth.

He waved a hand, and the ice encasing me melted in a splash of freezing water which pooled on the ground. I staggered, catching my balance before I slipped over. "Will she punish you for that?"

"Unlikely, given that she left you alone of her own accord," he said. "Provided you don't come back, you should be safe from retaliation. Go, now."

While Lord Lyle headed into the tunnel after the others, I ran shakily towards the way out, unable to believe he'd actually saved my neck. Then again, if the Wild Hunt was causing trouble on their territory, Winter had bigger problems than an ex-Gatekeeper and the Morrigan's offspring.

That is, if Lord Lyle hadn't manufactured the story in order to help me escape. He wouldn't have lied to his queen, though... right?

14

Once I left the cave, I broke into a run. Melting ice plastered my clothes to my skin, making the biting wind even more painful, but fear was a fairly effective motivator to keep me moving forward. For a second, I debated borrowing Lord Lyle's horse to make a quick getaway, but I didn't want to erase his brief moment of goodwill towards me.

Instead, I kept running downhill past the sprawling snow-covered estates of the Winter Court until I ran smack into a giant wall of fur.

"Whoa." Rearing back, I raised my blade at the bearlike creature and then startled when it turned into Puck. Damn if it wasn't an intense relief to set eyes on him again. "What the hell was that?"

"A bear." He beckoned, and a rather cold-looking faerie puppy shuffled after him from the bushes. "You ought to have specified how long to wait for you."

"You know the Sidhe don't have clocks." My words

came out through chattering teeth. "Anyway, I got the job done."

"You're soaking wet," he said.

"Well observed." I began to walk again, resheathing my blade with as much dignity as I could muster. "The queen is as charming as ever, but the bargain is fulfilled. Once the Morrigan sends help after her daughter, anyway."

If her captors had taken her into the Vale, as I'd suspected, then I'd have to leave it to the Morrigan to bring her back. Only a Sidhe could enter the Vale, and I doubted anyone here would be willing to give me more than a one-way trip.

"I saw two Sidhe ride past earlier," he commented. "One of them was the Winter Sidhe you met earlier. They looked quite agitated."

"Yeah, they had some kind of message for the queen." I declined to mention the details, since for all I knew, he didn't know anything about the Wild Hunt either. "It gave me a good excuse to leave early. The Sidhe do love their secret meetings."

He cast me a sideways look, his expression unreadable, while I wondered if he'd guessed how close I'd come to spending an eternity trapped in the Court as an ice statue. If he'd met the queen before, then maybe he did, but he asked no further questions. Instead, Puck kept a firm hold on Pepper's lead as we traversed the forests on the outskirts of the Winter Court.

"I've been dodging redcaps ever since I came here," he told me. "That's why I turned into the biggest and scariest monster I could think of."

"You looked like a big cuddly bunny rabbit. Minus the ears."

He sent me a flicker of a smile. "I've never set eyes on a real bear. Hence the improvisation."

"Is there anything you can't turn into?"

"People," he said. "With the exception of using a glamour, and that's not the same. Are we heading back to see the Morrigan now?"

"No." My briefly lightened mood dimmed. "I completed my end of our bargain, but I can't go to the Vale to make sure she keeps her word. She'll send a crow as a signal, but…"

"She'll keep her word if she dislikes the notion of being in your debt."

"Yeah, but… I still don't know who actually took Roseanne."

The whole point in our bargain was for her to send help so that we didn't have to risk life and limb in the Vale, so why did I feel like I'd failed all the same? Maybe it was the Unseelie Queen's interest in keeping the Morrigan's daughter as her very own harbinger and my subsequent narrow escape. I wouldn't set foot in the Court again if I could help it, but nevertheless…

A screeching cry rang out from among the trees, and I stiffened, hand going to my knife.

"That wasn't the Morrigan's signal?" Puck said.

"No." I slid out my blade. "I figured there'd be a banshee somewhere around here."

"Don't they normally live in the Death Kingdom?"

"Try telling anything in Faerie to stay where it's supposed to." Including me, for that matter.

I stepped into the undergrowth, trying to pinpoint the direction of the cry. Branches crunched beneath my feet, and then a stunning face appeared before me, mouth opening wide as though to scream again.

Her surprise at my appearance turned to delight. "Human prey."

"In your dreams." I thrust upward with my blade, only to find my wrist in the grip of a clawed talon which looked so much like Roseanne's half-shifted form that it threw me off for a moment.

Then her visage flickered around the edges, revealing an older face than the Morrigan's daughter's. Her other claw swung at my neck, but Puck flew at her like a feathery bullet, knocking her aim off. Blood and feathers rained on my head as the blow caught him instead, and a bolt of alarm shot through my core when he landed somewhere in the bushes.

"Damn you." I tried another strike, but my knife tangled in her claws, their leathery surface hard to pierce.

As I tugged my blade free, the faerie dog bounded forward and tackled the banshee flat onto her back. Bemused, I hurried to Puck's side. He'd turned human again, his face covered in blood and his eyes dazed. *Good. He's alive.*

Spinning back to face the banshee, I found her pinned beneath the faerie puppy. I strode over to finish her off, but an idea slid into my mind. Instead of sticking my knife in her, I grabbed a thorny vine from a nearby plant, hooking it around her clawed arms before she could wriggle away.

"Let me go!" she screeched. "What are you doing, mortal?"

I bared my teeth at her. "The Unseelie Queen is looking for a harbinger. I think you'll do nicely."

The banshee opened her mouth to scream, and I tore off part of my already ripped shirt and rammed it into her mouth before a noise escaped. She let out a horrified moan, which deepened when I pointed the iron blade at her exposed throat. A rash sprang to her porcelain skin when the merest tip of the blade brushed its surface.

"Go to the Unseelie Queen and offer yourself into her service in place of another harbinger," I commanded. "Or I'll let you gamble on whether iron poisoning will kill you before you bleed out."

Her eyes widened, darting towards the blade, before she gave a jerky nod of assent. I took a step back and watched her run into the undergrowth before I ran back to Puck, who'd managed to get to his feet. I found myself looking carefully to check he wasn't hiding any other injuries. "You okay?"

He touched a hand to his bleeding face. "Just a scratch. I'll patch it up when I get home."

"Okay." An awkward silence ensued before I forced out the words, "Thank you for getting in her way. Though it wasn't a wise decision."

"You're welcome." A grin tilted his mouth. "Speaking of bad decisions, does that mean you're going to tell me why you sent her to the Unseelie Queen?"

"Not until we're back home."

And probably not even then. I wanted to forget the queen's request that I bring Roseanne directly to her, given that I had yet to see the Morrigan's daughter safely home. If the banshee wasn't enough to satisfy her... then she'd have to come to the mortal realm in person before I gave up Roseanne.

"Agreed," he said. "We'd better get out of here."

Before long, we reached the path which connected the Winter Court with Summer, and it took all my willpower not to veer in the direction of the warm breeze emanating from the other side of Faerie in an attempt to dry off my sodden clothes. Being warmer and more inviting didn't make the Seelie Court any less likely to kill me on sight. The smell of rot lingered in the background, and I spotted the trampled remains of some poor creature lying in the undergrowth near the path. Hoof-shaped marks covered its chest, and the image of the redcap I'd run into before coming to Faerie appeared in my mind's eye. After Roseanne had been taken...

Puck gave me a bewildered stare. "Holly, what are you looking at?"

I dragged my gaze away. "I figure the banshee didn't kill that thing, but I'm not sure I want to meet whatever did."

A short cry made my head snap up, and a small crow flew past us.

"Is that the Morrigan's signal?" said Puck. "Then she's going after Roseanne."

My heart leapt. "Better hope she is, or else our next visit won't be as pleasant."

Pepper tugged on the lead and barked.

"Someone wants to go home." Puck gave a lopsided smile and walked in behind him. "C'mon. Let's get out of here."

The faerie dog led us along the path, which turned transparent as his paws found the invisible lines between realms. The trees faded around us, revealing a road beneath, and within another step, we were no longer in Faerie. Edinburgh's stone buildings surrounded us, while the sky overhead was streaked with pinkish highlights, suggesting it was early evening.

"Shit," I muttered. "It's getting late. I wonder if we missed more than a day or two."

Faerie's idea of time and space was flexible, and it was possible to lose a great deal of time there without trying. Not ideal when we'd been in the middle of a spate of serial murders when we'd left.

"No more than a week," Puck said in confident tones.

"That's still too long." Admittedly, since Roseanne was in Faerie, she'd have experienced time at the same rate as I had, but that didn't make her suffering any less acute. Regret speared my chest, and I reminded myself the Morrigan had promised to help her. She'd bound herself to me.

She had better keep her word.

Puck cleared his throat. "I think you need to change out of those sopping-wet clothes before you catch a cold."

"I'd better return Morgan's pet faerie dog first." I reached to take the lead from him. "Then I'll go home and warm up."

"Right." He watched me expectantly, though I hadn't a clue what he wanted me to say. I'd thanked him for saving my life, and he'd done the same when our positions had been reversed, and yet...

"Why did you come with me?" I blurted. "Can you tell me now? Because I don't know if you feel like I'm obligated to return the favour, but—"

"Not at all." His expression was serious for once. "Is it hard to believe I didn't want you to go into Faerie alone?"

"I wasn't alone." My heartbeat quickened. *He didn't want me to go alone? It wasn't a trick?*

Or was it? The guy was descended from a line of tricksters. He'd been anything but transparent so far, no matter how many times he'd saved my neck. For all I knew, this was one huge elaborate Robin Goodfellow-esque prank.

Pepper barked and tried to tug himself loose from my grip as though to argue against my point, half dragging me along with him, but Puck caught my arm before he pulled me flat on my face. My heart flipped again at his touch. His closeness. Was I misreading him?

"Sure you don't want to come back to mine and warm up?"

No. I wasn't misreading him. If his interest in me wasn't a joke, though... he didn't know my past. Nor, in all likelihood, my mother's either. He didn't know what she'd done or the legacy she'd given me.

"I should ask Ilsa if she found out anything more about those symbols," I said. "Depending on how many days we've lost, her witch friends might have another update."

Puck eyed me, some unreadable emotion flickering in his eyes, but in the end, he simply nodded. "Of course. See you soon?"

"Yeah. I'll... I'll text you."

Get a grip, Holly. Honestly. I'd pissed off the Unseelie Queen not long ago, but she at least was a known entity, if an unpleasant one. Puck, though? He'd flirted and teased me, shrugged off any rebuff, and even followed me into *Faerie* of all places. A stark contrast to most human and half-faerie guys I'd met, who tended to run for the hills the instant they got so much as a hint of my real identity.

What was I supposed to do with that? Any previous dalliances I'd had had been short-lived, impersonal, and entirely within my control. They certainly hadn't involved work colleagues, either, though the Gatekeeper's role was a solitary one by necessity.

These days, nothing at all was within my control, but that didn't mean I needed to add any more complications.

I halted outside the necromancer guild, sending a belated text message to Ilsa to tell her I was here before barging in. Pepper didn't have the patience to wait outside, though, instead yanking the lead out of my hand and sprinting through the doors of his own accord. I let him run, glad that I'd managed not to lose him in Faerie, at least.

Not long after, Ilsa emerged from the doors. "I saw Pepper running back to Morgan. He seemed happy to get out of Faerie."

"So am I, believe me." I sneezed.

"Whoa," said Ilsa. "You're all wet. Are you okay?"

I hadn't intended to tell her anything at all, but when I opened my mouth, I found myself saying, "I had a minor disagreement with the Unseelie Queen."

"Why'd you see *her?*" Ilsa's brow wrinkled.

"The Morrigan wanted me to deliver a letter to Her Majesty in exchange for helping me find Roseanne," I said. "Pretty minor, all things considered. How many days did I miss?"

"Three," she said. "You should know, there was another murder the day you left."

"Ah, shit." A guilty twinge hit me. "How many are we up to now?"

"Five, and you'd better come in out of the cold. Jas is on archive duty again, so we can hang out in there. The boss isn't roaming around at the moment."

I followed her into the guild, alert despite the exhaustion tugging at my bones. If I'd missed another murder, then Puck had, too, so Sal wouldn't be pleased with him. Unless Hawk had taken on the investigative role himself, of course.

Hardly anyone was in the guild's lobby, the novices presumably out on missions or taking the evening off, and Ilsa gave me the occasional glance as we made for the stairs. I was sure she'd guessed more than I'd said aloud about how my trip to Faerie had gone, but I was glad she didn't make any comments.

Of all my family members, she had the most experience knowing how it felt to live among the Sidhe without magic, though our brief friendship as kids had ended after my magic had shown up and my mother had forbidden me from playing with the other Lynns. I'd often wondered what it might have been like to have a sibling, but the sort of rivalry the curse had encouraged would have made it an unpleasant experience for everyone involved. These days, Ilsa and her siblings seemed to get on fine despite their bickering, but would that have been in the case if they'd grown up with a parent like mine?

I slammed a lid on the thoughts, relieved when the silence came to an end as Ilsa and I reached the archive room. Inside, Jas sat in the same chair as before, while Lloyd leaned against the desk and eyed my dripping coat and torn shirt. "What did you do, go for a swim in the river?"

"She went to Faerie, Lloyd," said Ilsa. "I told you."

"Nice." Jas's eyes gleamed with interest.

"Not sure I'd use that word," I said. "Did you translate some more of those witch symbols while I've been gone?"

"Not personally," she said. "I sent the images to Isabel—she's a coven leader and has access to more information than most—and she's struggling, to tell you the truth. Some of them straight-up don't have translations."

Weird. "What, are they really old?"

"Yeah, and blood magic has been out of style for a long while," she said. "Since it was banned. Some of us are trying to make it widely acceptable again, but that doesn't mean it's commonly known."

"Is that a good idea?" I asked. "Considering what you can do with it?"

"Oh, the mages will only legalise the symbols which aren't for dodgy purposes like controlling living and dead people," she said. "No ritualistic sacrifices either. The various spells will be ranked on a scale like necromancy."

That didn't reassure me as much as she probably intended. "That seems rife with potential for abuse."

"If witches can use blood magic legally, it'll open the doors for all kinds of innovations," she said. "Banning it didn't work, besides. It just ended up in the hands of unscrupulous individuals while the rest of us were left completely unprepared to handle the fallout."

"Is the killer one of those unscrupulous individuals?" I asked. "Do you know anything about the newest victim?"

"Not much," said Ilsa. "I heard they were Seelie…"

"The other victims were Seelie too," I said. "Not Unseelie."

"What's the difference?" asked Jas. "Is one the nice Court and the other the evil one?"

"Not quite," I said, really not in the mood to give a beginner's lecture on all things Faerie. "Neither is good or evil, but I wouldn't call them 'nice' either. Seelie is Summer, Unseelie is Winter. Their Courts correspond to those seasons, that's all. I used to work for Winter."

"So that's why there's bits of ice in your hair," said Lloyd.

I combed my fingers through my sodden curls, desperately wanting a hot shower. I'd make this visit quick. "Ilsa, have you spoken to the ghost of the last victim?"

"No, because the half-faeries didn't tell me his name," she said. "I figured they'd rather not know I contacted the ghosts of the other victims without their permission."

"Ah." Would it be too late by now? Most likely. "I'll ask the half-faeries myself, then."

"Hang on." Jas reached in a pocket and handed me a bracelet-shaped spell. "That's a drying spell. I use them after patrolling in the rain."

"Thanks," I said, surprised. "Ilsa—I'll message you if I find out the victim's name."

"Sure." Ilsa waved me off, and I left the archive room and pocketed the spell Jas had given me on my way out of the guild.

Dark shadows filled the streets as I walked home, so I stuck to the lights cast by the old-fashioned lanterns on the walls of the old buildings, daydreaming of a warm shower and bed. My guilt returned at the thought of Roseanne, trapped in Faerie while I had the chance to go home. It seemed selfish of me to stay home in comfort, even though there was little I could do from here, and I'd catch a cold if I didn't get into the warmth soon.

If my sojourn to Faerie had hammered home one fact, it was that I'd never been weaker or more human than I was right now. My pace quickened when I reached my street, only to come to a halt when I found a pile of clothes had been heaped on the front lawn. *My* clothes. Judging by their wrinkled state, it'd rained at least once since I'd been in Faerie. I dug in my pocket for my keys, but they jammed in the lock.

"Oh, fuck that." I gave the door a firm kick, causing it to rattle in its frame. "Hey! Let me in."

Another kick, then the door inched open and Meathead's flat face appeared in the gap. "Holly. You're back."

"What the actual fuck is going on?" I demanded. "Who changed the locks? I live here, in case you've forgotten."

"I thought you weren't coming back," he said. "Where've you been?"

"I was staying with a friend," I said.

"That faerie, right?" His eyes narrowed. "You sleeping with him?"

"No," I snarled, "but so what if I was? It's not illegal. It sure as hell isn't an excuse to throw me out of my house."

"Take it up with the landlord, not me," he said. "We don't want faeries in our house."

"And I don't want bigoted twats in mine, but we all have to make sacrifices."

He closed the door in my face, leaving me with the pile of sodden clothes in the garden and nothing more. Mechanically, I dug in my pocket and found the spell Jas had given me. Might as well use it if I wasn't getting a shower anytime soon.

My clothes dried the instant I activated the spell, as did my hair, while a rush of warmth banished the chill from my skin. That didn't mean I wouldn't get cold if I stayed outside and slept on the street, though, but I'd think about that later.

For now, I gathered my meagre belongings and went to pick a fight with the landlord.

15

The landlord didn't answer the doorbell, but the light in the downstairs window indicated he was at home. I hammered on the door with my fist, my other hand tapping on my phone screen in another attempt to call him and demand an explanation.

The call went to voicemail. Again.

"I signed the tenancy agreement, you thieving piece of shit!" I shouted through the gap in the door. "You owe me two months of rent if you aren't gonna renew the contract."

A message came through on my phone. I read the words *police* and *restraining order* amid the haze of rage that blanked my vision. It seemed "I was in Faerie" was not a good enough excuse for vanishing off the face of the earth, especially when it seemed my tattletale housemates had told him about Roseanne too.

Which put me in an impossible situation. Finding somewhere to rent had been hard to begin with, given that the faerie apocalypse had tanked the housing market as well as making whole areas uninhabitable. Didn't make what he'd had done *legal,* but I had no clout whatsoever.

Incensed, I walked away without really caring where I was going until I came to a breathless halt beside the entrance to half-blood territory. It was a safe bet no half-fae landlords would rent to a human if the others would even tolerate me as their neighbour. Which was debatable, given that some would consider my former Gatekeeper status as proof I wasn't to be trusted. The murders, and the fact that I'd got into Faerie recently where some of them would never see the realm of their ancestors, would not help matters either.

On the other hand, I might as well ask Sal about the most recent victim of the serial killer. As I headed for his house, however, I spied none other than Puck walking towards me. Had he heard about the murderer's latest victim too? In the brief time he'd been at home, he'd cleaned the blood off his face and changed into fresh clothes. My torn shirt and muddy jeans were the least of my concerns, but it didn't seem fair that he could take an unplanned sojourn into Faerie and still come out of it looking that good.

"Holly." His gaze travelled from me to Sal's house. "Did you hear?"

"About the newest murder?" I guessed. "Yes. I was on my way to ask who it was."

"Sal was the victim."

"What?" I stared at him. "He was the victim?"

He was the one who'd hired Puck to begin with. Now that he'd died, would the other half-faeries even want us continuing with the investigation?

"Yes," said Puck. "He died the day we left for Faerie, in fact."

"Crap." I didn't need to ask if he'd had his throat cut by an invisible assailant who'd inked sprawling marks on his skin beforehand. "Who's taken over from him, then? On the case?"

"That's the complicated part," he said. "Hawk was waiting for my return before deciding how to proceed."

"Typical." As if today couldn't get any worse.

"I thought you were going back home." He eyed my backpack. "Weren't you?"

"I got kicked out of my house while I was gone." He'd find out sooner or later if he found me sleeping on a doorstep, I didn't doubt. "I thought I might appeal to Sal's conscience, assuming he wasn't ticked off with me for vanishing in the middle of an investigation, but I guess that's no longer a possibility."

"You got kicked out of your house?" he said. "Why?"

"Because my landlords are greedy dicks and my housemates are worse," I replied. "They don't get Faerie. As far as they were concerned, I left without a trace, and why waste energy waiting for me to come back?"

"I have a spare room," he said. "Above the office. It won't be a problem for Hawk or me if you stay overnight."

"I won't owe you, Puck."

"This isn't a faerie vow situation, Holly," he said. "It's a favour for someone who needs my help. Nothing more."

My resolve began to weaken. The odds of finding anywhere to stay this late in the day were almost zero, and I'd be much better off waiting until morning and starting afresh after a night's sleep and a shower to wash every taint of Faerie from my skin.

"You saved my life in Winter," he added.

"That doesn't mean you owe me either."

"That's not what I meant," he said. "Regardless, the offer is open."

"Just for tonight." I spoke the words clearly and carefully, more a reminder for me than for him. "That's all."

"Of course," he said. "Look, Hawk would make the same offer even if I didn't, and he'd be more than happy to tell you everything we missed while we were in Faerie."

I rubbed my forehead. "Does that mean you'll start answering my questions?"

His expression lightened. "Sure, if it means you won't do anything foolish like sleep outside on the streets."

"It's not like I haven't done it before."

Surprise flickered in his eyes, and I averted my gaze before it inevitably turned to pity. Instead, I led the way to the gates out of half-blood territory and out into the regular street.

It was fully dark by the time the two of us reached the office, and Puck unlocked the door to let us both in. When a low-flying bird drew me to a halt on the doorstep, he gave me a quizzical look. "Holly, what is it?"

Just a seagull. Not a crow. I lowered my gaze. "If Roseanne makes it home during the night, she won't know where to find me."

"I'm fairly sure she remembers the way here. She can fly, remember?" He rested a hand on the door frame. "Holly, you sent the banshee to the Unseelie Queen because she was looking for a harbinger. Is that why?"

How on earth had he guessed? I was too exhausted to concoct a feasible cover story at this point. "I made the mistake of mentioning Roseanne in front of the queen and reminded her of her previous grievances against the death fae. It's up to her if she wants to risk starting a war with the Morrigan over her half-human daughter, which I'd wager she doesn't, so I figured I'd send her a banshee instead. After the banshee tried to kill both of us, I think she got off lightly, personally."

"And the letter you delivered?"

"I didn't read it."

"Then you have admirable self-control," he said.

"Or self-preservation."

"Except for the part when you made a vow that bound you to the Death Goddess in the first place."

"Ha ha." Mildly annoyed that he'd successfully improved my mood, I followed him into the warmth. Through the office, we found Hawk in a back room, which was a kind of kitchen–living room hybrid with modern fittings and more illusory landscape paintings on the walls. Hawk was cooking something that smelled incredibly enticing, considering it'd been ages since my last meal.

"Holly," said Hawk, displaying no surprise at seeing me enter the room along with Puck. "You got out of Faerie in one piece, then?"

"Of course," I said. "Puck offered to let me stay here for the night, so I hope you don't mind giving up your spare room. Turns out my housemates didn't appreciate me bringing faeries into the house and complained to the landlord, who changed the locks on the door while I was gone."

"Is that even legal?" said Hawk.

"No, but it's not like I can deny I brought faeries into the house." I wished I'd figured out a cover story, because

I was far from in the mood to answer any more questions on my former living situation. "It's fine. I'll go and look for another place tomorrow. I just need one night to recuperate."

"Good job I'm cooking enough for three, then," said Hawk.

"Don't turn down a meal from Hawk. It'll hurt his feelings," said Puck before I could object. "Besides, his cooking is divine."

"I'll take your word for it." I dropped my backpack and took a seat on the inviting-looking plush sofa.

I watched a leaping deer travel from one illusory painting to the next, from bright-green fields to lush forests. My eyes began to flicker closed as soon as my muscles relaxed, and I had to force myself to stay alert.

"I didn't know faeries could cook," I remarked, watching Hawk pile three plates with some kind of curry with vegetables next to a heap of white rice.

"Bit of a generalisation there," Hawk said, though he didn't sound insulted. "My mortal mother was South Asian and she was an amazing cook, and she gave me some of her recipes to try out when I moved to the mortal realm. There aren't many places to buy ingredients in Faerie."

"Unless your cuisine includes decapitated corpses and deadly plants."

"I prefer the non-deadly variety, personally." He set up a third chair at the table. "That's not an oblique hint that this is poisoned, for the record."

"Hawk, don't scare her off." Puck casually took one of the other seats.

"I don't scare easily."

I'd have seen if he'd slipped anything into my food, and I was almost too starving to care, so I took a seat and scooped some of the curry and rice into my mouth. A dozen spicy flavours exploded across my tongue, and Hawk grinned when he deduced that I liked it. "See, I knew you were hungry."

"I didn't get the chance to eat before I ran off to Faerie," I told him. "As soon as I recovered from bleeding nearly to death, I realised Roseanne was missing... that she'd been taken. Anyway, you were going to tell me about the latest murder."

"Did Puck tell you that to lure you into coming here?"

Yes, he had, but that wasn't the point. "I'd like to know the details, considering we were among the last people to see Sal alive."

He'd saved *my* life, in fact, using his healing magic. Yet he hadn't been able to save his own.

Hawk's mouth tightened. "You aren't on the suspect list; don't worry. Everyone knows you were nowhere near him when he died."

"Was he in his house?" I asked.

"No... actually, he was on his way to fetch the victim you found in the shed to half-blood territory, Holly. It seems someone ambushed him on the way."

Nausea turned my stomach. "So he never made it there. Was the body from the shed recovered and brought back to half-blood territory?"

"Yes, it was," he said. "I don't know about you, Puck, but I'd rather not discuss murders at the dinner table."

Puck gave a shrug. "I did tell you she wanted to know all the details."

I was pretty sure Hawk hadn't told me everything, but

I'd figure out more questions later, when I was less tired. In any case, the food was good, the lure of a warm shower beckoned me upstairs, and Hawk even offered to put my muddy clothes in the wash. I was pretty sure it was already too late for my shredded shirt, but I had a change of clothes in my bag along with all my other earthly possessions.

I took my backpack up to the spare room, which was bare but serviceable, containing nothing but a single bed made up with clean sheets. Either they'd always planned to rent it out, or they'd expected to have frequent guests. I was too tired to puzzle that one out, but I'd have to deal with my housing situation tomorrow along with asking more questions about the odd timing of Sal's death. Had it been simple bad luck that he'd been ambushed right after he'd healed me? Or had the killer been waiting at the scene with the abandoned body in the shed? With the death fae?

Did the people who took Roseanne kill him?

If they had, then surely Roseanne herself would be able to tell me once she returned. And if the Morrigan's help was on the way to her, she ought to be back by morning.

She will be. The Morrigan had promised to bring her back, and she above all would be bound to keep her word.

———

I woke in a tangle of sheets, disorientated and with zero idea where I was until I recognised the plain walls of the guest room. I'd slept heavily enough that I didn't remember dreaming or even falling asleep. My rucksack lay in a corner of the room next to a pile of clothes I didn't remember leaving out.

I climbed out of bed and crossed the room, finding my newly washed clothes from yesterday stacked near the door. Had Hawk left them there while I was sleeping? Or Puck? I hadn't heard the door open. Goosebumps sprang up on my arms. Even after yesterday's narrow escape, I still let my guard down too easily.

And yet… what other choice had I had last night? Even Roseanne hadn't—

Roseanne. If she returned to my old house, she'd realise pretty quickly that I was no longer there, but she might not be willing to come here alone. I needed to find her as soon as I left.

Thoroughly wide awake, I took the opportunity to repack my bag after dressing in my newly washed jeans and a clean shirt. Shrugging on my jacket, I shouldered the backpack and headed downstairs.

In the kitchen, I found Puck fiddling with a surprisingly modern coffee maker, his expression of concentration suggesting he was unfamiliar with how it worked. Given Faerie's aversion to technology, I figured he lacked experience in that area.

"Want a hand?"

He straightened upright. "Sure. Hawk insists on buying these contraptions and then throwing out the instruction manuals."

I took over from him, noting that he had at least managed to figure out how to make toast. Kind of. Several pieces of toasted bread ranging from blackened to mildly burnt lay stacked on a plate on the table.

I poured the coffee into two mugs, belatedly grabbing

a third in case Hawk showed up. "You haven't seen Roseanne?"

"No. I'd have woken you if I did."

"Would you?"

"Of course." He took the coffee mugs and placed them on the table next to the plate of toast. "Hawk isn't really a morning person. He'll be down soon. Did you sleep well?"

"Fine." Catch me letting on that I'd slept better than I had in weeks. In fairness, I hadn't been so exhausted in a long time, either, but the guilt about sleeping in comfort while Roseanne remained captive in Faerie began to gnaw at me again, and I hoped the Morrigan had seen to her release from her captives overnight.

I nibbled at a piece of toast, my mind running through the clues, and the pieces I'd been too tired to comprehend the previous day finally slotted together. "Shit."

"What?" said Puck.

I put down my mug. "Do you think the people who took Roseanne are also the murderers we're looking for?"

"I would say there's a chance, but until she's back, we can't be certain."

"Do the other half-faeries know?" I began to pace around the kitchen. "I don't think they do. They paid zero attention to her disappearance."

"Maybe not, but we can explain when we visit them," he said. "We can do that today if you have time."

"Of course I do," I said. "I also wanted to ask Ilsa to contact Sal's ghost, but I'm pretty sure it's too late for that. And I need to find somewhere to live, of course."

The person to talk to on both matters was Brook, but he hadn't seemed much of a fan of Puck the last time I'd spoken to him. I sat back down at the table, debating how to tell him that I wanted to see Brook alone, when Hawk entered the kitchen. "Hey, Holly."

"Hey." I picked up my coffee mug again and took a sip, figuring I'd need the energy if I was to convince the half-faeries that the harbinger they feared so much might be able to lead them straight to the killers once she returned.

"Are we ready to talk about the giant unicorn in the room?" said Hawk.

"What unicorn?" The image of the giant unicorn Hazel had ridden into battle right before she'd broken the Gate-keeper's curse came to mind, bringing a scowl to my mouth. My cousins always had to be so *dramatic*, though Hazel at least had had the sense to avoid Faerie now that she no longer had any magic. I could just see her rolling her eyes at me if she knew I'd walked into the Unseelie Court yesterday.

"Holly, I'm pretty sure you're human enough to under-stand he didn't mean that literally," Puck said. "Hawk, which unicorn would this be?"

"The murders?" I suggested. "Because Puck and I are going to speak to the half-faeries and update them on my newest theory. I think the person who took Roseanne might be linked to the killer, since she disappeared more or less around the same time as Sal died."

Hawk's eyes widened. "That's not what I meant, but… damn. I never realised the connection. I should have."

"What did you mean, then?" I asked.

"The Winter Queen."

My spine stiffened. "What about her?"

"You worked for her."

Ah. Of course it was about my former Gatekeeper status. "Puck told you." He'd probably told him right before we'd gone to Faerie, in fact. "Was it really that much of a surprise?"

"No," he said. "I figured you wouldn't know your way into Faerie if you didn't have some experience, but working directly for the queen? That surprised me."

"I thought everyone already knew," I said. "Yes, I worked as Winter Gatekeeper before my cousin Hazel broke the Gatekeeper's curse and set us all free."

That was the abbreviated version of the story, but it wasn't like I'd witnessed all of Hazel's erratic efforts to break the curse, which had culminated largely by accident when the queen of the Aes Sidhe—the *actual* faerie queen who'd enslaved our ancestor—had tried to usurp the throne of the Summer Court. The upshot was that she and the ex-Seelie Queen had both perished in the battle with an angry god one of them had summoned, and I'd found myself down one Gatekeeper's title.

"Is Hazel the one who works at the necromancer guild?" he asked.

"No, that's Ilsa," I said. "Hazel left the country as soon as the curse broke and is currently gallivanting around England. I think she's in Cornwall at the moment."

It was just like Hazel to go swanning off with her fae boyfriend and leave everything in complete disarray. While Summer had rebuilt itself with a new monarch on the throne, I was kind of glad I hadn't waded into *that* mess during our visit to the Courts. I didn't hold a grudge against Hazel, but I wished she'd at least attempted to clean up some of the chaos she'd left behind. The instant the curse had broken, I'd lost my home and most of my belongings, which would explain why my current home-less state didn't faze me that much. Been there, done that.

"Wow, it's all right for some people," said Hawk. "How'd you wind up in Edinburgh, then?"

"It's the city I have the most experience with." That, and I hadn't wanted to return to the small town in the Highlands in which I'd grown up. "Thought I might join the necromancer guild, but it didn't pan out."

Meaning I didn't have the ability to see ghosts, the minimal requirement to become a guild member. Wraiths didn't count, given their rarity and the fact that nobody except Ilsa could banish them.

"Holly doesn't work for the Unseelie Queen any longer," said Puck. "Our mission yesterday was to visit the Morrigan, not her, as I told you."

"Yeah, he told me about you signing a vow with the goddess of death," Hawk said to me. "Mad, if you ask me, but so is going into Faerie voluntarily."

"It'll be worth it when Roseanne is back." Speaking of which, I needed to check half-blood territory to see if she'd gone looking for me there. "And on that note, I should head off."

"You want to look at Sal's body?" Hawk guessed.

"Assuming it's still in the morgue," I said. "Might as well confirm the symbols are the same and see if the killer left any other clues behind."

"I agree," said Puck. "Hawk, can you get together a file on Sal?"

"What do you think I've been doing while you've been gone?" he said. "We're long overdue for another victim, actually, given the killer's usual time frame."

"Steady on," I said. "We need to confirm the details on the last one first."

We had no time to lose, so I grabbed a slice of toast to

eat on the way to half-blood territory. When Puck and I reached the gate, I scanned the trees for Roseanne, but not so much as a feather appeared. Nor did she show up on the other side of the gate or on the winding paths leading into the wooded area near the morgue.

We both came to a halt, seeing several hulking security trolls patrolling outside. Did they expect someone to come and steal the bodies?

"Hawk mentioned death fae were sighted around the territory," Puck said in a low voice. "They must have taken extra precautions."

"Roseanne and I got in through the back entrance last time," I murmured. "I picked the lock, and she flew in as a crow."

He gave a nod. "Shifting would mean avoiding attention."

"For you, maybe," I said. "Some of us can't shape-shift."

"I can help," he said.

"You can transform me?" I hadn't known he could use his powers on other people, but it must have been one of the tricks he hadn't revealed yet. "I'd rather not spend an eternity as a deer, thanks." That particular piece of magic had been a favourite of the former Seelie Queen, or so I'd heard.

"I won't turn you into a deer, Holly."

"Bloody hope not." Being frozen into an ice statue had been bad enough, thanks. "No, we need to drive them away from the doors."

"On it." He vanished in a swirl of leaves. I waited behind a thicket of trees as he transformed into some mischievous woodland creature to cause a disturbance that would lure away the guards.

Puck returned within two minutes in the form of a crow and flew ahead of me towards the morgue. The back door hung open, with no security trolls in sight.

"What did you do?" I whispered. "You know what, never mind."

Having a trickster faerie on my team had its perks, I wouldn't lie. When we entered the morgue, he flew at my side through the darkness to the main room, where the latest victim of the murderer lay on a table, his body encased in ice.

Like the others, Sal's throat had been cut, but it wasn't the symbols on his chest which drew my attention. Three wounds lacerated his neck, and while they'd all been inflicted by the same weapon, they looked… odd.

"They're half-healed," I whispered to Puck, who'd landed at my side in human form to look at the body. "Was he using… healing magic? While he was being attacked?"

"I think you're right," Puck whispered. "He healed himself, but the killer kept going until he was dead."

A sudden suspicion prickled at me. "Did the others have similar magic?"

"Why?"

"A theory." Not a well-formed one, admittedly. "Never mind. We'll talk later."

I retraced my steps to the back door while Puck flew out ahead of me in bird form. Not a single noise disturbed the silence until we came upon Brook waiting on the path leading out of the woods.

"I knew you'd be back," he said. "Haven't you done enough damage?"

"Damage?" Puck echoed. "We came back as soon as we returned from Faerie to check on the latest news."

"Sal hired you, and you disappeared at the same time as he was murdered." Brook's pointed features looked exhausted, like he hadn't slept in days. "You must know that doesn't paint you in an innocent light."

"We didn't intend to get stuck in Faerie for that long," I said. "Why, people aren't saying we killed him, are they?"

"I can't stop them from talking," he said. "Especially with that harbinger friend of yours—"

"The killer took her captive," I cut in. "That's why we risked our necks in Faerie to get her back. Don't you dare accuse her of working with the murderer when they're holding her as a hostage."

"Are you sure she didn't go with them of her own free will?" he said. "Look, I don't have any opinions on the girl. I never met her. But the others have their own views, and they're scared and angry. We've had death fae breaking into our territory every night, not to mention the killer is still at large."

"Sorry for our badly timed disappearance," said Puck. "If you wish for me to continue with my work in Sal's place, I would gladly do so."

"I also have theories," I added. "It's my belief that the killer is stealing the magic of their victims."

"Stealing their *magic?*" he said. "That's not possible."

"It's certainly possible using a certain type of witch-craft," I said. "And those symbols on each of the bodies indicated that's what they were trying to do."

"Why would a fae need to steal another's magic, then?"

"I think all the victims might have had healing magic." Fewer half-faeries had the ability than their Sidhe brethren, but it was more common in Summer faeries. It'd account for the killer's fixation on Seelie fae too. Besides, what else might the "absorb" symbol have signified?

His expression clouded. "This is out of my area. Puck, I will talk to you about potentially continuing on with your investigation, but Holly…"

I held up a hand as Puck began to object. While I wasn't thrilled at the idea of leaving the pair of them alone together, given Brook's previous comments about the trickster fae, I needed to find Roseanne, and it was pretty clear Brook didn't intend to listen to me. He hadn't even believed the killer had taken Roseanne through the Ley Line and trampled everyone in their path in the process.

I looked between them. "I'm going back to the guild to ask my cousin some questions."

16

I faced Ilsa and River across the desk in the necromancer guild's archive, waiting for Jas to return from a mission. Morgan was supposed to be on archive duty, though like the others, he was more interested in hearing my update than tidying the mess of books stacked beside the desk. I'd just finished telling them about our visit to the morgue and the conclusions I'd arrived at since yesterday.

"Healing magic?" echoed River. "Are you sure?"

"It's possible that all the victims had the same kind of magic," I said. "Puck is checking with Brook, but it's the most common secondary ability among half-faeries, except glamour."

Ilsa's gaze clouded. "Let's hope the killer has more sense than to target a necromancer, then."

"Wait." I looked between them. "River... *you* have healing magic?"

"I do, yes, but it only works on myself," he said. "It's not uncommon among the Seelie... less so among the

Unseelie. Some can heal anyone and not just themselves, but that's much rarer than the self-directed sort of healing power. I doubt the killer would dare to target the guild, though. It's too conspicuous."

"I'll tell Puck." I fired off a quick message. As Ilsa had warned, the phone signal in the guild was complete crap due to the number of wards on the place, and it took several attempts for my message to go through.

"You're still working with him?" asked Ilsa.

"Yeah, since the guy who originally hired a detective was murdered when we were both in Faerie, and we're out of favour with the other half-faeries." I hadn't mentioned where I'd spent the previous night, but I didn't want to diverge from the point.

She blinked. "I didn't know the last victim was the guy who hired Puck's detective agency."

"I never mentioned him by name," I said. "I take it contacting his ghost is out of the question? Has it been too long since his death?"

"Unfortunately, yes," she said. "Did you get any more details?"

"Puck's friend Hawk has the files on him," I said. "It sounds like he got ambushed on the way back from checking out the body I found hidden in a human's garden shed. The body belonged to a victim of the same killer."

"Who shoved it in a shed?" asked Morgan.

"A faerie masquerading as a human." Part of me wondered if I could have prevented Sal's death. If I hadn't gone to Faerie, we might at least have been able to summon his ghost to question, but would that really have made a difference? "Assuming the killer was trying to steal healing magic from their victims... is that possible, even with witch magic?"

"Normally, I'd say no," said Ilsa. "Stealing someone's talisman and claiming its magic is one thing, but I've never heard of anyone ripping out a faerie's innate magic. Then again, blood magic is capable of doing things which fall outside of our current understanding of what magic is capable of."

Puck's response to my message came: *You were right. Brook checked the notes and confirmed that all the victims had the same healing power.*

I'd got it right. The knowledge brought a rush of invigorating energy that almost banished the niggling worry that I'd screwed up this case altogether. "Jas mentioned the symbol meant absorbing or siphoning... and it's true. They all had healing magic."

Ilsa's mouth pressed together. "Siphoning healing magic out of someone seems an inefficient way of boosting one's power."

"It's also not what killed them, right?" said Morgan.

"Yeah, the killer slit the victims' throats." I'd wondered if their deaths had fuelled the magic inside those marks, and perhaps they had—we didn't have the meanings of all the symbols, just some of them. "Seems strange that a witch ritual so old that it isn't even in the textbooks can be used against faeries when our realms were completely separate until recently."

"I dunno. The Sidhe have been making trouble for thousands of years, haven't they?" said Morgan.

"For the witches, though?" That was Jas's area, not mine, but for all I knew, it was true. They'd certainly been screwing with *my* family for generations.

"I can think of *one* way to take a faerie's magic," Ilsa said. "When the Sidhe exile someone, they rip out their magic, talismans and all. It's supposed to be horrifically painful. They use an Invocation to do it."

A shiver ran down my arms. Losing my magic had been almost painless, a result of breaking the vow which bound me to Faerie, but I'd certainly heard of the pain inflicted on exiles who dared to betray the Courts.

"That's not what's happening here," River said, looking equally discomfited. "The killer is using *witch* magic… and killing the victims, which I assume is to prevent them from telling tales. Most exiled Sidhe don't die as a result of having their magic taken."

"If they're exiled to the Grey Vale, they usually end up dead anyway."

The Grey Vale, where the killers must be hiding. Yet they kept coming back for more victims. Was there an end goal, or would they keep going indefinitely? What were they even doing with the magic they stole?

The door opened, and all eyes went to the front as Jas walked into the room. "Why's everyone so quiet in here?"

"We're discussing theories about our faerie killer," said Ilsa. "Holly found out the victims all had healing magic."

"Healing magic?" said Jas.

"The killer is deliberately targeting half-faeries who possess healing magic," said River. "I didn't think it was possible to rip someone's magic out using a spell, but those symbols push the boundaries of what's possible, Ilsa said. Have you heard of a spell which can take someone's magic?"

"No, I can't say I have," said Jas. "Taking healing magic

from the victims… was the killer dying from a fatal wound or something?"

"If so, they could have just asked a faerie with healing magic to heal them without any ritualistic killings needing to be involved." I thought of how Sal had reluctantly saved my life at Puck's request. *He'd* known Sal had healing magic, and at that thought, my old suspicions began to return. Puck wasn't the killer, I was sure, but I'd also been certain he knew more about the situation than he'd been willing to admit.

"What I don't get is how these symbols were forgotten for so many years," said Ilsa. "Surely, someone wrote them down."

"Not everyone has the compulsion to document everything, Ilsa," said Morgan.

"Honestly, the symbols themselves don't necessarily need to follow the textbook exactly." Jas perched on the edge of the desk. "From what I've learned from the local covens, there are numerous variations on each spell which use different symbols for similar results. They used to vary widely between covens at one time, and even when they became standardised, not everyone followed the textbook."

"And there's always been people who conducted wild experiments," added Morgan. "Like blasting holes in the walls."

"Guilty." Jas gave a sheepish grin. "It's true, though. My old coven originally popularised blood magic and claimed to have invented the current symbols which are widely in use. That might have been an exaggeration, of course, but it's true that modern witch symbols tend to look pretty similar, including the ones used in blood magic. The killer, though… I'd almost say they're using symbols that are centuries out of date."

"What, so they're time travelling?" Morgan said sceptically.

"Faeries' sense of time works differently to ours, and most of them have been alive for several human lifetimes." I began to pace from one end of the narrow room to the other. "Maybe the last time the killer had contact with humans, those symbols were the popular ones. It doesn't necessarily matter which they use as long as they get the right result, does it?"

"Hmm." Ilsa left the desk and walked among the bookshelves. "Maybe there's a textbook in here which mentions magical symbols from older eras."

"You won't find anything on blood magic in here, Ilsa," said Jas. "Pretty sure Lady Montgomery still has all those books in her office, except for the ones I gave to Isabel and Asher."

Ignoring her, Ilsa continued to comb through the dusty shelves. With an eye-roll, I scanned the others. River was a Summer half-Sidhe with healing magic, so it wasn't impossible that he would find himself on the killer's hit list at some point. Maybe the killer would want to avoid breaking into the guild and drawing the ire of the city's most powerful necromancers, but that was by no means a guarantee.

"Is there a limit?" I asked of nobody in particular. "The killer is going to run out of half-faeries with healing magic to target eventually, right?"

"You're the expert," said Morgan. "What, do you want to set up an ambush the next time they show up? Using River as bait?"

River cleared his throat. "I doubt Ilsa would appreciate it if I offered myself up as bait. Besides, I'm not certain any of the victims have been part necromancer. I'd certainly be able to see any threat coming using my spirit sight even if they tried to mark me using those symbols which block their victim's vision."

"If anything, that's reason enough for you to give it a shot," said Morgan. "I'm not volunteering, but I doubt the killer is gonna stop until someone stands in their path."

River shot me an exasperated look as though it was my fault for putting ideas in Morgan's head. In truth, I didn't think it was a terrible idea for River to be the bait to lure in the killer. For one thing, he held a genuine Sidhe talisman of his own. Whatever magic the killers possessed, I doubted they had one of those at their disposal unless they'd swiped one from another exile.

Ilsa returned with a large book in her hands. "Why are you all so quiet? What are you plotting?"

"How do you know we're plotting?" Morgan said.

"Because you're never that silent unless you're about to do something reckless."

"Hey, it's not me," said Morgan. "It's River."

"River has healing magic," I said.

Ilsa's eyes narrowed a fraction. "Don't finish that sentence."

"She has a point," said River. "The killer has been sneaking around the city, relying on stealth and those magical symbols to avoid detection. They won't be expecting an ambush."

"What did you want to do?" said Ilsa. "Unless you plan on making a public spectacle of your healing abilities, the killer wouldn't necessarily know you had them."

"It's an idea, though," I said. "None of the other half-faeries with healing magic will offer themselves up as potential victims, but you can fight back, and we can be ready to help. If we go to half-blood territory and wait there, there's a good chance the killer will be on the lookout for a new victim anyway. It's been a couple of days since the last one, after all."

And, a voice in the back of my mind whispered, *if Roseanne manages to escape with the Morrigan's help, then they might come after her.*

Ilsa cleared a spot on the desk and opened the book she'd taken from the back of the archives. "We don't even know what we're up against yet."

"Death fae, for a start," I said. "Vale faeries who feed on life energy. Or death energy."

Beings like death stealers and sluagh were predictable enough, but using symbols to extract energy from the victim required the kind of finesse only the Sidhe possessed.

Lady Rive's words echoed in the back of my mind. *I believe the beasts of the Wild Hunt are trespassing in the Court.*

My blood iced over. I swore under my breath, and Ilsa's gaze lifted from the book. "What is it?"

"The Wild Hunt," I said. "They're Sidhe, right?"

"Yes, but not part of the Courts," said Ilsa. "They used to be close to the Unseelie, I think…"

"Before their leader robbed the Unseelie Queen."

"I didn't know that," said Ilsa. "Who told you?"

"The queen herself did," I said, not wanting to get into the details. "It was before I became Gatekeeper, but the Hunt's warriors dispersed after their leader was killed. I think some of them are still wandering the Vale, and at least one of them is the killer."

Ilsa dropped the book onto the desk. "You're joking."

"The Sidhe in the Winter Court mentioned some beasts from the Wild Hunt were causing trouble on their territory," I said. "Killing their livestock, that type of thing. I'm not sure if it's the same person, but they can walk between realms, can't they? And they work with death fae. The hounds of the Wild Hunt used to answer their call."

Ilsa pressed a hand to her forehead. "You're right. I can't say I've ever met any of them, but Ivy has. I should have asked her."

"Who's Ivy?" I asked at the same time as Morgan said, "Is nobody gonna tell me why it matters if it's the Wild Hunt?"

"The Wild Hunt used to carry the souls of the dead from the Courts to the Death Kingdom in order for them to be reborn into new bodies," I explained. "They scattered after the source of immortality broke... and after their leader was killed."

"Ivy is the one who killed him," said Ilsa. "Anyway, the Wild Hunt... there are even myths about them in the human realm. They say the Hunt used to travel along the spirit lines and could sometimes be seen by ordinary people on nights when the veil between realms was thin."

"You think one of them is committing the murders?" River asked me.

"The clues fit," I said. "In fact, I'm sure Roseanne was carried off by someone riding a lethally quick fae horse. The fae they left behind were trampled flat."

The Morrigan had been temporarily forced to serve the Huntsman, as had Roseanne herself... and if the survivors from the Wild Hunt remained supportive of their dead leader even after he'd betrayed the Courts, they might see her as their ally. That was why they'd kept her alive.

My throat went dry. How could I hope to stand up to the Wild Hunt, the legendary beasts that even the Courts feared to cross? I racked my brains, trying to remember my lessons, but I didn't recall my mother talking much about the Wild Hunt. She hadn't mentioned their connection to the Sidhe's immortality source, either, but then again, none of us had known it existed until over a year after its destruction and Fionn's death.

Had the Sidhe punished the other horsemen for Fionn's mistake too? Had they stripped away their magic and cast them out, or did they still possess the full extent of their powers?

Ilsa looked at me with worry clouding her eyes. "Nobody knows exactly what the Hunt's members are capable of. Pretty sure even most of the Sidhe don't know their identities either."

"I bet the Morrigan does… and the Unseelie Queen," I said. "In fact, some of the Unseelie Sidhe mentioned they wanted to name a new Huntsman. Can't say I know the queen's opinion on that, but maybe the former Hunt took offence when they found out."

"And started killing humans?" said Jas, confusion furrowing her brow. "Half-faeries, I mean? I can't say I know a thing about this Wild Hunt, but if they're old enough to have had contact with the older covens, then they're old enough to have contacted the Ancients too."

The word jolted me upright. "You might say that. The Hunt was in charge of the Sidhe's source of immortality, so I'd say they likely got up close and personal with the gods."

Her jaw dropped. "The Ancients... are you sure the killers weren't trying to use an *Invocation?*"

"Doesn't an Invocation need to be spoken aloud?" The magic belonging to the Sidhe's godly predecessors did sometimes involve symbols, but the sort that humans couldn't read. Like the marks shimmering on River's talisman—or the Gatekeeper's mark which had once gleamed on my forehead.

Ilsa, in response, reached into her pocket and pulled out her talisman, opening the Gatekeeper's book and flipping through its pages. "I should have known to consult the book sooner."

I rested my gaze on the back of its worn cover as if I could see through to the pages on the other side. "Consult the book about what?"

"Summoning rituals," she said without looking up. "There *are* sacrificial rituals which enable someone to summon a god, and most of them involve slaughtering someone in the process. I can't think of any which involve sacrificing multiple victims over the course of a few weeks, though."

"Bet they exist." Morgan shuddered.

Ilsa gave the book a shake. "Come on, I know you have more information than that."

Jas and I exchanged bewildered glances, though it wasn't the first time I'd seen Ilsa talking to her talisman. The book itself was conscious, after all, and it struck me as though for the first time that the magic of a god ran within its pages. The same god my mother had killed in order to use its lifeblood to make herself into an immortal. She'd failed, of course, but the Sidhe had once maintained their immortality in a similar manner.

How deeply had the Wild Hunt been involved with the gods? Nobody knew who'd *created* the Sidhe's original source of immortality, only that Fionn had unintentionally seen to its destruction while he'd been trying to create an army to dominate the Courts and the human realm all at once. The rest of the Wild Hunt had gone along with his plan, but I hadn't had the impression they'd had much choice in the matter. They obeyed the Huntsman.

Now that the Huntsman was dead, whom did they answer to?

Ilsa laid down the book again. "I don't know what they're doing. Even the book doesn't. Until we know *who* is responsible, we're in the dark."

"Then it's worth setting up an ambush," said River. "I'll be the bait. They won't expect me to have a talisman of my own."

"And they won't expect you to have backup," said Morgan. "We'll all be there. Right, Ilsa?"

Ilsa blew out a breath. "Okay. It's worth a shot."

"Yes, it is," I said. "We'll trap and interrogate them. Bring as much iron as possible."

And get Roseanne back.

———

After we'd hashed out the details of our ambush plan, I went to meet with Puck and Hawk. I'd texted Puck the brief details but had received little in response aside from a request to drop by at his office. Fine with me, because I'd got so caught up in plotting our ambush that I'd forgotten all about the thorny problems with my living situation. If I wasted the rest of the daylight hours speaking to landlords and letting agencies, though, I might miss my last shot at getting Roseanne back and catching the killer.

There was no set time at which the murderer might make an appearance, and I could only assume they were riding in and out of the Grey Vale via the Ley Line. Considering the Line went straight through the middle of the city, that gave the Hunt a lot of potential places to show up. To lure them into our trap, we'd have to draw their attention first.

I pushed open the door to Puck's office, where he and Hawk stood in conversation over the desk.

"*What* are your friends plotting?" Hawk wanted to know.

"We think we know who the killer is, and we're going to set up an ambush today," I said to him, figuring Puck had been in the middle of explaining when I'd walked in. "They're outcasts from the Wild Hunt."

His brows shot up. "Who?"

"Come on, you must know the Wild Hunt." I looked between him and Puck. "They're probably older than the *Courts,* for crying out loud."

"I know who they are," he said. "I also know their forces disbanded several years ago, and a large number of them were killed."

"Not all of them," I said. "Their leader died a few years ago, but I assume the survivors scattered throughout the Grey Vale."

"That's a big assumption to make," said Puck, "given how long it's been since any of them were sighted."

"Actually, one of them was causing trouble in the Winter Court not long ago," I said. "But that's not the point. They took Roseanne. In the vision I saw through the tracking spell, she was carried off by someone riding a fae horse. That's how they moved so damn fast."

"Causing trouble in Winter?" said Hawk.

A jolt of suspicion shot up my spine. He was taking this a little *too* calmly, and I was reminded that I didn't necessarily know where either of their loyalties lay.

"Never mind that," I said. "They're too scared to get near the queen, so I reckon they'll be easy enough to lure into a trap."

I opted against mentioning Ilsa's theory on sacrificial summoning rituals involving both magical symbols and spoken Invocations to summon the gods. We had no proof of that... yet.

"You never said how you intend to lure them into a trap," said Puck. "They've entirely avoided detection so far. Besides, they're targeting half-Sidhe from Summer who have healing magic, aren't they?"

Hawk's mouth tightened. "They are, and none have survived so far."

"Luckily, we have one," I said. "My cousin Ilsa's boyfriend, River, has healing magic. He also has a talisman, so he's agreed to act as bait before we strike."

Puck's eyes widened. "He has? Does he know what he's offering to do?"

"Stand on the Ley Line and advertise his healing magic for the world to see," I said. "Ilsa has strong enough spirit sight that she'll notice the instant one of the Wild Hunt crosses over the Line. That's when we'll jump in and corner them."

"It's not a bad plan," Hawk said. "Risky, but so is waiting for them to strike first."

"Exactly," I said. "You don't have to come, either of you, but we intend to capture and interrogate the killers before we hand them over to the authorities."

And then? I'd pocket the payment and use it to buy myself a roof over my head. Once I'd found Roseanne, anyway. Why the hell was the Morrigan taking so long to find her?

"So the rest of us will be spectators?" asked Puck. "I don't like the idea of going into this without being able to see our attackers until they're on top of us. Do you trust your cousin with your life?"

"I—" Did I? I wasn't sure that was a question I could answer. After all, I was pretty sure the feeling wasn't mutual, given my family history. "I trust her to get the job done. If necessary, she can track the Hunt through the spirit line."

Shock blanked his expression. "She can travel on the spirit line? How's that possible?"

"Ask her yourself." I didn't want to tell the whole story about how she came to wield a talisman containing the power of one of the gods. In fact, the Wild Hunt's horsemen must have similar talismans which enabled them to ride on the paths of the dead and cross between realms unless the ability came as a natural part of their Wild Hunt magic. I didn't know nearly enough about them, and a prickle of worry ran between my shoulder blades as Hawk and Puck exchanged grim looks.

I'd braced for a refusal, so it came as a surprise when Puck said, "I'll come with you. Hawk, are you waiting here?"

"I'll go to the authorities first to make sure they're ready to take in the killers."

Does he not have magic of his own? I'd never received a conclusive answer on that one, but Puck was clearly the fighter of the two of them, while Ilsa and River could make use of his help. More than they could mine, anyway.

I rested a hand on my iron blade, doubts whispering in the back of my mind. Should I even be there for the ambush? River and Ilsa had all the firepower, the guild's necromancers had the training, and all I had was a knife. If I got captured or killed, I might throw off our whole plan.

That won't happen. Besides, Roseanne was counting on me. If nothing else, I'd get her away from them. With or without the Morrigan's help.

17

The daylight had begun to fade by the time we assembled near the Ley Line. I assumed the others had had to shake off the rest of the necromancer guild, not wanting to be followed, and to gather as much iron as they could lay their hands on. Puck and I joined Ilsa and River down the road from the guild, where Morgan and Jas came to join us after convincing Lloyd to stay at the guild with the faerie dog.

From what I gathered from their whispered conversation, none of them had fought against a Sidhe before, and the Wild Hunt were a virtual unknown compared to the regular Winter and Summer Sidhe and had more in common with the Morrigan than any other fae. Maybe that was why they'd taken her daughter, if not because their leader had once held her under his spell.

I, however, *had* fought Sidhe and won. Before I'd lost my magic, anyway. That gave me no guarantee of victory today, but finding the Wild Hunt was our first priority. We positioned ourselves on an abandoned street which lay directly on the Ley Line, not far from half-blood territory but also not near anyone who might accidentally end up getting caught in the backlash.

River carried his faerie talisman strapped to his waist, its bright glow hidden by the sheath, but I couldn't help wondering if the killer would easily fall for our ruse when even glamouring the sword wouldn't hide its magic from a Sidhe warrior.

The first minutes of pacing up and down the Line in groups were laced with tension, but after a while, everyone began to grow fidgety.

"Maybe they aren't coming," Ilsa said.

"River, use your healing magic," said Morgan. "Anyone want to volunteer to stick a knife in him? I'll do it if nobody else wants to."

"I draw the line at being stabbed," said River. "I doubt the killers are watching us right this instant. They're picking their victims via some other means."

"Then we should have waited for them to find out about your healing magic first," said Morgan.

"How?" said River. "What am I supposed to do, fall on my own sword and hope one of them happens to be watching me?"

Puck, who hadn't said much so far, shook his head at their bickering. "Whose idea was this?"

"Mine," I muttered. "Look, I really thought... what's going on over there?"

The sound of an uproar drifted from the direction of half-blood territory. I turned that way, glimpsing several figures running around the area, pursued by a slithering shape formed entirely of shadows.

The death fae had come out to play.

"Bet their allies won't be far behind." I walked in their direction, brandishing my knife.

Puck kept pace with me easily. "Are you sure it's a good idea to run into the middle of a fight with the death fae?"

"Have you learned nothing about me in the last few days?"

A smile appeared on his mouth. "Usually your recklessness has a method to it. Why were you so certain your plan would work today?"

I glared at him. "If you must know, I was counting on the Morrigan keeping her word and returning Roseanne. That would drive the killers to come back to this realm and make them doubly likely to fall into our trap. Too bad the word of the queen of the death faeries turned out to be unreliable after all."

Unless, of course, she'd been on their side the whole time.

Our group ran into view of half-blood territory, where a giant slavering furred beast was bearing down on a terrified-looking teenage half-faerie. Oh, great. As if death stealers and the sluagh weren't bad enough on their own, they'd brought hellhounds too.

Hellhounds precede the Wild Hunt. They must be close. In fact, maybe this attack was a diversion so they could seek out their next victim. Didn't mean I'd let them get away with it, so I launched myself at the nearest death stealer, stabbing its tentacle before it looped around the neck of a fleeing half-faerie. As the iron deflated the beast, I ran towards the teenager the hellhound had targeted. In the same instant, a giant furry monster appeared on the road where Puck had been standing, tackling the hellhound from the side. Puck's green eyes shone from above the beast's sharp teeth as it bit into the hellhound's neck, killing it in an instant.

Puck's beast form bared its teeth at me in a bloody grin before shifting back to human form again. He spat blood onto the road. "That thing tastes foul."

"It also looks more like a bear than you did," I said. "Let's find the rest of these bastards."

The half-faeries were doing their best to fight off the death fae with magic and blades, while Morgan, Jas, and Ilsa assisted with their own necromantic powers. Meanwhile, River fought with a regular blade rather than his talisman, wearing gloves to protect himself from the iron. Smart idea, given his need to keep his talisman hidden until we'd lured our targets into our trap... wherever they were hiding.

Anyone watching through the Ley Line would be able to see the commotion on the other side as the death fae fell beneath the half-faeries' attacks. Hawk hadn't been kidding when he'd said they were more actively attacking half-blood territory recently. Growing bolder. Yet their masters remained as elusive as ever.

Ilsa ran past me, her talisman in her hand and her forehead aglow with bright magic. "Holly, we're gonna lure them away."

"Where?" I spotted River backing away from a sluagh. A deep-looking cut marred his arm—and as I watched, it began to heal, the skin gleaming beneath a lantern hanging from a nearby wall.

Puck flew to my side, his crow form covered in hellhound blood. I didn't know he could get so downright nasty in his fighting methods, but I was glad to have him on my side. The sun had almost fully set in the last few minutes, shadows spilling through the streets in the gaps between the lights, and while the Ley Line remained difficult to see, it wasn't hard to imagine the dark paths of Faerie on the other side.

Puck shifted into human form, took my arm, and yanked me backwards into an alleyway. A rebuke rose to my tongue, cut off as the sudden pounding of hooves echoed through the air.

The Wild Hunt is here.

An enormous black horse rode into view, too fast for me to track with my sight, its rider little more than a blur of motion as it passed our hiding place. I remained absolutely still, my heart leaping into my throat as River stumbled into the horse's path with a feigned gasp of alarm.

Or it might not have been faked. On the back of his giant horse, the Wild Hunt warrior towered above the six-foot-something half-Sidhe. From this view, I couldn't see anything but River's pale face and his widening eyes as the horseman circled him so fast that he seemed little more than dark smoke. Within seconds, vivid marks were inked onto the exposed skin of his face and neck.

The horseman had marked him without seeming to move at all.

I inched forward, and Puck's hand gripped my arm. Hard. His voice was barely a breath. "You can't win this, Holly."

"He's not supposed to be an *actual* sacrifice, arsehole."

Despite my whispered tone, the horse's ears pricked at the sound—and then a blast of vibrant blue-white necromantic power shot through the air. The horseman vanished into smoke, and the bolt of magic struck the spot immediately in front of River. In the brightness, he looked dazed, ink trickling down his neck like blood. He hadn't even had time to draw his talisman.

Ilsa ran into view, her hands aglow with whiteness, presumably the source of the magical attack. In a nearby alley, I glimpsed movement that likely belonged to Jas and Morgan, who were waiting to strike with their ambush— except our target had vanished into thin air.

Not for long. Pounding hooves echoed down the street once again, and no fewer than *three* horsemen rode into view. All were dressed in the same dark clothing, all were masked, and behind one of them sat the pale and terrified Roseanne.

My heart plummeted. *They took her. I knew it.*

"Half-blood." The leading horseman's voice was cold and echoing, putting me in mind of deep dungeons and empty rooms. He paid Ilsa no attention, his gaze fixed on River. "You dare to bring necromancers to fight against us?"

River raised his head, one hand frantically swiping at the marks on his neck. His gaze was fixed in the distance, panic stiffening his features. The marks had erased his sight, just like the other victims.

"You're the outcast Sidhe, aren't you?" he said. "Why is the Wild Hunt slaughtering half-fae of the human realm?"

The horseman didn't reply, simply riding forward with his horse gliding like liquid beneath him. In seconds, he came up behind River and drew a line across his throat—

River's blade glittered like the sun when he drew it, blocking the horseman's attack before it made contact with his skin. Even blinded, he had the speed and skill of a fae warrior, and the other horsemen remained transfixed for a second at the sight of the talisman glowing like a beacon with green Summer magic.

"You have a talisman," the horseman said. "*You* were chosen by the Summer Court? A half-blood?"

"Yes, I was," River said. "Why are you killing half-faeries? Why are you using witch magic to mark their bodies for sacrifice?"

"It isn't witch magic, foolish half-blood." The horseman's hand moved, holding up some kind of pencil-like instrument which glowed faintly around the edges. *Is that what he's drawing the symbols with?* I'd lost sight of my allies, but with three enemies facing us down, they'd have to be careful not to get trampled to death.

River faced the horseman, his talisman glittering in his hand. "Regardless, you're breaking the laws of both realms."

"No law constrains us," he said. "Not the Courts and not the human realm. We will take back what is ours."

He swung his blade. River blocked the strike, but even he had trouble keeping up with the horseman's preternatural speed. I glimpsed Ilsa helplessly backing away, unable to risk jumping into the fray without getting trampled beneath those hooves. They were faster than any Sidhe I'd ever set eyes on before.

As for me, I fixed my attention on Roseanne, wondering if I'd be able to grab her from the horse's back while the rider was distracted. Why had the Wild Hunt forced her to ride with them? Did they think she wanted to join them, as she'd been forced to serve Fionn, or were they trying to leverage her against the Morrigan? The old bird owed me a damn favour and had yet to repay me. *Now would be a great time, Morrigan.*

I pulled my arm away from Puck and edged through the shadows towards the third and final horse—at the moment, completely still, as though he and his companion were waiting for instructions from their leader before striking. From the deafening clash of metal, River was doing a pretty damn good job of fighting off his attacker without being able to see his target, but it wouldn't last. *Come on, Morrigan.*

A sharp pain in my wrist made me glance down. A crow—Puck—had landed on my arm and pecked me hard, an indication not to move. I shook my head and whispered, "I won't let them take her again."

The horseman slammed his blade into River's, forcing him back—and Ilsa appeared at his side, her Gatekeeper's book aglow in her hands. "Trust me, you don't want me to use this here. None of you do. Surrender, or I swear I'll open the Gates of Death on top of you."

My mouth fell open. I *hoped* she was bluffing, because the last time she'd done that, she'd damn near screwed up the Ley Line badly enough to kick off another faerie invasion. Admittedly, my mother had been the one who'd forced her hand, but Ilsa couldn't use the talisman to its full extent on the Ley Line without risking ripping open the boundaries between realms and causing worse than the Wild Hunt to descend upon Earth.

In any case, I was out of time. I crept up on the horse carrying Roseanne and came to a halt when the rider's head tilted to the side. "Want to show your face, little human?"

My hand clenched on my blade. "You took my friend, and I want her back."

Roseanne twisted in her seat, alarm flickering across

her face, but the horseman simply laughed. He was bigger than the leading rider, broad under his armour with a mask covering his face. Dark hair blew loose beneath his heavy-looking helmet, but he didn't have any exposed skin beneath all the armour. Not to mention the horse, which rotated in my direction, its hooves coming at me with blinding speed—

Puck flew into the horse's face in a shower of screeching and feathers while I leapt out of the way and made a wild lunge for the saddle. My fingers locked on the side of the saddle, and when the horse did a flying leap, I used the momentum to pull myself onto its back. Roseanne screamed.

"It's only me!" I leaned forward, hanging on to the saddle for dear life. "Not my finest rescue mission, I'll admit."

"Let go!" she yelped. "You're gonna die."

"Not a chance." I hung on grimly, expecting the rider to turn around and attempt to stab me.

Instead, he sped up. The horse rode hard, jolting me unpleasantly with every movement, until the streets blurred into darkness and I no longer had a clue whereabouts we were. Regardless, I let go of the saddle with one hand and grabbed Roseanne's arm.

Roseanne trembled all over, her face bright with tears. "Holly, please let go."

"I'm getting you out of here." I'd need to time my jump well, but the instant we hit the ground, we'd be free.

The slight problem was that the horse ran so fast, I was pretty sure its hooves weren't even touching the ground any longer. If I somehow made it crash, the armoured Sidhe would survive the fall, but Roseanne and I were all too mortal. Time for a new plan.

I let go of Roseanne, who made a startled noise when I swung my leg around and shuffled past her so I could perch directly behind the armoured horseman.

At last, he moved, drawing a sword. The blade missed my leg by inches and would have skewered me if we hadn't been moving at a speed which reduced the buildings to a dark smudge. I fell back in my seat to avoid the blade then lunged forward with my own knife. The iron simply glanced off his armour, which was made of some kind of metal-like material I didn't recognise. Not iron, surely.

I raised myself to a half-standing position behind him, and the horseman twisted around in his seat. His blade whipped past my neck as I fell on top of him, intentionally landing across his lap. Pain struck my arms and legs where I crashed onto his armour, but I twisted onto my back and stabbed my blade directly into his eye.

The horseman bellowed with pain, and I held on with my free hand when the horse hit the ground with a jarring movement. Roseanne screamed again. "We're gonna crash!"

"I've got it!" I grabbed the reins from the rider's limp hands and swung my leg around so that I was sitting upright. A shove sent the rider toppling off the horse, but I didn't stop driving it forward, not until we touched the ground again on a wide cobbled street and the horse finally slowed.

My breath rushed out, my heart hammering. I hadn't the faintest clue where the rider had landed, but that didn't matter. I'd won.

Roseanne slid off the horse and dropped to the ground while I climbed down to crouch beside her. "Hey. You okay?"

She trembled, and I drew my arms around her, causing her to startle at the contact. Nevertheless, she held on to me for a brief moment before breaking away. "Where are we?"

"Haven't a clue." I breathed hard, watching the horse canter away, perhaps in search of its fallen rider. "Bloody hell. So much for the Morrigan actually helping."

Roseanne startled. "What about her?"

A bright flash ignited on the Ley Line, dazzling my eyes. A very familiar brightness. *Ilsa's talisman.*

"Can you run?" I asked.

Roseanne nodded, and we hurried down the street towards the direction of the flash. As we ran, I gave her the gist of our plan.

"You're mad!" she gasped out, clutching a stitch in her side. "They're gonna come back and kill you."

"Pretty sure that dude isn't going anywhere."

The other two, though... we'd left Ilsa and the others to fight them off, and that flash had looked awfully like Ilsa's talisman.

I skidded to a halt in a street near half-blood terri-tory. River sat on the pavement, his sword in his hand, while Jas wiped at the inky marks on his neck with a cloth. Nearby, Morgan spotted us first. "Hey, Holly's alive. Did you seriously jump onto a fucking *faerie* horse?"

"Where's Ilsa?" I asked.

"They took her." River's expression was bleak. "I'm sure they took her. I couldn't see..."

"Hold still," said Jas. "I'll get those marks off you. Damn, those bastards move fast."

"I saw a flash," I said uncertainly. "What…?"

"Where's the third horseman?" asked Morgan.

"I stabbed him in the eye." I indicated my bloodied blade. "Got lucky. Where'd Puck go?"

He hadn't tried to follow me, surely.

"I have no idea." River grimaced, rubbing his eyes with a hand. "Jas—stop it, I can see. I'll clean off the rest of the ink later. Where do the Wild Hunt keep their base?"

"Either the Grey Vale or the Path of the Dead, I'm guessing." Every instinct warned me to get Roseanne out of harm's way, but Ilsa's absence tore a hole in my chest. The plan had been my idea, after all, and I'd been a fool to consider it would ever be easy to best the Wild Hunt. I couldn't let Ilsa be the one to pay the price. "Wait, did Puck follow the horseman?"

"I don't think he did," said Jas. "I saw a bird flying out of the street we were in… towards half-blood territory. I think it was him."

"He picked a fine time to pull a disappearing act."

Maybe he'd gone to help the half-faeries deal with the aftermath of the attack, but something about his absence made me uneasy all the same.

Roseanne tugged at my sleeve. "I'll go with you."

"Okay, but stay close," I said. "I won't let them take you again."

Her eyes glittered with tears. It struck me that this might have been the first time anyone had promised to keep her safe, or at least meant it.

If I'd achieved nothing else today, at least I'd done that much.

18

Part way to half-blood territory, dark wings fluttered overhead, and Puck swooped down as a crow before turning human again. "Holly. I thought… they took you."

"I thought you ran off." It was about time he showed up. "Where have you been hiding?"

"Hiding?" he echoed. "I was looking for you."

"They took Ilsa," I said. "They took her captive. Are you telling me you somehow managed to miss that?"

Roseanne clutched my arm. "What is River doing?"

I turned around, my heart sinking when I saw River step through a shimmering line in the air onto a path which was part there, part not. Morgan and Jas stared after him, neither of them able to prevent him from walking into Faerie.

"Shit!" I yelled after him. "Dammit. He went after Ilsa alone."

"Don't follow, Holly," said Puck. "If the Wild Hunt took her, he won't get her back."

"I got Roseanne back," I pointed out. "Thanks for having faith in me."

He paled, his face streaked with blood from his earlier attack on the death fae. "I do have faith in you, but the Wild Hunt…"

"I thought you had no experience with them." I studied his face. "Right, Puck?"

"No, he knew," Roseanne whispered in my ear. "He knew…"

And there it was. He'd known what we were up against all along. The truth slid into me as keenly as a sharp blade. "You knew. Did you come here to watch us die? Is that it?"

"No!" he said. "Not at all. I can explain."

"But I don't have to listen." Yet River was long gone, and I couldn't follow him without the aid of another faerie. I dragged my gaze back to Roseanne. "Tell me… do you know who he is?"

She shook her head. "No, but he intentionally got out of their way during the fight."

Puck's mouth thinned. "I am not in the service of the Wild Hunt, Holly, I can assure you of that."

"Forgive me if I don't take your word for it." I moved closer to Roseanne. She'd been their prisoner, but Puck had no such excuse for his behaviour. Lowering my voice, I asked, "Do you know where they're based?"

"No… they never stopped." Her hands clenched. "They never stopped riding. They didn't give me an opportunity to get away."

"Bastards," I said. "I'm not sorry I stabbed that dude in the eye."

"You *stabbed* one of them?" Puck said.

"Want to join him?" Confusion swirled within me like tides of a dark and unknown sea. "Was *anything* you told me the truth?"

"Yes," he said. "Yes, almost everything, but I couldn't challenge the Wild Hunt. As per an oath I swore a long time ago, I am unable to harm them. I was barely able to shift for long enough to distract the horse and let you climb onto its back."

"An *oath?* To whom?" I stared at him. "Where did you really come from?"

Puck drew in a breath. "I used to live in the realm of the Aes Sidhe, an offshoot of the Summer Court. I was… I suppose you might say I was employed by their queen. Because my abilities were unique, I wasn't subject to the same rules as the others and was able to leave their realm, for short periods at least. When the Aes Sidhe's Court fell apart after the death of its leader, I left and came to Earth. So did Hawk."

My mouth hung open. The Aes Sidhe? Seriously? Until recently, most of us had thought they'd died out centuries ago, but it turned out they'd been banished from Summer when their leader had tried to usurp the Erlking's throne and had retreated into the shadows. Puck literally *had* been living underground for years, and he must have resurfaced after the Aes Sidhe's leader Etaina had died along with the former Seelie Queen, in the same battle which had ultimately ended in the shattering of the Gate-keeper's curse.

"So you knew how the Gatekeeper's curse started." I couldn't believe I was even having this conversation. "You knew Thomas Lynn."

"Not personally."

That didn't matter. No employee of Etaina was innocent. She'd woven a trap for Thomas Lynn which had ensnared every single one of his descendants, and unlike Hazel, I didn't believe Thomas had been as much a victim as the rest of us. After all, he'd chosen to make a deal with Etaina in exchange for his own freedom and doomed generations of his successors to serve the Winter and Summer Courts. Hazel might have undone his mistake and ended the curse, but from my perspective, they'd all been as bad as each other. The Aes Sidhe, Thomas Lynn, the scheming Sidhe who'd played with our lives like puppeteers… and now, Puck.

"Did you fight on their side in the battle, then?" I asked. "Did you fight against the Courts and against my family?"

"Of course not," he said. "We left the Court when the Aes Sidhe's territory was cleared out."

"And went into hiding in the human realm," I concluded. "I suppose that was the easier option for you."

I might have done the same in his position, but I found it hard to reconcile his claims that he knew nothing of the Gatekeepers with the knowledge that he'd lived in the same realm as the originator of the curse and had worked for the queen who'd tormented generations of my family.

"It's not like that," he said. "The point is, Etaina once had all her followers swear an oath to protect the Wild Hunt."

"Why would she even do that?" I frowned. "She's dead. I saw her die. Besides, the Wild Hunt had nothing to do with the Aes Sidhe except for collecting their dead, I assume."

"Not quite," he said. "I can't say I was in Etaina's confidence, but she spent a great deal of time with the Wild Hunt when they came to her. I believe they were teaching her."

"Teaching her?" I echoed, nonplussed. "What the hell were they teaching her, death magic?"

No... *blood* magic. I'd bet it was them who'd taught her the ritual she'd unwisely used to summon the god which had led to her own destruction. Hazel had mentioned finding similar tools in the queen's lair, but it wasn't as if I'd ever set foot in the realm of the Aes Sidhe myself.

"I don't know the details," he said. "That's the honest truth, Holly. I certainly didn't know the Wild Hunt were behind these murders. Not until it was too late to do anything about it. All I wanted you to know was that an old vow prevents me from harming the horsemen of the Hunt. If that's too much for you to deal with, then I understand."

I looked away. Roseanne slumped against a nearby wall, her expression despondent. I knew the feeling. I'd spent my life dealing with faerie trickery, but I hadn't expected Puck's admission to hit me that hard.

"Don't send him away," said Roseanne. "We'll need his help when they come back to get us."

"Why did they want you?" I asked. "The Wild Hunt, I mean? Do they mean to challenge the Morrigan?"

"Hardly," she muttered. "The Morrigan doesn't give a shit what happens to me."

"She promised to help me get you back," I said. "I made a bargain with her, and believe me, she's going to have to answer for why she didn't keep her word."

"You made a bargain with her?" she said. "Why?"

"Because it was my only option."

Tears spilled from her eyes. "You shouldn't have done that for me."

"It wasn't a big deal." I mean, if you discounted the part where I'd almost been turned into an ice statue, anyway. "Did the Hunt mention where they were going next? Because they took Ilsa, and now, River's gone after them alone."

Roseanne straightened upright. "Shit. If they kill River, they'll have killed seven half-Sidhe."

"Seven?" I echoed. "What's significant about that number?"

"I don't know, but they specifically said they needed seven for the spell to work, whatever that meant," she said. "They tried not to let me overhear anything else."

"Seven." The number echoed in the back of my mind. Etaina had captured a mortal man every seven years, sacrificing him to her dark god, and Thomas Lynn had been the last. Hazel claimed he'd managed to wriggle out of being sacrificed, but that didn't explain *why* she'd wanted to summon a death god. "Seven deaths… seven sacrifices. Are you sure you don't know what spell they were trying to use?"

"I wish I did," said Roseanne. "They definitely need seven victims."

"And we're up to six." Counting the guy whose body I'd found in the shed, anyway. "I guess we'd better hope that River gets the better of them first. He has his talisman, and so does Ilsa. That'll help."

"You're just gonna stay here?" asked Roseanne. "We're going home?"

"I can't follow them into Faerie." Yet I didn't have a home to return to unless I counted Puck's spare room. "By the way, the landlord kicked me out of my house when I went into Faerie."

"He did *what?*" Roseanne leapt forward. "It's because of me, isn't it?"

"No, it was my fault." I didn't look directly at Puck when I spoke, though I knew he was listening. "I disappeared, and he thought… my housemates saw me with Puck and assumed I'd gone off with him."

"So where are you living now?"

"I spent last night in Puck's spare room." Humiliation burned my cheeks. I'd thought losing my magic and the protection of being Gatekeeper was the lowest I could possibly sink, but the universe insisted on proving me wrong. I'd lost my house, I'd lost most of my allies, and now, Ilsa had been captured by the Wild Hunt, who were one murder away from casting some horrible spell I had no way of stopping.

If I lost Roseanne again, it would be the last straw. I turned to Puck, whose open expression threatened to unravel me. Especially when Roseanne shuffled closer to me. "I don't mind staying with him. I… I don't think he means you harm."

"That's not what concerns me." But she was right. Rescuing her had been the priority, and I might have to put my trust in Puck again in order to keep her safe. He hadn't unleashed any Aes Sidhe–style illusions or traps on me last time.

Puck, however, had his attention fixed on a point behind me. I turned around, seeing Hawk walking towards us. "What's he doing out here?"

"Looking for us." Puck beckoned him over. "Hey, Hawk."

"Were you involved too?" I asked him. "With the Aes Sidhe?"

"He told you?" said Hawk.

Puck's lips pressed together. "I had to explain why I couldn't challenge the Hunt. They took her cousin."

Hawk swore under his breath. "The one who works for the guild?"

"She has a talisman," said Puck. "Her partner went to search for her, though, and he's Seelie… with healing magic."

"He fits the murderer's criteria," Hawk concluded.

"Do *you* know what spell they're trying to do?" I asked.

"What spell?" he said. "Nobody said anything about a spell."

"I did," said Roseanne. "The horsemen specifically said they needed to kill seven half-faeries. I don't know why, but I'm guessing it isn't good news."

"No, it isn't," I said. "Not if they were taking blood-magic lessons from the queen of the Aes Sidhe."

Hawk winced. "If Puck made it sound like we were in on it, we really weren't. Frankly, I have no idea what her relationship with the Hunt was. I don't get the impression she told even her most trusted soldiers."

"If they're experts at blood magic, though, I guess it explains why they know symbols which predate the modern covens." Ilsa would be fascinated, assuming they answered any of her questions before they killed her. My chest tightened. "Besides, if you know anything that might keep us alive, then I'd appreciate it if you shared it."

"We don't," said Hawk. "Most of the Aes Sidhe are

playing catch-up on the last few centuries since they went underground. Those of us born too late to remember the outside world are even more scattered."

"There are a few right here on half-blood territory," added Puck. "Brook being one of them."

"That's your history?" I looked between him and Hawk in disbelief. "Seriously?"

"It's not much of a history," said Puck. "As usual, my reputation precedes me."

"But he knew what you were." He also hadn't told *me*, which put my plan to leave Roseanne in his care on shaky ground. Assuming he didn't outright refuse. "Okay, forget all that. The Wild Hunt's horsemen's ritual is as precise as a faerie vow, in the sense that it consists of an exact series of steps which need to be completed in order. Every victim needs to be sacrificed in the right way, with the right symbols, or else it won't work."

"And they're one step away from the end," Hawk said.

"You've got it," I said. "If you're staying here, then you can do one favour for me and keep an eye on Roseanne."

Roseanne shot me an alarmed look. "You're leaving me behind?"

"I have to." I looked at the other two. "I want you to swear to me that you won't allow Roseanne to come to any harm while I'm gone. If you break your word, I'll have your head."

"I promise," Hawk said. "Puck—I'll watch the girl. You fix this."

What he meant by "this" I had no idea, but Puck said, "I'll go with you. Are you going to find a way into Faerie?"

"We need to tell the Sidhe what the Wild Hunt is up to." If he insisted on coming with me… I'd deal with that later. "I guarantee they won't be happy when they find out."

"You think they'd be willing to help us out?"

"Given that the Unseelie Queen still carries a grudge after all this time?" I gave a grim nod. "We'd better hope so."

In truth, I'd rather have eaten a redcap's blood-drenched hat than set foot in the Unseelie Court again, but it was that or face the Wild Hunt alone. Besides, the Morrigan owed me, and she knew it.

To start off with, we needed a way *into* the Court. While Hawk took Roseanne back to the office, Puck and I tracked down Jas and Morgan.

"Thought you left," said Morgan. "Where are those Wild Hunt fuckers?"

"In the Vale, I expect," I said. "I'm going to the Courts to ask the Sidhe for their help."

"Seriously? You're mad." Morgan dug into his pocket. "Dammit. Lloyd's messaging me again."

"Same here," said Jas. "Pretty sure he's on his way here, in fact."

"Good," I said, "because I need to borrow the puppy."

"Why?" said Morgan.

"I don't have time to fly up to the middle of nowhere

to find what's left of our family's old route into Faerie," I said. "We need to get in right away."

"So you want to borrow Pepper?" said Morgan. "You'd better not take him anywhere near the Wild Hunt."

"We won't," Puck said. "We need to warn the Courts, but I doubt we'll find the Hunt there."

No. They're in the Grey Vale. How I'd get *there* I'd figure out later. Unlike River, I didn't have Sidhe family members who might be willing to help me cross into the Vale without expecting anything in return. I didn't have a talisman either.

"How do you know Ilsa has a talisman?" I asked Puck in an undertone while we waited for Lloyd to show up. "I never told you."

"I saw her use it, remember?" Puck said. "There was no mistaking it for anything else. Besides, I guessed something of the sort must be involved when you mentioned she retained her Gatekeeper's title. She wasn't bound to the Courts."

"Or the Aes Sidhe," I added.

His posture tensed. "Holly, I swear I had nothing to do with the vow which bound your family. The queen herself told nobody of her relationship with Thomas Lynn. I gather that she did not wish us to know the humiliation of how the Erlking tricked her."

"Tricked her into giving up her glorified servants, I know." I paced the street, turning my back on him. "I don't blame you personally. I'm just a little sick of the Sidhe fucking us over. Why'd the Hunt even take Ilsa? They have no use for her talisman."

Her talisman belonged to one of the Ancients, but since my mother had killed the Ancient in question, it wasn't as if they could do anything with it when it answered to her alone. Short of opening the Gates of Death, of course, but I was pretty sure the Gates couldn't even be accessed from within Faerie. Not that I was an expert on the subject.

At that moment, Lloyd walked into view with the faerie dog in tow. Behind him walked Keir, the strikingly handsome vampire Jas was reportedly dating, who made straight for Jas.

Meanwhile, Lloyd veered in our direction. "Did you say you wanted to borrow the puppy? You aren't going to vanish for days this time?"

"I hope not, but you know Faerie."

"No, I don't," he said. "And frankly, I'm glad of it."

I took Pepper's lead from him, and the puppy whined and tried to hide behind Lloyd's legs. "Probably a good thing. You'll live longer."

Puck stepped up to my side. "Thanks. We'll be back soon."

The others waved us off, and I handed the puppy over to Puck. Within seconds, he'd worked his magic on Pepper and had him happily trotting into the middle of the Ley Line.

In an instant, Puck and I reached the path leading between the Courts. Sunlight dappled the leafy path, while the vibrant trees shone with Summer magic. It never seemed to go fully dark here, not unless the Sidhe willed it to, and they disliked change.

No signs of the Wild Hunt materialised. I hadn't expected to find them this close to the Courts, but my heart skittered with nerves all the same. "I'm going to ask a couple of the Winter Sidhe to pass on my message to their queen, and then I'll go and see the Morrigan. Are you going to wait here?"

"I can do more than that," he said. "When the Aes Sidhe scattered, some went to Summer and some went to the borderlands. They know of the Wild Hunt, even if they are as powerless to challenge them as Hawk and I are, and if I can get their attention, they might be able to ask for the new Erlking's help. Whether he'll actually send it in time is another matter entirely."

"Same with Winter, pretty much," I said. "Want to take the puppy with you?"

"Are you sure?"

No. If I let Pepper run off with him, I was essentially leaving my way home in Puck's hands. That was entirely too much trust to put in someone who'd deceived me once today already. On the other hand, if he did do a runner and leave me stranded, I'd be able to beg Lord Lyle to deposit me back on Earth if I really had to.

"I'm sure."

Puck took a step closer, his gaze searching my face. "I'll wait for you here."

"I'll hold you to that."

I turned away before I changed my mind, heading towards Winter. A familiar cold breeze swept a swathe of bright leaves into my path, the trees ahead of me shedding their coatings. I walked on, wrapping my coat tighter around myself. If the Unseelie Queen turned me into an ice statue again, I wouldn't be any use to anyone, but she alone had the resources to bring the Wild Hunt to justice. Given her opinions on the deceased former Huntsman, she was more likely to send someone to help us than the new Erlking of Summer.

I began to walk, treading a familiar path until the trees frosted over and the soil crunched beneath my feet. The smell of rotting leaves and decay lingered in the air, the chill biting my exposed skin. I came to an abrupt halt near a snowy clearing when Lord Lyle melted out of the trees in front of me, his pitch-dark eyes looking down at me from where he sat atop his horse.

His voice was cold. "I told you not to come back."

"I found the Wild Hunt members responsible for attacking the Court," I told him. "It turns out they're also committing murders in the mortal realm."

"You found them," he said. "Where are they?"

"Hiding in the Grey Vale," I said. "I think that's where they are, anyway. They kidnapped my cousin and are holding her hostage. I request the aid of the Winter Court to get her back."

"You want an audience with the Unseelie Queen?" he said. "Come with me."

I didn't budge. "Oh, no, I'm not cosplaying as an ice statue again. I don't have *time*. My cousin's been kidnapped by the Hunt, and there's a strong chance they'll either use her talisman to kick off Armageddon, or her boyfriend will become the seventh half-faerie they kill as part of some unknown ritualistic sacrifice."

"Seven!" His dark eyes widened. "What ritual? Tell me at once."

"I have no idea what they're trying to do," I said. "They've killed six Summer half-faeries in order to take their magic, and they're on the brink of killing a seventh. They're using symbols—witch magic, with possible links to the Ancients—"

Lord Lyle's horse reared back, almost tipping him off.

He regained control in time to catch his balance but not before I saw the fear flickering in his eyes. *He's afraid.* It wasn't the first time I'd seen a Sidhe show fear, but on top of my own powerlessness, it left me reeling.

The noise of more hooves pounding came along the nearest path, accompanied by the rustle of bushes. Lady Rive approached, her horse snowy white and her outfit impeccable.

"What is the mortal doing here?" she said. "Is she the one who sent a banshee to the Unseelie Queen as a foolish joke?"

I should have known *that* would come back to hit me, but I'd been desperate enough to keep Roseanne out of the hands of the Unseelie Queen that I hadn't cared. "I'm here to warn you of an impending attack from the survivors of the Wild Hunt."

"She claims they're conducting a ritual," said Lord Lyle. "If she lies, she will face our wrath, but she knows things she should not."

"The Wild Hunt members have killed six Summer half-Sidhe," I said. "Now, they have their seventh victim, and they've also kidnapped my cousin, who wields a talisman belonging to an Ancient herself. If they kill the seventh... I have no idea what will happen, but I'm guessing your queen won't like it."

Anger flared in her eyes, and her mouth tightened. "Why was I not informed of this?"

"Of what?" I looked between her and Lord Lyle. "I only found out tonight... or whatever time it is here in Faerie. It's taken us this long to catch the killers. Nobody knew they were part of the Wild Hunt nor that they were killing to advance some other goal—"

"Not that." Lady Rive scowled down at me. "Nobody informed me one of your family members holds a talisman."

"What?" I said blankly. "You mean Ilsa? I thought everyone knew. I told the Unseelie Queen myself."

"Which Lynn is that?" said Lady Rive.

"Ilsa, the former Summer Gatekeeper's sister." I pushed aside my annoyance that the Sidhe still couldn't be bothered to remember our names. "She had no magic of her own before the talisman bonded to her when… when my mother's attempt to break the curse went wrong."

That was a mild way of putting it, really. Besides, Ilsa's talisman wasn't the Wild Hunt's goal. They'd taken her for some other reason, perhaps to lure River into a trap. Didn't mean it would be anything other than catastrophic if the talisman of the Gatekeeper of Death ended up in the wrong hands, but given Lord Lyle's reaction, he knew exactly what they were trying to do with their ritual.

"Never mind the talisman," said Lord Lyle, to my relief. "It sounds as though these exiles from the Hunt are attempting to enact an ancient ritual."

"To do what?" I looked between them. "What kind of ritual requires seven sacrifices? What exactly are they doing with the magic they're stealing from the victims?"

"Taking it for their own, I would guess," said Lord Lyle.

"Or putting it into a talisman," said Lady Rive. "Pray tell, what do you expect us to do about these rogues? We have no knowledge of their location."

"They're hiding in the Vale, but it's up to you," I said. "It's clear they're already testing your boundaries, attacking your livestock and trespassing in the Court. Wouldn't your queen want to know?"

"Even if the Unseelie Queen agrees to send someone to help," said Lord Lyle, "it's unlikely that she will do so for your sake. She is rather irked at you."

"I take it she doesn't know you helped me escape?"

"You saved the mortal?" said Lady Rive. "Lord Lyle, your actions insult the Court."

"*I* used to serve your Court," I said through gritted teeth. "In case you've forgotten. Can you save your bickering until after we've caught the exiles? If you'd rather not help, then tell your queen I've gone to request the help of the Morrigan instead."

"You think the Morrigan will help you?" said Lady Rive.

"She owes me." I met her steely gaze with my own. "Tell the queen or face the consequences later; it's all the same to me. Good luck."

"I would not depend upon her, mortal," said Lord Lyle as I turned away. "I will inform the Unseelie Queen of the Wild Hunt's actions, and the rest will be up to her."

That was the best I'd get. "Fine."

I turned away from the path to the Court and headed for the Kingdom of Death instead, searching for a path trampled by generations of hooves pounding on the soil. The Wild Hunt had once ridden down this very path, silently spiriting away the broken bodies of the dead from the Court to the Morrigan's domain and through to the Path of the Dead which led to the cauldron of resurrection.

It crossed my mind that the Wild Hunt might be hiding

somewhere on the path and not in the Grey Vale at all, but I wouldn't do myself any favours by searching for them alone. It'd be a nice bit of irony if they had chosen the path as their hideout, given that my mother had met her end there. She'd killed the Ancient to whom Ilsa's talisman owed its magic and then used its lifeblood to form herself a new immortal body, but in leaving her mortality behind, the former Winter Gatekeeper had become vulnerable to iron like all Sidhe and had perished at Ilsa's hands. There had been no cauldron of resurrection for her to be reborn from, so her second death had been her last.

After the cauldron had shattered, the Path of the Dead had been abandoned, but the imprints of recent hooves stood out against the trampled soil. I held my breath as I reached the Morrigan's lair and the smell of the freshly and rotting dead washed over me.

Here we go. The Morrigan had a lot to answer for. Did she know the Wild Hunt had taken Roseanne? Was that why she'd failed to help me get her back? Or might she be on their side? Surely not given her history with them, but it was anyone's guess.

I walked across the bridge to the Morrigan's cave and met the ogre on the other side. "I've come to speak to the Morrigan about our bargain."

"I wouldn't cross her today," said the ogre. "She's in a foul mood."

"So am I." I peered around him into the cave. "She has yet to fulfil her side of our bargain. I'm here to remind her."

"Your choice." As he shuffled aside, I marched past him and into the cave towards where the Morrigan sat hunched on her throne, her wings tucked against her back.

"Back again so soon?" she said.

"You made a promise to me." The vow tugged at my chest, reminding me of its presence. "I kept up my end of the bargain and delivered your letter—at a risk to my own life, I might add—but in the end, I found your daughter myself without any help from you."

"Do you want me to congratulate you?" she croaked. "In that case, there is no need for our bargain to exist any longer."

"I beg to differ." I narrowed my eyes at her. "Did you know I found her in the company of the Wild Hunt? I got her back, but they captured my cousin in her place."

"How unfortunate."

"I want you to help me get her back and to stop their scheme in its tracks."

"That is far out of the reach of our agreement."

The vow twinged as if agreeing with her, but I ignored the painful tug in my chest. "No, it isn't. As long as they remain at large, she's in danger."

"There are a great many dangers in this world and others, Holly Lynn. Especially when one is mortal, as you are."

I raised my head. "Are you afraid of the Wild Hunt?"

"How dare you!" She expanded her wings the best she could with the chains binding her, and her crows descended around her like clouds of smoke. I took a step back, but anger drove me to hold my ground.

"Fionn enslaved you," I continued. "The leader of the Wild Hunt once had total command over you. You're scared of the others for that very reason, aren't you? You're scared to even send help to rescue your daughter in case it rebounds on you. I was told you kept your word, but you didn't even try, not when you realised what you were up against."

"Do you wish for me to sever your soul, Holly Lynn?"

I folded my arms, my heart thumping against my ribcage. "You wouldn't need to resort to threats if I wasn't right."

"His followers are nothing," she spat. "The Wild Hunt no longer exists."

"They're trying to enact a ritual," I told her. "They're killing Summer half-Sidhe in order to absorb their healing magic. That doesn't sound like nothing to me."

"Fools," she snarled. "They're fools."

"What are they trying to do?" I asked. "If you won't help, you at least owe me an explanation."

"At a guess, they plan to invoke the god of death," the Morrigan croaked.

"The god of death? I take it that doesn't mean you?" No. She was commonly referred to as the goddess of death, but not an Ancient. Not like the Sidhe but not like their predecessors either.

Like the one with whom the queen of the Aes Sidhe had once made a bargain, sacrificing a mortal every seven years… until Thomas Lynn had broken the cycle. When the queen of the Aes Sidhe had tried to contact the god again, it hadn't ended well for her.

Please tell me that's not who they're trying to contact.

"No," said the Morrigan. "I imagine you've set eyes on that particular god very recently, in fact."

"Not exactly." I hadn't *seen* the god. I'd heard a voice, a terrifying presence from within a void which had ultimately swallowed up the beings who'd opened it.

Along with my Gatekeeper's magic.

The Wild Hunt were trying to rip open a void to contact *him?* Why didn't these people ever have normal hobbies?

"Think, Holly Lynn," said the Morrigan. "What do the Sidhe want above all else, and the Wild Hunt most of all?"

"To be eternal again, but they must know that the god of death isn't going to offer himself on their altar as a sacrifice to bring back their immortality." Was *that* the intention? To slaughter another god to remake the cauldron of resurrection? It wouldn't be the first time a Sidhe had tried to create a replacement—or even some humans, like my mother—but that didn't mean it'd *work.*

No, it was more likely to end in catastrophe, and the rest of us would be collateral damage.

Hadn't Puck said the Wild Hunt had had some kind of arrangement with the Aes Sidhe before they'd split from Summer? I already knew the Aes Sidhe's queen had made an agreement with the god of death, so it wasn't impossible to imagine that she'd told the Wild Hunt how to do the same. The problem was that the Wild Hunt hadn't been there in the battle when the god had made an actual appearance. They didn't know how close Faerie had come to utter destruction.

I needed to put a stop to them first... which meant getting the Morrigan on my side. I faced her, hunched on her throne, and said, "I want your help. You owe me, and I'll stay here until our vow is fulfilled."

"What are you asking, human?" she said. "I am bound here unless you wish to set me free. If you want to risk the wrath of the Unseelie Queen, then I will not object. It would be nice to stretch my wings again."

"Nice try, but no." If I set her free, the Hunt might force her into another bargain. "I need to be able to stop them. Give me everything you have."

"You do not know what you ask, mortal."

"Nevertheless. Give it to me."

I'd hoped she might have some kind of weapon hidden away in her cave, something that might put me on an even footing with the Wild Hunt. I certainly didn't expect her to reach out a clawed hand and grab me, chains and all, yanking me into the shadows enclosing her throne.

I hardly had the chance to draw breath before darkness closed in over my head.

20

The Morrigan's shadows enveloped me from behind, folding around me like an opaque cloak and swamping my senses. The cave vanished from sight, and I could no longer hear the sound of her birds' cries. *What is she doing to me?*

I opened my mouth to ask, but I couldn't even draw breath to speak. The darkness was absolute, a suffocating, cold pressure on my skin. Then the chill went *under* my skin, alighting in my veins like electricity. I gasped aloud, but the shadows held me captive, preventing me from breaking free. Darkness itself moved under my skin—magic, but nothing like the Winter magic I'd wielded before.

When the cloud of the Morrigan's shadows lifted from me, revealing the cave, a touch of darkness remained behind. Instead of a cool-blue glow which signalled Winter magic, I held up my hand to reveal a shadowy orb of energy hovering above my palm.

"Did you just—?" I faltered as the shadow vanished

under my skin, bringing a rush of sharp energy. She'd given me her magic. Or some of it, anyway. The Morrigan didn't look diminished at all, though, instead wearing a smile on her craggy face as she watched me marvel at the power in my hand. Cool shadows sprang to the surface of my palms, yet the chill felt invigorating rather than numbing. "How long will it last?"

"Until you use it up," she said. "Rather like one of those talismans the Sidhe revere so much. If you tell anyone else what I loaned you, I will rip out your soul piece by piece."

Nice. "You're assuming the Sidhe won't guess anyway when I show up to fight the Wild Hunt with magic I shouldn't have."

"The Sidhe can draw their own conclusions," she said. "I would ask that you do not squander my gift if you wish to save your friends."

Yes… it *was* a gift, and from the Morrigan of all people. Was one promise worth so much? Part of me was sure there must be some trickery involved, but I could worry about that once I'd caught up to the Wild Hunt. I let the shadows in my palms grow and then drew the magic underneath my skin again. Falling into a defensive stance, I hit at an invisible enemy.

My hands shifted to claws, curved and sharp and not unlike the ones chained to the Morrigan's throne. Alarmed, I gave them a shake. "They aren't stuck like that, are they?"

"No." She sounded more amused than anything else. "I'd advise you to learn fast if you want to be of any use in the coming conflict."

Reassuring. Yet she'd been more help than I'd ever have anticipated. She'd loaned me some of her power, a gift I doubted even any past Gatekeepers had had access to. Did she not care what I might use it for, or was she confident that I'd burn through the magic she'd given me before I could cause any trouble?

I shook my hands again, willing the magic to withdraw, and to my relief, the claws became my hands again. My gaze went to her face, searching for any signs of hidden trickery. It might be that she spoke the truth—she couldn't lie, after all—and the worst that would happen was that I'd lose my powers at the worst possible moment.

In any case, the vow no longer bound us, which had erased her debt to me. It was an extreme length to go to in order to be left alone, but honestly, it wouldn't have surprised me if that was all she wanted. She didn't even want her own daughter around, let alone anyone else. As one of the last true immortals, she had nothing to want and nothing to fear—except for the Wild Hunt, apparently.

"I am grateful for your gift," I said. "I'll use it wisely."

She said nothing in response, so I left the cave, my hands trembling. Fuck. I had the power of the death goddess running in my veins. Gift or curse, it didn't matter.

I broke into a run across the bridge and through the Death Kingdom, uncaring of anything or anyone I ran into. Redcaps scattered in my wake as I disturbed a nest and then brought out my new claws when they objected. They didn't try to fight, fleeing in terror as they recognised me as a death faerie.

A grin came to my mouth, inexplicable, as the wild magic inside me raged on. Damn, I'd missed feeling strong. I'd missed feeling like I could survive the horrors that Faerie threw in my path and meet them as equals on the battlefield.

I was so lost in my flight that I hardly noticed I'd returned to the Path of the Dead until I came close to colliding with Puck coming the other way. His eyes flew wide, and I belatedly remembered my new claws as I caught my balance before I accidentally skewered him.

"Hey, Puck." I shook my hands, and the claws withdrew. "I didn't know you'd come here, to the Death Kingdom, to find me."

Pepper hid behind Puck's legs, whimpering, while he stared at me. "What happened to you?"

"I asked for the Morrigan's help," I said.

"What did she *do* to you?" he said. "You were flying."

Whoa. I hadn't noticed I'd grown wings as well as sprouting claws. "Yeah. I'm not allowed to tell anyone what she gave me, but you can probably guess."

As with any promise of secrecy, if someone else guessed the truth of their own accord, we'd be able to speak freely. It was one of the few loopholes in the Sidhe's uncompromising magic.

"That can't be possible." Puck crouched down to whisper something to the faerie puppy, who stopped trembling but continued to watch me warily.

"It is," I said. "I'll run out at some point, but it should be enough to drive off the Wild Hunt."

"I hope you're right." From his tone, it sounded like he hoped my new magic *would* run out, which I found a little insulting. The Morrigan wouldn't let me run amok with her powers forever, though, right?

"How'd it go with Summer?" I asked.

"I sent a message to the Erlking and then asked a

couple of acquaintances to pass on a request to the fae in the borderlands for aid," he said. "I debated asking for passage into the Vale, but I have some doubts that the Wild Hunt is hiding there at the moment. If they're still looking for victims and your half-Sidhe friend hasn't found them yet…"

"You think they might have gone back to Earth?" I asked. "I actually thought they might be on the Path of the Dead. Part of it overlaps with the Ley Line."

"You know the way?" He rose to his feet, holding the puppy by the lead.

I gave a sharp nod. "Yeah. I do."

I did *not* want to go back, but Ilsa had stared death in the face on that very path once before. That time, I'd arrived too late to help her, but she hadn't needed me, anyway.

This time… maybe she did.

The well-trodden path took us uphill through the fog. In no time at all, or so it seemed, the trees pulled back until they flanked a single long, twisting path leading into the distance. It was easy to envision the Wild Hunt riding up and down this path, over and over again, for centuries. I found myself imagining the pounding of hooves as I walked, Puck and the faerie dog running alongside me as we followed the track along the Ley Line.

We came to a halt in an overgrown clearing, its trampled grass indicating its recent occupation. The confidence born of my new magic fled as I looked upon the place where my mother had made her second attempt at domination and met her second, permanent end. The same place where the source of the Sidhe's immortality had shattered. No signs of the cauldron of resurrection lay here any longer, or if they did, they'd long since been buried beneath the weeds. The Wild Hunt, too, were nowhere in sight.

"Wrong guess." I paced across the grass and spotted a few blackened pieces of branch lying in a heap. "I think they were here recently, though. I can see the remains of a fire…"

"You don't think River managed to take Ilsa back and the Hunt gave chase, do you?" Puck walked into the clearing, his brow furrowing as he took in the trampled earth and grass which was all that remained of the site of the Sidhe's resurrection.

"Maybe," I said. "If he did, they still need a seventh victim. And there's not a ton of half-bloods in Faerie."

Regardless, the Hunt hadn't chosen their previous victims from Faerie, which meant the odds were high that they'd gone back to Edinburgh to find a seventh victim or to chase down River and Ilsa if they'd escaped. I'd better hope the Courts did send help, because if they didn't, we'd potentially missed a few days without anything to show for it.

Except for the magic filling my veins with shadows.

My heart began to beat faster. Roseanne was back home, too, and I would not let her end up at their mercy again.

"We have to head back home," I said. "Can Pepper get us out from here? We're on the Ley Line… I think."

"Better move back a little." He turned away from the clearing and began to retrace his steps down the path. "Pepper, can you get us to Edinburgh from here?"

The puppy barked and tugged on the lead, running forward. Puck reached out and grabbed my hand, startling me, and then we walked out of the Ley Line and onto a deserted street. I let go of him, looking around.

Pitch-black darkness filled the street, a streetlamp's glow on the corner the only visible landmark. Did that mean it was the same night we'd left? *Please say it is.* I didn't want to imagine the horrors the Wild Hunt might have inflicted on the city if we'd been gone any longer.

"Please tell me you know the way back." I scanned our unfamiliar surroundings, unable to make out more than the facades of a row of terraced houses.

"I don't, but he does."

Pepper barked, tugging on the lead, and we obligingly followed until we came to more familiar ground. My heart plummeted at the sight of half-blood territory, where thorny branches formed a barrier around the fence which hadn't been there before.

"What's going on in there?" I walked up to the gates, which didn't open at my touch. Instead, a thorn would have speared my hand if it hadn't shifted into a claw at the last second. "Hey! What's going on?"

"We're under siege!" came the muffled reply. "Who's out there?"

"Holly and Puck," I replied. "Have you seen the Wild Hunt?"

"Have I seen the *what?*"

"Let me through," said another voice. A moment later, Brook's face appeared in a gap in the thorns. "Where have you been?"

Damn. "Faerie. How many days—?"

"We've been under attack for the past day and a half!" he shouted. "The death fae keep coming in waves."

Shit.

"It's the Wild Hunt," I said. "They captured my cousin, but I don't know where they took her—and they're looking for a seventh victim."

I doubted it'd improve morale if I told them they planned to make a sacrifice to summon the god of death, but I found myself hoping, selfishly, that the Hunt had left Roseanne and Hawk alone. Nevertheless, if they'd killed their seventh victim, we might already be too late.

"The *Wild Hunt?*" he said. "That can't be them. They've gone."

"Who else commands hellhounds?" I glanced at Puck. "Seriously, we need to find them. River and Ilsa must have escaped; otherwise, the Wild Hunt wouldn't have left their hiding spot... but where are *they?*"

Unless they were lost in Faerie somewhere, but I hadn't seen them on the Path of the Dead or near the Courts. That left the Grey Vale, of course, but that was hardly a suitable place to conduct a ritual, given that the Sidhe had stripped the magic out of the place. The Hunt would need a spot high in magic, like the victims they'd killed near the Ley Line.

"What are you talking about?" Brook frowned. "I can't come out of here. We've barely managed to keep out the dead as it is."

Ah, screw it. "Look. I can't explain in detail, but the Wild Hunt is trying to enact a spell to summon a god of death, and to do that, they need to sacrifice a seventh Summer half-Sidhe with healing magic. So anyone who fits that criteria should probably go into hiding. If anyone else wants to help us fight them, though, it'd be appreciated."

"The Sidhe should be on their way," added Puck.

"We've requested the aid of both Courts, but there's no guarantee they'll arrive in time to be of use. We need to be ready."

"You can't be serious," Brook said weakly. "The Wild Hunt… the god of death…"

"It's up to you," I said. "We've wasted too much time already. Puck—"

"Your friend's pet wants to return to the guild." Sure enough, Pepper was attempting to make a quick getaway. "Might your friends be hiding there?"

"I'd say there's a fair chance." Ilsa and River were both guild members, after all. "Let's go."

Leaving Brook behind, we made our way in the direction of the necromancer guild. *I hope the Wild Hunt hasn't attacked them.* Admittedly, the place was a haven of death energy, but it was also faerie-proofed, with iron laced into the very walls to keep out the dead and the fae alike.

The lanterns became more frequent as we reached the more inhabited areas of the city, the shimmering wards on the guild's exterior easy to pick out. Pepper broke free of Puck's grip and ran into the guild, and less than a minute later, Morgan stuck his head out. "You found Ilsa?"

"No, we didn't." My heart gave an uneasy flip. "Why, is she still not back?"

"No, and neither is River," he said. "I hoped you might have found her."

"We went to get reinforcements," I said. "The Sidhe are on their way, but the Wild Hunt left the Path of the Dead, so I assumed they came back here."

Puck swore and took a step back. "Can you hear that?"

I listened. The distant sound of pounding hooves hit my ears an instant later.

Where did that come from?

"I think they're riding on another spirit line," said Puck. "Damn... look."

I rotated on my heel, seeing nothing behind me. Then I looked up. The outline of several horsemen appeared etched against the sky, riding along an invisible path. Another spirit line... oh, *shit.*

"They're riding the spirit line above the necromancer guild." They wouldn't find many half-faeries in the guild... but they *would* find a shit-ton of magical energy to draw on for their summoning ritual.

Panic rose, but the shadows under my skin reminded me of their presence. Morgan gaped at me when my hands shifted into claws, but I didn't have the breath to spare for an explanation. "I'm going after them. If I were you, I'd take cover."

Then I ran at the spirit line and leapt into flight.

21

Wings stretched out behind my shoulders, carrying me into the air and above the street. It was like flying on one of the Wild Hunt's horses, except this time, I was fully in control. I flew higher and higher, the wind buffeting my hair and snagging my strange new dark, feathery wings. Despite my experience with magic, I'd never actually *flown* before, not with wings at my shoulders and a kind of grace I'd never achieve on the ground.

I hovered above the necromancer guild, searching for the spirit line which I knew went straight through the building. Even the Morrigan's gift didn't make the line visible to me, but I'd heard the horsemen. They must be close.

I flew lower, wings beating, envisioning the glowing line beneath my feet. A shimmering light caught my eyes, and I picked up speed—until a massive tree reared up in my path and I came to an abrupt halt, landing on surprisingly solid ground.

I stumbled back, confused beyond measure to see a giant oak tree sitting on top of what was supposed to be the middle of Edinburgh—except the city had vanished from sight. Instead, a path stretched to either side of the tree's sprawling roots, which spread to at least the size of a house. This must be the spirit line... but where were the horsemen?

Puck flew up to me as a crow and landed in human form at my side. "That was a close one."

"Nobody mentioned a tree would get in my way." I turned on my heel, squinting into the distance, but murky white mist covered both sides of the path as well as the ground beneath my feet. "*Why* is there a random tree here, anyway?"

"This spirit line is unusual," said Puck. "Or so I hear. I don't see the horsemen..."

"I heard them, though." Had they been pursuing Ilsa, or had she already escaped their clutches? "They're on the spirit line."

"Or they moved to another one. If you walk too far in that direction, you might end up stranded in the middle of nowhere."

I halted in midstep. "I'll fly, then. There must be a way to track them down."

As if conjured up by my thoughts, none other than Jas ran onto the path behind me, accompanied by Keir, Morgan, and Lloyd.

"Thought I'd find you up here," said Jas. "Nice job flying, by the way. New trick?"

"A temporary one," I said vaguely, mostly so Morgan wouldn't get any ideas about asking the Morrigan to loan him some magic too. "You do realise the Wild Hunt is somewhere on this path, right?"

"That's the idea," said Jas, eyeing the large tree. "I've used this path before, so I know all the hiding spots."

"You do?"

"Yeah." There was an odd note in her voice I couldn't quite pin down, and she dragged her gaze away from the tree and to the path ahead. I glimpsed a faint light shimmering in her hands and the swirling marks on her wrists disappearing underneath the sleeves of her long coat.

"Blood magic?"

"A few basic marks to make the fight easier." She walked ahead down the spirit line, her gaze fixed at some point in the distance. "They aren't far away."

No wonder she'd understood the magic the killer had used, since she'd been using blood magic on herself. Except, of course, she hadn't used it to kill people… or summon a god of death.

I only hoped she and the others knew what they were up against, because there was no turning back now. While Jas led the way, we followed until she veered off the path. At first, it seemed as though she'd stepped into empty air… then the mist at the side of the path cleared, revealing an area the size of a large room. A liminal space.

In a clearing, two horsemen stood with their backs to us, their horses secured nearby. As we walked, I saw the target of their attention: a woman tied to a tree trunk in front of them.

Ilsa. I didn't see River anywhere, but when Ilsa's gaze locked on us behind the horsemen, recognition flared in her eyes. The horsemen said something to her which I didn't quite catch.

"I told you," Ilsa said in reply. "The god whose power resides in my talisman is already dead. You can't use him to fulfil your twisted bargain. You're wasting your time."

"My mother already tried that and failed," I added. "She's right."

The horsemen spun on me, drawing their swords, but I'd already shifted my hands into claws and leapt at both of them. My claws missed as the horseman on the right twisted out of the way with preternatural speed. Puck flew at him from the other side while Morgan let Pepper the faerie dog free to jump into the fray, Jas moved in a speedy blur—she must have used blood magic to give herself a speed boost—and Keir's hands alighted with necromantic power.

Yet every one of their attacks missed. Puck, of course, couldn't land a direct hit on them, simply flying into their eyes as a distraction, and Morgan and Keir's necromantic magic fizzled out, while Jas's spells had a similar lack of effect. We might outnumber them, but they were Sidhe, and none of our magic equalled theirs.

Except, perhaps, for a death goddess.

This is what I asked for your help with, Morrigan.

Wings sprouted from my shoulders, my clawed hands extended, and the others exclaimed in shock as I flew forward on a tide of shadow. The two horses reared back, and in unison, both horsemen leapt back onto their steeds.

"Goddess," one of them said. "No. You wear her face, but you are a mere mortal."

"You got that right."

As I lunged at him, his blade glanced off my clawed hand, and with the other, I raked my claws across his face.

A bellow of rage escaped him, and he hit out with the back of his hand. I landed on my back, the feathers on my new wings cushioning my fall, but the breath rushed from my lungs. Damn, he was strong.

I rolled to my feet and drew my iron blade, but he glided easily out of reach. "Hey, that's not fair. If you get a horse, I should too.

Not that it would have improved my reach, given that he towered over me even on the ground. The second horseman urged his horse to stand in front of Ilsa, while the others faced him with their own magical attacks at the ready. With my new magic, I'd better be able to take down this guy.

One hand shifted into a claw, I wielded my blade with the other, striking and dodging the horseman's attacks. As I fought, I drew on all my years of training to be Winter Gatekeeper, where I'd learned to use my few strengths as a human against the Sidhe—yet I'd never fought an opponent like this before. If not for the shadowy magic flowing under my skin, a single blow might have killed me, or my slowed reactions would have thrown me into the path of his blade. As it was, my wings kept me out of range of his worst attacks, while my claws were as strong as a blade in themselves. I dealt two more vicious slashes to his face which drew blood, but he refused to slow despite the blood trickling into his eyes.

Puck shifted forms over and over, turning from a bird to a bear to a leaping flame in an attempt to throw off his aim, but between us, we made no headway. The Wild Hunt were simply unbeatable with any regular magic, and the best I'd ever be able to do would be to hold them off until one of us collapsed from exhaustion. Without the

Morrigan's resilience to back up her magic, winning outright wasn't an option.

While Puck turned into a bear again and attempted to shove the horse out from underneath him, I found myself at Ilsa's side. She'd managed to untie her bonds, but her talisman's magic was designed to use on the dead, not on immortal horsemen who never tired.

"You okay?" I asked her.

"Sure," she said. "It's my own fault I got recaptured. River and I were separated when they came after me, and the next thing I knew, I was knocked out and tied to a tree."

"So he did manage to find you." The time we'd lost in running around Faerie hadn't been a complete waste after all.

The horseman's blade struck my claw, drawing blood, and then swung at my head. Puck distracted him first, flying into his face as a crow and blinding him. I gave him a nod of thanks and returned with another swipe of my claw, only for the horseman to block with a bone-shaking hit.

I took the blow on the back of my newly clawed hand and skidded back several feet, where I landed on Ilsa's other side. Nearby, the other horseman had his hands full dealing with Morgan, Jas, and Keir at the same time, though it was the faerie dog who was causing the most chaos by leaping at the horse and getting underfoot. Nevertheless, nobody had managed to deal the warrior any damage.

"Ilsa." I caught my balance. "What're the odds of us being able to lure them away to the Ley Line?"

"Not good. Why?"

"The Sidhe are coming to our rescue."

"Really." Her tone dripped with scepticism. "Unless they swore a vow, I wouldn't count on their help."

"Fair point, but we can't fight forever."

Ilsa raised her talisman. A bolt of magic shot from the pages of the book and struck the nearest horseman, but he hardly stumbled. Instead, he reached out and grabbed Puck's bird form by the wing. As he did so, Puck transformed from a bird to a snake and sank his teeth into the horseman's hand, who shook him off with a bellow of rage.

Puck landed on his feet next to me, a grin on his bloody mouth. "Biting gets around my vow. That's good to know."

"Traitor!" bellowed the horseman. "I know you. You're one of the Aes Sidhe."

"At your service." Puck gave a mocking bow. "Care to leave us alone now?"

"Only when your blood runs down the spirit lines, trickster."

My anger spiked. *Dammit, Morrigan, the magic you loaned me was supposed to help me win.* I focused hard on the shadows spreading under my skin, turning my hands to claws and causing wings to sprout from my back. A stinging sensation came from beneath my blade. Was the iron hurting me?

In a wild gamble, I reared back and flung the knife at the horsemen. He glided out of the way, but in that moment, the rest of the Morrigan's magic broke free. Shadows filled my vision, and I leapt into flight, drawing the attention of both horsemen.

"Go!" I screeched, sounding alarmingly like the Morrigan. "Leave the Gatekeeper and flee, or your lives will be forfeit."

My words rang through the air, and to my shock, the horses obeyed even if the horsemen would rather not have. Both of them spun around, galloping out of sight and back into the spirit line.

I gaped after them. I hadn't expected it to *work*.

"I hope they went back to the Ley Line," Puck remarked. "Otherwise, we'll have a hell of a job tracking them down again."

"They're fucking fast." Keir moved to Jas's side, who was applying a healing spell to a cut on Morgan's face. They'd been damn lucky to escape any worse injuries. I tracked down my iron blade and put it back in its sheath, but the dark magic shimmering around my clawed hands was already dimming. I'd better hope I hadn't burned it out, because I'd need it again when we tracked the warriors down.

Ilsa, meanwhile, put her talisman back into her pocket. "Thanks for coming to find me."

"Hey, we deserve our shot at saving you for once," Morgan said. "Where's River?"

Her expression clouded. "I don't know. We ran out of Faerie into Edinburgh and then… the Hunt caught up."

"They had you captive on the Path of the Dead, right?" I asked.

"Yes, why?"

"We just missed each other," I explained. "Also, the half-faeries in the city have been under siege for a day and a half."

She groaned. "I figured I'd missed some time."

"And we've all been worried about you," added Morgan. "The Sidhe better come and get those fuckers."

"We'll find River first." Ilsa stepped out of the liminal space and onto the path leading back to the guild while the rest of us followed her. The horsemen had indeed vanished from sight, but the whole city was covered in a mass of criss-crossing spirit lines, and there were countless places for them to hide.

Jas took the lead while I walked alongside Ilsa.

"They didn't take the book from you?" I asked.

"They tried," she said, "but I don't think it was their main goal, since the god whose magic is inside it is already dead."

Thanks to my mother, who'd slaughtered the god and used its blood to make herself into a temporary immortal. If the god had lived, then we might be in a world of trouble now, but that wasn't to say the horsemen wouldn't find a way to succeed in making their seventh sacrifice anyway.

"No, but it turns out their seven sacrifices are intended to summon the god of death," I said. "They arrived too late to the battle which broke the Gatekeeper's curse to know why that's not a good idea."

Ilsa groaned. "For fuck's sake."

"Yeah." I hardly believed I'd managed to scare them off like that. Either the Morrigan had massively underplayed how much power she'd loaned me, or she had more to spare than I'd ever imagined. Which made me glad I hadn't ended up on her bad side, if nothing else. I turned to Puck to see what he thought of all this and found him staring at me as though concerned I might burst into flames at any moment. "Do *you* think the Sidhe will keep their word?"

"I think if they do half of what the Morrigan did, those horsemen won't stand a chance."

I blinked. "It's not like I actually killed them."

"Still." His gaze went to my newly clawed hands and then to my face, and I found myself wondering what I looked like to him. A terrifying death goddess, maybe. Would he have made his offer for me to stay at his house if I'd shown up like this?

I shook off the thought, annoyed at myself for even thinking it.

Ilsa cleared her throat. "Now that we've averted the apocalypse, can you help me find my boyfriend before he becomes a sacrifice to the god of death?"

"Gladly." Jas led us back down the spirit line towards Edinburgh. How she saw where she was going was beyond me, but it must be some kind of witchy sixth sense which was as out of bounds to me as the spirit sight was and as invisible as the faerie realm was to most humans.

Within a minute, the giant tree appeared again. Jas led us around its roots and then walked out of the spirit line, where we emerged onto an unfamiliar street somewhere in Edinburgh's Old Town. While the others veered towards the guild, I found myself looking back at the spirit line, wishing I could see where it intersected with the other lines so I could figure out where those horsemen had fled to.

"Want to go back to half-blood territory to warn them?" asked Puck.

"Might as well."

River must be somewhere in the city, but the horsemen might have gone looking for another victim instead. In any case, we needed to warn the others that the Wild Hunt was loose in the city again, so we made our way towards the Ley Line and half-blood territory.

As we turned into a deserted street, we came to an abrupt halt when a lone horseman barred our path. Without his horse, he walked with a faint limp, and when he looked directly at me, I saw one of his eyes was nothing more than a bloody hole.

And he held an unconscious River in his arms.

22

"You," I said to the horseman. "How'd you survive being stabbed in the eye? Are you made of steel?"

Even an iron blade to the eyeball hadn't brought an end to him, but he hadn't been with his fellow Wild Hunt members when they'd held Ilsa captive. Instead, the scumbag had taken River. From what I could see, he was unconscious, not dead, without any symbols inked on his face—but when the horseman casually tossed him aside onto the pavement, he didn't stir.

"You've been difficult to track down," the horseman growled. "You will pay for what you did to me, human."

"I gave you what you deserved for kidnapping my friend." Tempted as I was to take out his other eye, he'd be wise to my tricks this time, and he'd find it easier to fend me off now that we were no longer precariously balanced on the back of a faerie horse.

Instead, I left my blade sheathed and drew on the shadowy magic flowing through my veins, shifting my hands to claws and bringing feathery wings to my back. At my side, Puck shifted into his largest bear form. I prepared to draw on the terrifying magic I'd used to send the other horsemen fleeing—but before a single syllable could leave my mouth, the horseman said, "Your trickery won't work on me."

Then he spoke another word not in English but in a language that struck me like a sharp musical note. The word slid through my mind, not leaving any comprehensible trail behind, but it instantly brought me to a complete halt. I didn't need to be able to understand the word to know he'd told me to *stop* and that since he'd spoken in the language of the gods, the magic imbued in the word itself compelled me to obey.

An Invocation. Words no mortal could speak aloud without being driven to madness, with few exceptions. Even the Morrigan's magic couldn't force my limbs to move, to make my body respond as the horseman strode towards me and pointed his blade at my neck.

Puck crashed into him from the side, knocking him off balance. Shifting from bear to bird and then to a leaping flame, he sent the horseman staggering back when the fire seared his exposed hands.

In the light of the flames, the horseman's arms and hands gleamed with swirling symbols. Blood magic. He'd used it on himself, too, but he hadn't inked anything on River. No, he hadn't taken him for a sacrifice but as bait to lure *me* in. Evidently, even the ritual to summon the god of death didn't matter to him as much as his revenge on me for stabbing him in the eye.

"How did you avoid him?" I gasped at Puck.

"Flew out of reach," he replied. "We have to get River out of here."

"I don't think he's this dude's priority."

The horseman recovered from the unexpected flames, bearing hardly a mark on his singed hands. Then again, I'd assumed stabbing him in the eye would finish him off, and my assumption had been dead wrong. He came at me with his blade thrusting to kill, and I raised my claw to block him, relieved his spell had temporarily broken. If he spoke another Invocation, though, I doubted I'd be lucky enough to escape again.

Holding his sword in my grip, I staggered back a few steps. "What *is* your problem? Why are you randomly slaughtering Winter's livestock? Were you trying to piss off the Unseelie Queen?"

"The Courts spurned us," he said, his voice like gravel. "They will pay, as will she."

"Your leader turned out to be an impostor, in case you've forgotten," I said. "Were you aware of his identity the whole time? Did you know Fionn killed the real Huntsman?"

"What business is it of yours, mortal?" He wrenched the blade free and attempted to strike again, only for me to block with a clawed hand. If he wondered where my newfound powers had come from, he didn't ask. "Fionn was our leader. If he broke ties with the Courts, it didn't matter to us. We served him alone."

"Even when he made you invade Earth." Another blocked blow jarred the bones in my arms and rattled my teeth in my skull. "When he had you slaughter humans in droves and throw the Courts into upheaval. When he murdered children and enslaved the Morrigan—"

"The Morrigan got everything she deserved," he growled. "The Courts will too."

"Tough talk coming from a glorified undertaker."

The side of his blade slammed into my clawed hand, drawing a spasm of pain. A trickle of blood dripped from underneath the layers of thick feathers, but I didn't relinquish my grip. I could see Puck's crow form looking for an opening, but his vow remained intact. He couldn't harm the horseman.

Besides, maybe he was as curious as I was about why the Wild Hunt's warriors had gone so far off the rails. Or off the Path of the Dead, as the case may be. Fionn had been scum, but I'd thought he'd duped everyone into thinking he was the genuine Huntsman and not an impostor who'd stolen the job from the real guy. It sounded like at least some of the Wild Hunt's members had been in on the truth, or else they didn't care what he did as long as he didn't take away their power.

"We owe the Courts nothing." Another blow blocked. More crimson droplets scattered onto the pavement. "We owe the queen everything."

"What queen?" I said blankly. "Not the Morrigan?"

"No," he snarled. "Etaina, the Lady of Light and ruler of the Aes Sidhe. She was far more grateful for our service than the Courts ever were."

The blade jarred in my grip. "You worked for her back when Fionn was still alive. Against the Courts' orders, I'm betting."

Puck had said as much. Not that he was capable of speaking in his bird form, simply flying around the horseman's head in an attempt to peck at his remaining eye.

"Not at all." The horseman swatted at Puck, forcing

him to fly out of range. "The Courts had no say in our agreement with the Lady of Light. We entered into our bargain freely."

"Some of the Aes Sidhe would beg to differ."

Puck's flight became more agitated, but the horseman's mouth twisted into a sneer. "They're lucky the queen's sacrifices to the god of death had to be human, not fae. One mortal every seven years. Until your ancestor ruined everything. Yes, I know who you are… Gatekeeper."

"If you expect me to feel guilty for the way my ancestor wriggled out of being sacrificed, then you're talking to the wrong person."

Thomas Lynn had been spared thanks to his own bargain with the so-called Lady of Light, but the god had been furious to have missed out on the payment for his soul. Once Etaina had summoned him again, centuries later, she'd been one of many who'd paid the price for the years of sacrifices he'd missed out on.

Yet the horseman's claims brought another question to mind. If Etaina had sacrificed many mortals to the gods, then what had the gods given her in return? Had the Wild Hunt received anything from their bargain?

The horseman lunged forward with his blade. I readied myself to meet his blow, but he veered to the side at the last second—straight at River.

"No." I jumped into his path—but he spoke an Invocation. The word slid through my mind, and I stopped in midmotion, my body locked to the spot. His blade kept on coming, aimed at my neck.

Puck flew in front of me, and the blade struck him instead. My scream went unheard as the spell held me captive, heedless of the shadowy magic roving beneath my skin. Puck. *Puck*. He dropped like a stone, landing on the pavement in a splatter of blood and feathers.

"That's one pest taken care of." The horseman raised his blade over River again—only for the half-faerie to spring to his feet, raising his talisman. The green light swirling around the blade knocked the horseman's weapon aside, while the spell on me broke for long enough for me to stab my clawed hands into his neck.

The warrior snarled, shedding blood droplets, and threw me off. I hit the ground, winded, and rolled to check on Puck. He'd turned human again, lying on his back, crimson staining his front where the side of the blade had sliced him open. As I fumbled to find his pulse, River and the horsemen exchanged a few more blows. The faintest beat fluttered against my hand, fading by the second.

Then the sound of loud hoofbeats rang out from nearby.

"They ride again." The warrior spun towards me, his one good eye fixed on my face. "I will see you soon, Gatekeeper."

In one swift movement, he vanished into the night while I crouched over Puck's limp body. Dammit, I had the power of the goddess of death at my fingertips. She could rip out souls and put them back. If anyone held the power to forestall death, it was her.

"I'm sorry," River said. "I can't use my healing ability on others."

I barely spared him a glance. "You have the spirit sight, don't you? You can see if he's alive or... or not."

"Yes, but I can't bring him back. Not like that."

"Not without breaking the rules, you mean." I extended my hands above his body. The Morrigan's power rushed to my fingertips, and I pushed the shadows at Puck, demanding they restore his bleeding life force.

Heal him, damn you. If she can repeatedly heal from iron chains, then she can do the same to him.

The wound on his chest began to glow, and shadows slithered over his skin. They slid into the wound, dampening the glow, and a sudden weariness slammed into me. My knees hit the ground. Then—

Puck drew in a halting breath and sat up. "Holly... what did you do?"

"Saved your life." I rocked back into a sitting position, my throat dry, my hands human again and shaking hard. "I—are you okay?"

He held a hand to his chest, stunned. "Why did you do it?"

"Not 'how'?" I coughed. "Not sure I can answer that one, either, but I did it because I could. Because it was within my power."

It was that simple, and that complicated. I might have said I was sick of killing and that I wanted to be the good guy for once. Or I might have said that despite everything he'd kept from me, everything we'd been through in the last few days, I'd come to care whether he lived or died. I'd come to care about him.

That knowledge restored some of my flagging energy. I climbed to my feet, feeling oddly detached from reality, as though I knew on some level that I'd be lucky if the Morrigan let me walk away intact from our next meeting if she found out what I'd done... but that could wait until later.

"What the hell was that?" River demanded. "What did you do?"

"The Morrigan gave me a present."

His eyes were wide. "You brought him back from the dead. I saw."

"I healed him," I corrected. "Major difference there."

I'd saved him. That was all there was to it. I'd think about the consequences later, assuming I lived that long.

River's brow crinkled. "Damn. I think the horseman went to join his friends. Or to find an easier victim to kill."

I grimaced. "I don't know if you heard everything he said…"

His eyes narrowed. "I heard it all. He used an Invocation to stop me from fighting back when he brought me here. He knew you'd be searching for me."

"Bastard," I said. "Good news. Ilsa is safe and back at the guild. We drove off the other two horsemen, but that dude seems to be doing his own thing. He's the guy I stabbed in the eye when I went to get Roseanne back, so I guess he was more interested in revenge."

"I gathered," said River dryly. "I'm glad Ilsa's okay. They didn't take her talisman?"

"She still has her talisman," I said. "She said the Wild Hunt wouldn't have much of a use for it—"

At that moment, an alarmingly bright current of energy came from the direction of the Ley Line. In fact, it looked awfully like the light of Ilsa's talisman.

Or maybe not.

From River's expression, he thought the same as I did. "We'd better go."

The three of us moved towards half-blood territory

while I did my best to ignore the growing suspicion that I'd broken some major rules when I'd healed Puck. There was a good reason even necromancers never raised the dead permanently. In fact, their job was mostly the opposite, to lay the unquiet dead back to the earth, to banish ghosts and calm zombies… but nothing in their rule book mentioned magic like the Morrigan's.

Didn't mean they wouldn't lock me in jail if they found out. I was pretty sure the Morrigan was actually banned from this realm by the order of the Mage Lords, in fact—but it wasn't like she'd used her magic here. I had instead. And I'd keep using the power she'd given me until the Wild Hunt surrendered.

The pounding of hooves greeted us near the Ley Line, where screams rang out from half-blood territory. Bright magic flared up, green and blue, as the half-faeries fought against the intruders. They might outnumber the horsemen for now, but if they'd found a seventh sacrifice again, it would all be over.

River picked up the pace and ran towards the battling faeries while I followed with my wings and claws at the ready. Puck flew at my side in his bird form, and we found ourselves face to face with three giant hellhounds.

The hounds of the Wild Hunt had come out to play.

23

The three hellhounds moved to circle us, their huge, shaggy forms casting wide shadows on the street and their sharp teeth dripping with drool. I made sure not to tread in said drool—which contained a deadly poison—and averted my gaze from their pit-like eyes. They fed on death, which meant they grew bigger with each one that died—and from their sheer size, they'd feasted upon several of their fallen dead already.

I dodged a hellhound's snapping teeth and lashed its flank with my claws while River skewered its head on his blade. Puck shifted forms and flew to meet the second one, doing his rapid shifting trick and turning from bear to snake to thorny briar and searing flame. The hellhound spun around, baffled, but the third loomed overhead, its eyes looking into mine.

Oh, shit. You weren't supposed to look into their eyes… but no effects came from its death stare. Of course. *The Morrigan must be immune.* It made sense that a death goddess couldn't be affected by death magic from others. Grinning, I swept my claws across its face and dispatched it with a stab to the back of its neck.

Puck brought the third down with a few well-placed swipes, and its huge body collapsed on the road. Leaving their bodies, River ran to the street's end. "Ilsa!"

My heart lurched. Ilsa stood with the Gatekeeper's book in her hand, facing a dark cloud of magic. *Wraith.* It looked as though the horsemen had brought some friends from the Grey Vale.

Even the Morrigan's magic didn't give me a clear way of fighting wraiths, so I went in search of the horsemen. More death fae did battle with half-faeries, from sluagh to death stealers, but the echo of hoofbeats had gone silent. Had they left?

Puck took flight with a piercing shriek. Wondering what had startled him, I hurried over and spotted the unmoving body of a half-faerie lying in the road. *Hawk.*

"No." A gasp rushed from my lungs. "If he's here, then Roseanne…"

Puck shifted to human form again, his gaze reflecting my own dread back at me. Only then did I see the swirling marks inked on Hawk's face and neck.

"Tell me he didn't have healing magic too," I whispered.

Puck's silence answered for him. He hadn't shared the details of his friend's magic, but if the horsemen had killed the seventh victim they needed, then the god of death was only a single step away. If they'd done the ritual correctly, we were in serious trouble.

"Go beyond the Gates of Death!" Ilsa yelled at the wraith, a bolt of power shooting from the book in her hands and pushing the wraith backwards. Movement stirred in the streets around us, and the three horsemen melted out of the shadows, surrounding Hawk's body.

One of them held a squirming Roseanne in his grip.

No. Our rescue had been in vain, and Hawk had paid the worst price of all to bring them their seven sacrifices. I took a step forward, and the three horsemen spoke a single word, their voices chiming in unison. The word slithered through the air, and all of us froze to the spot at the same time—even the wraith. Only the three horsemen kept moving, surrounding Hawk's inert body. My gut tightened. *Why did he leave the office? Why?*

"That's better," one of the horsemen said. "It is time for us to give our final offering to the god of death."

"Thank you for your service, mortals," the other added.

The shimmering form of the Ley Line appeared beneath our feet, revealing Faerie's paths on the other side. One more step, and the force separating us would be impossible to traverse. My mind screamed for their spell to break, but my limbs remained frozen.

I have the power of the Morrigan. I ought to be able to break the command of a scumbag like him.

Shadows burst from my hands, fighting against the word that held me captive. My body moved—one step then two—and then Edinburgh vanished from sight.

Leaves cushioned my feet, marking the path between realms where the two Courts met, but I'd left the others behind. Only the three horsemen had travelled through the Ley Line, carrying Roseanne and Hawk's body along with them.

One of the horsemen strode forward, holding the same odd pointy instrument I'd seen earlier. Its glittering end shone like a torchlight as he crouched beside Hawk's body and began to draw more swirling lines on the ground. The ink glistened like a snail's trail, forming symbols of magic etched in the blood of the Ancients which shaped the magic to their will. It made a horrible kind of sense that they'd opted to complete their ritual within Faerie itself in order to ensure it worked.

Think, Holly. My movements were sluggish, the remnants of their spell clinging to me, but the Morrigan's magic clearly *did* have some degree of resistance against the Ancients, perhaps stemming from her own near-immortal status. My hands turned to claws, and I gave a wild lunge at the two horsemen inking symbols onto the ground.

The third moved, and I caught his blow in my clawed hand instinctively, the momentum forcing me to brace my feet on the leafy ground to keep from being pushed off balance.

"I wondered if you'd be foolish enough to follow us here," growled the one-eyed horseman. "Your blood will satisfy the god of death too."

His two companions didn't spare me a glance, continuing to daub swirling marks around Hawk's body. Fear twisted within me. I'd left my allies behind, effectively pitting myself against all three of them alone.

"You're making a huge mistake." I spoke loudly enough for all three of them to hear. "Don't you know what the god of death did in the brief time he had access to the Courts? Both queens who tried to make deals with him met tragic ends, including your precious Etaina, and the Courts nearly fell apart."

"Don't you dare insult the Lady of Light," snarled the one-eyed horseman. "Your family is the reason she died."

"My family survived because they didn't break a promise to the god of death," I said. "It was she who tried to sacrifice their souls."

"Mortals are good for nothing more."

"Gonna have to disagree with you there, mate."

His friends ignored us, continuing to daub swirling symbols around Hawk's fallen body with their tools. Then again, I'd already failed to beat this dude in combat even with the Morrigan's strength at my disposal. He didn't need the others' help to bring me down.

"Also—" I raised my clawed hands in anticipation of a blow. "You don't treat your gods any better than you treat the rest of us, in my experience. Do you think the god of death will happily do your bidding after Etaina locked him out of this realm for centuries and then expected him to act as though no time had passed at all?"

The god had required the sacrifice of a mortal life every seven years in exchange for whatever Etaina had asked him to do before Thomas Lynn's rebellion, and I frankly preferred not to find out what new appetites he'd developed in the intervening years.

"The blood of the Ancients fuels our magic," said the one-eyed horseman. "And the lifeblood of a god will enable our immortality to return. We will reforge the cauldron of resurrection."

"By killing the god of death?" He had to be kidding. "You can't. There's no way you're strong enough to. Etaina wasn't."

"Etaina was betrayed." He extended his blade, and the

marks surrounding Hawk's body glowed even brighter than before.

"You're deluded." I willed the Morrigan's shadowy magic to expand my wings and turn me into a mirror of its owner. *Once more. Just once.* "Stay back."

His surviving eye narrowed. "You are not the goddess of death," he spat. "You're an impostor."

The lights intensified, and then a slash appeared in the air like a door opening… to somewhere that wasn't Faerie at all.

"No!"

I took flight and slammed down before the other two horsemen. They straightened upright, weapons at the ready, but the gaping hole in the air commanded their attention.

"Shut that hole you opened." I waved my clawed hands at both of them. "Close it, or—"

"Or die," finished Roseanne, leaping onto one of the horsemen's backs. Her clawed hands dug into his neck, causing him to collapse with a pained cry that rang up and down the path.

His companions released noises of outrage, advancing on both of us. That was when Hawk lifted his head, his eyes opening a fraction. *He's not dead?*

Had he faked his death? There was no time to ask him how, not with the slash in the world gaping open… yet nobody waited on the other side. Of course. Hawk, the cunning bastard, had fooled them into believing him dead, and without a seventh victim, no god had answered their call.

Yet the gaping hole to another realm remained, and a vicious breeze came from within, slamming into all of us. Roseanne hung on to me for balance as the strong gust of wind knocked even the horsemen back. As though some great beast within was roaring in triumph…

Then several voices spoke in unison, saying words which slid through my mind like rain on windows. *Sidhe.* They rode down the paths on either side of us, horses gliding to a halt, and they continued to speak words which gave the impression of locking doors, of bonds too tight to break.

The gap in the air glowed around the edges, the breeze fading as it began to close. The Sidhe had the stunned horsemen surrounded in seconds, while several people appeared on the path around us. Ilsa, River… and Puck, whose eyes widened at the sight of Hawk sitting up amid a mass of swirling symbols on the leafy ground.

Hawk rose to his feet, a grin on his face, as Puck ran to his side. "How are you alive?"

"He faked his death," I told him. "Causing the ritual to fail. The god didn't come when they called because they didn't have seven sacrifices."

"You gave me the idea," he said. "You said those rituals can be pretty exact in how they work. Take one element away, and they fall apart."

"Hey, I wasn't in on it," I said in response to Puck's accusing look. "I thought we were screwed too."

"Yet you still *followed* them here."

"Someone had to. They had Roseanne." I glanced over at the horsemen, who stood within a circle of angry Sidhe from both Courts, predominantly Winter.

"I wasn't in on it either," Roseanne said. "Holly… you look like… like my *mother*. Why do you have claws?"

I shook my hands, and the shadows withdrew from sight. "I borrowed a little something from the Morrigan."

Her eyes bulged. "How?"

"I may have guilt-tripped her a little over Fionn and her broken promise." I assumed we were even now, but that didn't mean I looked forward to our next meeting. "It was supposed to have a limit, so it probably won't last much longer."

"Holly." Ilsa walked over, River keeping pace with her. "We're heading home. Want to come?"

"Yes, please." I nodded to Roseanne, who nodded vigorously herself. "Puck?"

"Right behind you." He and Hawk joined us, and our group followed River out of the Ley Line.

We landed next to half-blood territory, where I wasted no time in striding right up to the thorny gate.

"Show's over, folks," I said, loudly enough for anyone on the other side to hear me. "The Wild Hunt is in the Sidhe's hands now."

Nobody answered for a long moment. Then Brook's face appeared in a gap between thorny vines. "They're gone?"

"To the Unseelie Court's jail," said Roseanne from behind me. "All three of them. They won't come back."

Brook opened the gate a little. "You did this? You brought them to an end?"

"I told the Unseelie Court to take care of them." No need to mention the gift the Morrigan had given me. "Your nightly attacks by death faeries ought to be over too. You're welcome."

The gate opened another inch or two, and Brook said, "Tell me... is there anything I can do to repay you?"

"Sure." I nodded to Roseanne. "I'm looking for a new rental house. For two people."

"What do you think?" asked Brook.

Roseanne gave the house in front of us an appreciative once-over. "I like it."

I had to agree. The neat cottage was small, perched on the end of a road at the edge of half-blood territory, and within my price range. If I continued to get work after the money I'd snagged as a bonus for ridding the city of the Wild Hunt and their death fae, that is. The garden was overgrown with weeds, curtains of ivy covered the walls, and when we went inside, the facilities were decent by post-invasion standards. No issues we couldn't fix, anyway.

The best part? It contained exactly zero bad-tempered mercenaries. The landlord was half-fae, too, and while the general superstitions around the Morrigan's daughter remained intact, Brook had grudgingly vouched for me. The others would just have to deal with it.

I nodded to Brook. "We'll take it."

As he left the room, Roseanne gave me an uncertain

look. "Am I allowed to sign the paperwork if I'm under sixteen?"

"Leave it to me," I said. "Or rather, leave it to Brook, and if necessary, I can remind him what we did to help drive off the Wild Hunt."

Besides, most half-faeries were either orphans or abandoned by their faerie parents, so I should be able to declare myself Roseanne's guardian without any trouble. Considering she'd ended up on her own for years by those very same rules, I should be able to use them in our favour this time around.

In any case, Brook had no objection. After we signed the paperwork, I found Ilsa of all people waiting outside the house. I'd been texting her during our tour, but I hadn't expected her to trek all the way over here. Her gaze landed on Roseanne first, whose expression gained the wary countenance of a trapped bird.

"I don't know if we've ever been properly introduced," said Ilsa. "I'm Ilsa. You're Roseanne?"

"Yeah." She fidgeted shyly, but the lack of open hostility from Ilsa won out. "Holly's my legal guardian. Kinda."

"Only because the laws are contradictory if not non-existent when it comes to half-faeries," I added for Ilsa's benefit. "If you expect me to pay for all your food after you're old enough to work yourself, then you're mistaken. You can always sign up to do a paper round."

Roseanne shot me a grin. "Do you think the locals want a crow delivering their mail?"

"Sounds like an essential service if you ask me." I knew better than to think either of us was cut out for an ordinary job, though, but it was nice not to worry about money or having a roof over our heads for a bit.

Ilsa smiled. "Glad you worked something out. I need to go and join my patrol again before the novices get themselves lost up near Arthur's Seat."

"There's a ghost all the way up there?"

"Ghosts get everywhere," said Ilsa. "That's one constant."

Another constant was Ilsa's ability to be at the centre of everything. She'd recovered from her capture at the Wild Hunt's hands in no time and hadn't given away my own role in the action when she'd reported to the guild. I appreciated that, at least.

Strangely, the Morrigan's magic hadn't entirely gone away. Shadows lurked under the skin of my arms, liable to shift to claws at my command. The others didn't know, save for the ones who'd witnessed my use of her power, but I had to wonder what the Morrigan had been thinking. Unless she'd majorly underestimated how much magic she'd loaned me.

As Ilsa walked away, my phone buzzed with a message from Puck, asking me if I wanted to go and cause some mischief. What was that supposed to mean?

"Why are you frowning at your phone like that?" Roseanne wanted to know. "Is it Puck?"

"How'd you guess?"

"You got that look on your face." A smile tugged at her mouth. "You like him, don't you?"

"I don't know what he wants." I didn't know what I wanted, either, for that matter, but if I met with him in person, maybe he'd explain what this mysterious text was supposed to mean. "I think he's inviting me to join in some kind of trickster game."

She snorted. "Yeah, and he's not trying to get your clothes off."

"Watch it, you."

As we walked, a torrent of autumn leaves blew past, vivid and striking and the same colour as Puck's hair. He wanted to play a game, did he? I followed the leaves' path, along with Roseanne, until we came to a familiar street. Several doors down was my old house. I glimpsed the mercenaries inside through the living room window, and I backed out of sight to avoid making eye contact with any of them.

"What's he come here for?" I whispered to Roseanne.

"You think I know?" Her eyes gleamed. "I bet they'll regret kicking you out, though."

A strangled yell which sounded like Meathead came from inside the house. I took a step forward and then halted when the window flew open and countless wasps flew out, buzzing in circles around the house. I took a few more steps back to avoid them, but they seemed to mysteriously avoid every area except for the mercenaries' house, diving through every available window and eliciting screams every time they entered. Something crashed loudly, like a piece of furniture falling over, followed by shattering glass. Several high-pitched howls ensued while Meathead and Train tried and failed to escape their pursuers.

The shower of leaves blew past again and reformed into Puck, casually standing alongside me. "Hey, Holly. Glad you got my message in time."

I grinned. "Nice job there."

"I thought that was appropriate. I wonder if the land-lord will believe their stories about how and why they wrecked their house."

"I doubt it." They deserved the inconvenience of being hassled by the landlord after they'd royally screwed me over.

"I can help," said Roseanne eagerly. "How about I put worms in their beds?"

"Feel free, but don't get caught," I warned.

While she flew towards the house in bird form, Puck remained at my side as we headed back to half-blood territory, his hair as bright as the leaves he'd turned himself into. A self-satisfied smile appeared on his face at seeing the chaos he'd unleashed.

"I don't think I ever thanked you for saving my life," he said.

"Didn't you?" I waved a hand in the direction of the house. "I'd say this is more than enough compensation."

"You didn't get your money back, though?"

"Brook and the local mercs paid me enough for solving the murders." We'd split the money between Hawk, Puck, and me, but I'd be set for the next couple of months, and then Roseanne and I would have to start looking for mercenary work again. Which was fine with me. The idea of fighting death fae with a partner was more appealing than going it alone.

"Good." His mouth parted as though he wanted to say something else, but then his gaze fixed on a spot over my shoulder. "I think you have a visitor."

I turned around. None other than Lord Lyle stood at the end of the street near half-blood territory, as though waiting for someone. His gaze landed on me, and I groaned inwardly. What the hell was he doing here?

"I think he wants to talk to you," said Puck. "I'll make sure Roseanne doesn't get caught."

"I shouldn't be long," I said, "but just in case… thanks again for dealing with those dickheads."

I waved goodbye to Puck and went to meet the messenger. It must have been important if he'd come all the way here to Earth, but it wasn't like I'd been near Faerie since my last trip.

Lord Lyle greeted me with a jerky nod. "Her Majesty has requested your presence."

Why did the Unseelie Queen want to see me? To turn me into a statue again? No thanks. "What does she want?"

"She wishes to commend you for fighting against the Wild Hunt rogues and seeing to their capture."

I frowned. "Last time I went to the Court, I ended up being turned into an ornament."

"This time, you will not be harmed," he said. "She does not lie, and nor do I. I will take you to her, and then at your request, I will bring you back home."

"This had better not be a trap." I exhaled in a sigh, sending a brief glance in Puck's direction. "Fine. I'll get this over with."

I knew better than to draw out the inevitable when it came to Faerie, after all. Lord Lyle led the way into the heart of the Ley Line, at which point the street vanished from sight. In its place appeared the entrance to the Unseelie Court. I blinked in surprise, though it saved time for him to land directly in front of the Unseelie Queen's domain.

The ogres guarding the entrance moved aside at Lord

Lyle's command, leaving us a clear route into the Court. I was hardly dressed for an audience with the queen, but last time, she hadn't commented on my ratty clothes or obvious human appearance. If she complained, maybe I'd shift to bird form instead and see how she liked that.

In the centre of the cave, the Unseelie Queen sat waiting for me, as stunning as ever in a blue dress which matched the velvety blue of the fake sky on the cave ceiling. Glittering lights filled the rest of the space, and she beckoned imperiously with a pale hand. "Holly Lynn. I hear you played a part in apprehending the Wild Hunt traitors."

"I did," I said. "Are they in jail?"

"They are awaiting their execution," she said. "You did most of the job already."

I hadn't done it as a favour to her, but if she wanted to believe that was the case, it'd make my life a lot easier. Even if I did carry some of the Morrigan's magic... which she didn't seem to have noticed yet. I did my best to keep my expression neutral. "I hope they never gain a chance to enact their dark magic again. Did you know it was possible for such rituals to be used to contact the gods?"

"Of course I did," she said in impatient tones. "Do you think me a fool?"

"No, I don't." I'd hoped to find out how widespread the knowledge of blood magic was among the Sidhe, but from what I'd heard so far, it was pretty much unheard of outside of the Aes Sidhe, and even they had remained mostly oblivious to their queen's secret deals with the Wild Hunt. And with the god of death, too, come to that.

The Winter Queen would not appreciate me making

any comments to that effect, so I let the subject drop and waited for her next comment.

"Have you spoken to the Morrigan?" she asked.

"No..."

"I would like to know what she thinks of the current events," she said.

"Wasn't it in that letter?" I asked curiously. "Did she know the Wild Hunt were on the loose in Winter?"

"Ask her yourself," she said. "Leave, now, and visit her at once."

One did not argue with a faerie queen, so I said, "All right, I will."

A knot in my chest loosened as I left the cave, even if I did have to walk to the Death Kingdom again. I couldn't put off visiting the Morrigan any longer, and I wasn't supposed to keep her magic long-term. If she reacted badly to my revelation that I still had it, then at least I had something to defend myself with.

Lord Lyle met me outside. "Did the queen have any requests?"

"I have to speak to the Morrigan," I said. "Can I count on you giving me a lift home afterwards?"

"As I promised, mortal," he said. "I shall wait on the path."

"Good enough."

I made my way to the Death Kingdom with relatively few issues, reaching the Morrigan's overground cave having encountered nothing more dangerous than a handful of redcaps. I strode across the bridge to her cave unchallenged, and it wasn't until I reached the other side that the ogre security guard's absence hit me. Weird. I peered around the corner into the cave, which seemed oddly empty. In fact…

I entered the cave itself and came to a dead stop. The throne was empty, the only person present the ogre who guarded the cave. He sat hunched beside the empty chains which lay sprawled over the throne, the Morrigan herself nowhere to be seen. Even her pet birds had vanished.

My mouth fell open. "What happened to the Morrigan?"

"She's disappeared," he said in mournful tones. "I came in here, and she was gone."

"When?" My heartbeat quickened. *Tell me I didn't do that.*

"Two days ago… I think."

I took a step backwards, horror dawning. Accounting for Faerie's time slippage, she'd vanished around the same time as the battle with the Wild Hunt. Had I overused her powers and caused her to pay the price, or had she made her escape through some other means?

"How did she break her chains?"

"They aren't broken," he said. "They're… empty. She's gone, and the Winter Queen will slaughter us all."

My mouth went dry. "She won't. Not if I have anything to do with it."

Yet I had no idea where to start searching for the Morrigan. Assuming she was gone, and not… dead.

Unable to stand the sight of the empty cave a moment longer, I stumbled outside into the Death Kingdom. Even the foul smell of the bodies piled in the moat hardly pinged on my radar. All my attention was fixed on the sky for any sign of a shapeshifting bird.

Instead, a transparent figure appeared, hovering in

front of me. *Sidhe.* Not someone I recognised... but a ghost all the same.

"She is not here," said the ghost. "Where is the goddess of death?"

"Believe me, I wish I knew."

Oh, boy. The goddess of death, devourer of souls, also ruled over this part of the Winter Court. What her absence meant for Faerie I wasn't entirely sure I wanted to know.

In the time it took me to cross the river again, two more ghosts had appeared, drawn to me as though I carried a glowing necromancer candle. Instead, I held nothing save for the faint shadowy magic still flowing in my veins.

I'd done this to her. Somehow, I'd taken more of her magic than she'd intended to give away, and now... she was gone. The shining lights of another dozen ghosts shone among the trees. They hadn't reached the Courts yet, but when they did? The Sidhe would have a reckoning to face.

Change was coming.

ABOUT THE AUTHOR

Emma is the New York Times and USA Today Bestselling author of the Changeling Chronicles urban fantasy series.

Emma spent her childhood creating imaginary worlds to compensate for a disappointingly average reality, so it was probably inevitable that she ended up writing fantasy novels. When she's not immersed in her own fictional universes, Emma can be found with her head in a book or wandering around the world in search of adventure.

Find out more about Emma's books at www.emmaladams.com.